ALSO BY PETER PRINGLE

Food, Inc.: Mendel to Monsanto—
The Promises and Perils of the Biotech Harvest

Those Are Real Bullets, Aren't They? Bloody Sunday,
Derry, 30 January 1972
(with Philip Jacobson)

Cornered: Big Tobacco at the Bar of Justice

S.I.O.P.: The Secret U.S. Plan for Nuclear War
(with William Arkin)

The Nuclear Barons
(with James Spigelman)

Dan

PETER

Day of the delion

AN ARTHUR HEMMINGS MYSTERY

PRINGLE

Simon & Schuster

NEW YORK   LONDON   TORONTO   SYDNEY

SIMON & SCHUSTER
1230 Avenue of the Americas
New York, NY 10020

First Simon & Schuster hardcover edition May 2007

SIMON & SCHUSTER and colophon are registered trademarks of Simon & Schuster, Inc.

For information about special discounts for bulk purchases, please contact Simon & Schuster Special Sales at 1-800-456-6798 or business@simonandschuster.com.

Designed by Suet Chong

Manufactured in the United States of America

1 3 5 7 9 10 8 6 4 2

Library of Congress Cataloging-in-Publication Data
Pringle, Peter.
Day of the dandelion : an Arthur Hemmings mystery / Peter Pringle.
p. cm.
I. Title.
PS3616.R55D39 2007
813'.6—dc222   2006051298

ISBN-13: 978-1-4516-2396-3

For
Eleanor and Victoria

One of the most cherished dreams of plant breeders has been to find a way to transform corn and other cereal grains into superplants able to reproduce themselves. . . . The term for this type of vegetative miracle is "apomixis."

—United States Department of Agriculture

Prelude

THE MONASTERY OF ST. THOMAS,
Brunn, Moravia, Winter 1884

he abbot knew he was dying. Since the beginning of December, he had been unable to summon the strength to take even a few steps in the monastery garden. Each morning Frau Dupouvec, his housekeeper, wrapped his swollen legs in thick cotton bandages to stanch the fluids his failing kidneys could no longer remove. After a slight improvement in the summer, his sight had dimmed again; now he could read only a few pages without severe eyestrain and, sometimes, painful headaches. In recent days, the leaden cold of the Moravian winter had seeped through the stone walls of the prelate's quarters and seemed to settle most cruelly in his bones, his very being.

The monks at the Monastery of St. Thomas in Brunn were urgently praying for their beloved abbot's recovery. They could not bear the thought of losing him and had convinced themselves that he would get better. When ill health had overtaken him before, he had always rebounded. The crippling backache that had prevented him from tending his precious seedlings in the monastery garden had come and gone. The eye ailment had arrived and then disappeared. Moreover, he seemed far too young to die; he was only sixty-three. His predecessor, a frailer sort, had lived to be seventy-five. The abbot himself knew better than his devoted brothers, however. He knew that he would not survive to see another summer, perhaps not even another spring.

For several months he had not received visitors, but before Christmas he told Frau Doupevec and Joseph, his manservant, that he would make an exception for a young Russian botanist from St. Petersburg named Ivan Ivanovich Petrovsky.

A year earlier, Ivan Ivanovich had written the abbot asking for permission to quote from his essay *Experiments in Plant Hybridization.* The abbot had been surprised and immensely pleased by the request; it was the only recognition for his breeding work on garden peas he had received from his peers. At the time, he was too busy with the administrative duties of the monastery, but now his workload had diminished and he had sent the Russian an invitation.

The day of Ivan Ivanovich's visit, in early January 1884, a surprisingly sunny day, the abbot appeared to have made an astonishing recovery. He was walking on his own, without the aid of Joseph's arm. He was reading without eyestrain, the headache had gone, and mercifully, even the fluids had stopped leaking into the bandages around his legs.

The abbot asked Joseph to light the stove in the Orangery, where he would receive his visitor. He also wanted to take the Russian on a tour of the monastery gardens to show him where he had planted his peas, where he had potted his seedlings, and where he had observed the strange activities of the bees in his apiary.

Joseph warned his master not to linger outside—the January sunshine was deceptive—but the abbot had rebuked him with uncharacteristic sharpness, "I am well aware of the meteorological readings, Brother Joseph."

Frau Dupouvec had also protested, "Father Abbot has not even put on walking boots in five weeks, let alone ventured into the garden," she said sternly. But the abbot had insisted. Since it was not wet outside, merely cold, he would wear his felt boots, which would be loose enough for his tender, bandaged legs.

When the Russian arrived, promptly at ten o'clock as invited, the abbot was sitting upright in his favorite, wingbacked chair in the Orangery, facing out toward the garden. He was dressed, as usual, in his ankle-length black soutane, and Joseph had managed, after a struggle, to pull on the abbot's felt boots. For the sake of good relations with Frau Dupouvec, the abbot had allowed her to place a gray woolen blanket over his lap even though the Orangery was now warming up nicely with the heat from Joseph's fire.

Ivan Ivanovich was a tall man with curly brown hair, a high forehead, and a bushy beard. He wore a stiff white collar, a black frock coat, and high leather boots, the traditional dress of the tsarist professorial class. Behind the spectacles, clear blue eyes gleamed eagerly.

As the Russian entered the Orangery, the abbot rose to greet him with the wide familiar smile that Frau Dupouvec had not seen in several months.

"I am so pleased you have come," said the abbot with outstretched hand.

"I am honored to meet you, Father," replied the young Russian, bowing. "Very honored indeed."

From a respectful distance, Joseph and Frau Dupouvec watched as the abbot and the young Russian engaged immediately in a discussion of the genus *Pisum*. From the bright enthusiasm on the abbot's face and his energetic gesticulations, Joseph recognized each stage of the beautiful pea experiments. And when the abbot began shrugging his shoulders and raising his hands in gentle frustration, Joseph understood he was talking about his more recent encounters in the garden, with a plant that seemed to defy all his theories about heredity—the orange hawkweed, or *Hieracium*.

The abbot was talking heatedly and now loudly enough for Joseph to hear. "I must admit to you, my dear friend, how greatly I was deceived in this respect. I cannot resist remarking how striking it is that the hybrids of *Hieracium* behaved exactly the opposite to those of *Pisum*. They did not vary in shape or color, or in any respect, in the next generation. They were identical to their parents. Suddenly, I found myself in danger of having to renounce my experiments completely—and, therefore, my theory of inheritance."

Ivan Ivanovich let out a cry of protest. "But no, Father, you must not allow such oddities to dissuade you from your theory. I, for one, perfectly understand what you have discovered, and I believe that you have, indeed, unearthed a provable theory of inheritance. Your valuable work must continue and be repeated by others, as I am sure it will be."

The abbot adjusted his heavy frame in the chair, shifting his legs just a fraction, a movement that clearly caused him considerable discomfort. Then he again addressed his Russian visitor.

"I confess to you, dear friend, that part of my reason for seeing you today, besides thanking you for your mention of my essay, is my hope that you will continue my work. There is no one here at the monastery with sufficient interest, or expertise, to keep the experiments going. In fact, there are some, I fear, who will seek to destroy my scientific legacy as soon as I am gone."

The abbot paused.

"I have an idea about the strange behavior of *Hieracium*. Evidently, we are dealing with an individual phenomenon that is the manifestation of a different law of nature from the one I have uncovered. It appears that the seed of *Hieracium* can be made by the plant without fertilization. I have found only one other plant that behaves in this way, the common dandelion, of the genus *Taraxacum*. Dandelions, like hawkweed, do not reproduce as males and females normally do. The mother cells can produce the seed on their own, without fertilization by the pollen. In short, these plants do not have sex, like other plants."

The abbot paused again, carefully weighing what he was about to say.

"Ivan Ivanovich, my friend, I wish you to do me the honor of accepting my garden notes and other work that I have so far prepared on this matter. I would be happy to assist you in transporting these materials to St. Petersburg. May I ask bluntly, do you accept this assignment?"

The young Russian was stunned. He had not expected any such outcome. He had wanted simply to pay his respects to this remarkable old man who, as an amateur gardener, had apparently discovered a fundamental law of nature. For a long moment he was silent.

Then the abbot asked him again, this time more anxiously and yet still graciously. "It would make me most happy, I assure you, if you would accept this assignment."

Ivan Ivanovich quickly pulled himself together. He would accept, of course.

"Father, I am honored that you have considered me worthy of such a task. I will conduct the necessary experiments with all means at my disposal."

"Good, that is settled then," said the abbot, with obvious relief. "Now I must tell Joseph to prepare the materials, and we will walk in the garden, briefly, before lunch."

One

*A*t *precisely one minute* before three o'clock in the morning, when the only sound in the botany laboratory was the low hum of the DNA analysis machine, Karen Lichfield, the last of the researchers still working at this unforgiving hour, removed the disk from her desktop computer, placed it in a plastic cover, and prepared to leave her experiments. With a red marker, she wrote in large letters on a piece of paper, "T3. Do Not Touch," and taped it to a steel incubator containing rows of glass test tubes. She punched her security code into the pad on the wall and let the metal door shut behind her as she entered the main laboratory. A biohazard symbol on the door at eye level warned about the dangers of the poisons she knew firsthand, plant toxins so potent that they could make people bleed from their eyeballs.

She carefully locked the computer disk in her personal locker, shook off her white lab coat, and hung it quickly on its appointed hook. At the sink, stained brown from years of use, she turned on the

water and scrubbed her hands vigorously with the acrid soap, as researchers working with toxins were required to do at the end of each
day. She dried her hands on a sheet of paper towel, then reached for
her yellow fisherman's jacket and her blue backpack, telling herself
with each ordinary task that she must try to remain calm and breathe
normally.

The thick wooden door to the lab opened easily, and before it
swung back into place, she carefully inserted a white plastic tab, used
for labeling experiments, into the Yale lock, a primitive measure she
and her colleagues employed on more innocent occasions when they
were simply taking a break and did not want to be bothered about
the door key. The security guard downstairs in the exhibition hall
would now think the door was shut; on his closed circuit TV, the
status of the lab would show on the screen as "secure." She took a
long, deep breath and looked down the darkened balcony, reassured
that no one was there. Then she walked quickly over the flagstones
and down the steps into the silent cavern of the Museum of Natural
History.

It was a journey she had made countless times, often at this late
hour because her experiments demanded attention. But on this
night, when she had agreed to play this dangerous game, her departure was timed to coincide with the security guard's tea break, which
began promptly at 3 a.m. She knew, because she had practiced it
several times, that it would take just under a minute for her to walk
from the laboratory to the guard's desk, where he would be watching her on his monitor. Now she struggled to keep each function of
her body under control so that the guard would not recognize her
rising panic.

"Late one tonight, then," the guard said, giving her a friendly
smile, as he always did.

As she signed out on the time sheet, she could feel her hand
shaking.

"Yes, late one tonight," she repeated, trying not to look at him for fear he would see in her eyes something was bothering her, something different from all the other late nights at the museum over the last three years.

"Goodnight then, my duckie," he said, as he picked up his lunchbox and the evening's *Oxford Chronicle,* preparing to walk down into the basement kitchen for his break.

"You be careful on that bicycle, now. Watch out for those puddles."

The guard was her friend. He considered her personal safety one of his many responsibilities, more important, in some ways, than the safety of the museum's ancient specimens he was hired to protect. He didn't think it was right for a young woman, however important her scientific work, to be biking home on her own so late at night. His fatherly warning was always the same when she left the museum, no matter what the hour or the weather.

Walking across the exhibition hall to the service door at the back of the museum, Karen listened for the metal tips of the guard's shoes on the stone steps as he moved slowly downstairs to the staff kitchen. He was a nice man, she knew, a nice, considerate, widowed man who had several grandchildren of his own, and who had no idea that what was about to occur on his watch could so change both their worlds.

She shook her head, trying to concentrate, and checked the time on her digital wristwatch—3:03 a.m. Perfect, Karen thought as she pushed the bar on the service door. The opening cast a shaft of pale light across the darkened parking lot. She stepped outside, and as the door swung back, she placed her backpack in the way to prevent it from closing. She knew the open door would register "not secure" on the guard's TV screen, but he would not return from his break until 3:30.

Under the steady rain, she walked down the muddy path to the bike rack, her eyes slowly growing accustomed to the darkness around her. She took her bicycle lamp off the front of the basket on the handlebar, held it out into the parking lot, and switched it on twice, paused, and then twice again, as she had been instructed. Then she waited, shivering, although the night was warm. The shiver was only to shake off the rain, she told herself.

After a few seconds, endless seconds it seemed to her, a car head-light flashed twice and then twice again. She could just see the outline of the car, a small one, a Punto maybe, or a Panda. She heard the car's door open and then close with a firm click and could see the outline of a man walking toward her, his footsteps grinding the loose gravel at the edge of the parking lot. She walked back along the path, ahead of the man, and pulled open the service door, the light from the museum shining now on her companion for the first time.

His appearance startled her and she jumped back from him. He was of medium height and dressed entirely in black—T-shirt and jeans and black gloves, thick black gloves reinforced, like a goalkeeper's. A black ski mask covered his head and she could see only his taut mouth and cold gray eyes—a human, barely. He was carrying a small black bag, like a tool bag, and he moved with such ease and stealth that she felt clumsy and ordinary beside him.

She had not expected this catlike creature to come out of the night and she wanted to stop him right there, on the museum threshold, and tell him that there had been a terrible mistake, that she was not Karen Lichfield, or that she did not work in the botany laboratory, or that she was not the person who had arranged to meet a man in the parking lot and let him into the museum; that he should go away, right now, back to his car, or she would report him immediately to the security guard. But the man grabbed her arm with both his hands, a strong grip that made her wince in pain, and motioned to her with a flick of his head to go forward. This was how they would communicate, silently with head and hand signals, she realized, and she immediately nodded back. Then he grabbed her arm again and pushed her, roughly, inside and in front of him, clearly wanting her to lead the way. She felt his physical power and realized that there was no turning back, no backing down from her agreement to let this strange man into her private world.

The two of them slipped into the shadows of the exhibition hall, past the museum's dinosaur skeletons, the cases of fossils, and the stuffed birds suspended with their wings outstretched from the iron trusses of the glass canopy. Karen had walked through these exhibits many times, and at this time of night, but tonight, when she was moving silently with this man in black and when she was alert, watching and listening for any movement or sound, these ghostly creatures only added to her anxiety. Silently, she led him up the steps to the balcony and along the flagstones to the door of the laboratory. She turned the brass handle and the door opened. The plastic tab fell to the floor and instinctively she picked it up, a common tool of her trade, stowing it in a pocket of her yellow jacket.

She glanced around the familiar room, now strangely unfamiliar, as if she were seeing it through new eyes, the eyes of this stranger she had allowed to share it with her. Here was Oxford's botanical research, ancient and modern, amateur and professional. Smart new DNA analysis machines sat beside Victorian mahogany cabinets that had once housed the museum's butterfly collection. The drawers now contained small white cotton bags of exotic plant seeds studied by the young woman and her colleagues. In one alcove, antique brass microscopes, once the pride of the lab but long out of use, still stood among Leitz inverted epifluorescent microscopes and confocal laser devices. Shiny steel incubators and rows of test tubes lay on metal-topped antique pine tables with finely turned legs donated by alumni or a friendly benefactor. Plastic bags of dried plant specimens collected over centuries in distant tropical lands, each bag coded with a white tab, lay in piles, waiting to be examined and catalogued.

The man tugged at her arm, jolting her into action. As arranged, she led him to the professor's office, separated from the working floor by a partition with small glass panes, like the barriers that once separated factory managers from the work floor. This was an office with all the comforts of old Oxford. The desk was of polished oak, the armchair a rich brown leather. In the oak bookcases modern scientific journals sat beside leather-bound ancient monographs, and in one corner of the office stood an old steel safe, about the size of a commode, with a small brass wheel, polished and gleaming from constant use.

Karen pointed to the safe and the man nodded. He tried the door into the professor's office, which rattled but remained firmly locked. He looked at Karen for the key, but she shook her head. The man opened his bag and took out a roll of masking tape. He ripped off four short strips and stuck them in a crisscross on the pane of glass nearest the door handle. Then with one swift blow of his gloved fist he broke the pane, slipped his hand through, and opened the door. Karen watched as the man moved inside, cautioning her with a wave of his arm to stay behind.

He closed the door and unpacked his bag: a metal dial with a numbered face like a combination lock, two cloth pouches, and a pair of surgical gloves, the tools of a master craftsman in his underworld. The stranger took off his black gloves, revealing the long blond hairs on the back of his hands. Gray eyes and blond hair, Karen thought. It would not be enough if she ever needed to identify this man. Effortlessly, he rolled on the surgical gloves, well beyond his wrists. She watched as he placed the metal dial on the front of the safe, where it stuck, like a limpet. Then he pressed his ear against the disk as he gently turned the brass wheel. Karen watched the man and tried not to make any noise around this noiseless person.

After he had turned the wheel several times, this way and that, he gently pulled the safe door open and Karen could see the white cotton seed bags inside. The man scooped them into one of his cloth pouches, which he placed in his bag. Then he took out a small plastic box of slides, placing it also in his bag. He removed his surgical gloves, which came off with a loud snap, and he eased back into the lab.

Karen's watch read 3:22 a.m. The guard would return to his desk in eight minutes. She mouthed the words, "We must go," and urgently pointed to the exit. As they hurried through the lab, the man paused, as though he had forgotten something, placed his black bag on the lab bench, and opened it.

She pointed again to her watch and shook her finger, but he ignored her, picking out the little white seed bags, one by one, about a dozen in all. He held them up to show her, pointing to their coded tags. The codes began with the letters NS, and also with the letters SP. She nodded her approval. He opened the box of slides and held them up to the light, one by one, and showed her the labels. Again the codes began with NS and SP.

"Yes, yes," she mouthed, nodding her assent and pointing to her watch, more frantically than before. "We must go, now," she whispered, tugging at the man who slowly, too slowly, carefully replaced the slides into the box and then put the box into his bag, as though they were delicate pieces of jewelry. Then he took her arm again and pushed her in front of him, to lead the way out.

Karen let the front door of the laboratory close behind them, and this time it shut with a loud click that seemed to echo through the empty museum. Outside the laboratory door, they stood for a moment and listened for any sound of the returning guard, but there was silence. Satisfied, the two moved quickly along the balcony and down the steps into the exhibition hall.

As they reached the bottom, Karen froze, halting the stranger with a touch on his bulky shoulder. From down in the basement came the sound of a metallic shuffle, a slow, tired shuffle as the guard made his way up the stairs.

Karen signaled to the man to stay in the shadows instead of moving out into the hall, where she knew the TV monitor on the guard's desk would spot them. The sound of the guard's footsteps suddenly stopped, and then started up again, at first just one click, then several, quickening and disappearing. She could tell the guard was going back down the steps into the kitchen. She guessed he had forgotten something. She moved out into the hall, this time pulling the man with her by the arm. They walked swiftly toward the back of the building. At the service entrance, still wedged open with her backpack, Karen pushed the door, letting the man outside. As she bent to pick up her backpack, the man, in an unexpected gesture, held out his gloved hand. What was he trying to do, thank her? Say goodbye? She did not want his gratitude, she did not want his farewell. But he insisted, holding his hand outstretched, and she took it. The man squeezed her bare hand, his strong fingers digging into her skin. She winced as she looked into his eyes that were the color of flat steel. As she struggled to release her hand, Karen felt a tiny prick, like a needle or a shard of glass. She let out a cry of pain and the man released his grip.

"Goodbye," he mouthed and he was gone, down the muddy path, disappearing across the darkened parking lot.

She looked down at her hand and under the dim light of the service door could just make out a tiny red dot of blood. She ran her finger over the dot and felt something hard under the skin. A splinter of glass, perhaps, had lodged in the man's glove when he had broken the window into the professor's office. She could feel a sharp edge under her skin where the blood was.

Then she ran, stumbling down the path to her bicycle. She heard a car engine start and she thought of the man all in black, a man she had never seen except for the thin lips, the dead eyes, and the blond hairs on the back of his hands. She had never known his name. She had barely heard him say only one word—*goodbye*. She did not know if he had an accent. She did not know where he came from, what country even.

As she pulled out her bicycle and began to pedal furiously down Parks Road, she wondered whether the security guard had heard the service door close as he came up from the basement, or whether he had heard the car engine start, or had seen her as she rode off on her bicycle. She was shivering again. She wiped the rain from her face, rain now mixed with tears of fear and anger at herself for letting the man in, for changing her life in a few short minutes, in ways she could not be sure of now.

At the traffic lights at Longwall, a uniformed constable was standing on the corner and she stopped for the red light, although she would normally not have bothered this early in the morning, with no traffic. The policeman in his shiny yellow rain jacket stared at her and she realized that she had not put her front lamp back in place. She saw his face in the street light, a young face, a boy's face, tired and wet at the end of his night's duty. She willed him not to come over, not to question her. As she struggled to clip the lamp onto the front basket, the traffic light turned green, and she pedaled into the last hour of darkness, pushing the bike hard, punishing herself in the rush to get away. Under the street light she looked down at the back of her right hand, still hurting from the fierce grip of the man's glove and still with a spot of blood, now streaked with rain, from the prick to her skin.

Two

After his traditional Monday lunch in Balliol College, Professor Simon Goodhart, the vice-chancellor of Oxford University, retired to his rooms hoping to be alone for the afternoon to ponder the decision he had just made to resign from his exalted post. For forty years, since he arrived as a student at Balliol, Professor Goodhart had lived and worked in Oxford, capping a modest career in the history of science by becoming vice-chancellor. These days, this once-coveted office, a stepping-stone to a knighthood, was concerned mainly with the tiresome, and uncertain, task of raising money. Professor Goodhart had surprised his colleagues by being unusually successful, in this regard. His latest acquisition, as he liked to call it, was the promise of tens of millions of dollars from Panrustica, plc, the world's largest life sciences company, based in Zurich. They had offered to fund the School of Botany for ten years in return for exclusive rights to the department's research.

Professor Goodhart did not pretend to understand the finer details of this research, but the company had made it clear, by their generous offer, how much it was valued in the commercial world. At Oxford, he understood only too well what the funds could do for the School of Botany, which was virtually bankrupt. He had vigorously supported Panrustica's proposal, and his promotional activities on the company's behalf had deeply divided the academic staff, the younger ones seeing a link with business as the only way to survive in an age of harsh cuts in public funds; the older ones decrying the loss of academic freedom and what the science professors called the purity of their profession. Goodhart himself had thrived on the controversy, pointing to the deal one of Panrustica's smaller competitors had done with the University of California at Berkeley. Berkeley had simply pocketed 25 million dollars, Goodhart stressed to his colleagues; nothing sinister had happened. He enjoyed his contacts with the corporate world, and he loved being summoned to the ministry in London to discuss government policy. And more than anything else, he admitted, but only to himself, he loved the publicity. For the first time in his life he had been on television, several times in recent months. He had been profiled in the newspapers, in mostly flattering ways, and as he walked around Oxford, ordinary people recognized him and sought his views, and not just on the tedious topic of university funding.

What none of his colleagues knew was that Panrustica had recently sweetened their proposal with a personal one for Professor Goodhart. They had suggested that he might like to abandon his long university career and join the company's board full-time. At first, he was astonished at their brashness. It was a bribe in any language—and he politely refused. But a certain Mr. Richard Eikel, an American who was the company's chief counsel, kept coming back and raising the compensation he would receive. It now stood at the princely sum of half a million dollars a year—unheard-of riches in British academia.

There would be an apartment in Zurich and an expense account for unlimited trips back and forth from England. At last, he would be able to treat his wife, Pamela, to the Continental experience, as she put it, that he had always promised her, one day. Most summers, the Goodharts, having put five girls through private schools, could not even afford a week in Normandy, let alone a time-share house in Provence. Zurich might not be Paris, but it was Continental, better than Paris in some ways for their age.

Goodhart had decided to accept the appointment. He would not miss the stifling confinement of historical research, or stuffy dons stranded in their limited universe, or indolent students protesting about things they knew little about, and definitely not the mediocre meals at high table. Indeed, he would not miss the whole damned effete university existence.

He knew the dons would call it a bribe. Let them, he told himself. He now saw it as the just reward for years of exemplary service to the university and for his groundbreaking innovations for raising funds. On the board of Panrustica, plc, he had persuaded himself, his contribution would steer corporate policy on the environment and world health in a new, exciting, and socially responsible direction. Tomorrow he would lunch with Mr. Eikel, at Oxford's Randolph Hotel, and formally accept his seat on the board.

To ready himself for this event, and plan properly for the storm that he knew would follow, Professor Goodhart had told his secretary, Ms. Anna Bridgland, that he had to study the confidential draft of a Cabinet Office report supporting the Panrustica deal. She had promised to see that he was not disturbed.

In this moment, a glance in an antique curved mirror on his office wall added to his satisfaction. Professor Goodhart saw a man of distinction, silver-haired, a few lines across the forehead, but still handsome nevertheless. He smiled contentedly, adjusting his pose for the minor distortions in the glass, and then sat in his favorite chair overlooking the quadrangle to begin his personal reflections. But he had been alone for barely five minutes when there was an urgent knock on the door.

Ms. Bridgland was unusually flustered, her hands clasped tightly to her slight bosom, a deep frown on her face, as though she had experienced something dreadful.

"I'm so sorry to interrupt you, Vice-chancellor, but the police are here. There's been a break-in at the University Museum and er, er, some things stolen."

"The police? Well, let them in, Ms. Bridgland."

Goodhart rose to his feet as she ushered in Detective Inspector Charles Davenport of the Oxford Constabulary, the police liaison officer with the university. Davenport was a veteran of the Oxford force; he had seen vice-chancellors come and go. The relationship between himself and Professor Goodhart, each of them would say, was stiff but cordial.

"Sorry to bother you, sir," Davenport began. "It's the museum, the School of Botany lab. We were called at ten o'clock this morning and notified of a break-in."

"A break-in?" asked the vice-chancellor, his brow furrowing.

"Yes, sir, some plant seeds have apparently been stolen from a safe on the first floor. Normally I would not have bothered you with such a trivial incident, sir, but there was a note on file from you that any security issue associated with the botany labs should be reported directly to you personally."

"Seeds?" asked the vice-chancellor, his voice rising.

"Yes, sir," said the inspector, producing his notebook, for reference.

"Do sit down, Inspector."

"Two intruders, most likely a man and a woman according to the muddy footprints, sir, entered the University Museum through the service door between three and three thirty a.m. when the security guard was on his tea break. The footprints led across the main hall, past the museum's fossil collection, and the dinosaurs. You know the ones I mean, sir."

"Yes, yes," said Goodhart, impatiently. He was sitting at his desk listening intently to the inspector's report and writing furiously on a notepad.

The footprints ended at the steps leading to the second floor, Davenport said. Even so, he was in no doubt that the intruders had climbed the steps and then entered the laboratory's main door, which was apparently open. There were no signs of forced entry.

"They knew what they were doing, definitely, sir," said the inspector. "No visible damage, either to the door or the lock, only to the partition into the professor's office."

The vice-chancellor nodded again and scribbled "No Damage" in large letters on his notepad.

"Professor's office? You mean Professor Scott's office?"

"Precisely, sir."

"But the seeds, inspector. Seeds were taken, you said?"

"Yes, sir, it appears so."

"Seeds," the vice-chancellor wrote on the notepad, underlining the word several times.

The seeds were in white cotton bags, said Inspector Davenport. The safe had been expertly opened, again without damage.

"White bags in safe," the vice-chancellor wrote on his pad. He had a good-enough picture of the little white bags, tied tightly at the neck with cotton. Professor Scott had shown him dozens of these bags of seeds during a tour of the museum depository only three weeks earlier.

The stolen seeds were coded with the letters NS and SP, said Davenport, looking up again at the vice-chancellor.

"Apparently they stood for the Russian cities of Novosibirsk and St. Petersburg, sir."

"Russian, eh? How do we know that?"

"Information from a lab employee, sir," said the inspector. "A researcher named Karen Lichfield is helping with our inquiries. That's what she told us."

Nothing else in the depository appeared to be missing, Davenport reported, although there were items of considerable value, antique microscopes and such, the usual lab paraphernalia, and, of course, desktop computers. They were all accounted for and were being checked.

"When did this happen, did you say?" asked the vice-chancellor. He had now stopped writing on his pad and was orienting himself rapidly. This could be much worse, he knew, than the loss of expensive microscopes or even the prized museum exhibits that drew visitors from around the world.

"We think very early this Monday morning in the small hours, sir, as I said, when the security guard was taking his tea. It was only discovered when the staff came back to work after the weekend."

"Any ideas, any clues as to who, Inspector?"

"Only that it could have been an inside job. A jealous researcher trying to sabotage a colleague's work. We have seen that type before, especially towards the end of the academic year. We've cordoned off the building, again according to your special instructions for botany labs, sir, and will have two constables on duty. I just wanted to drop by, as a courtesy, sir. We would like to start interviewing the staff . . . with your permission, of course."

The vice-chancellor hesitated, weighing several options.

"I must inform the ministry before we do anything, Inspector. After all, they own the seeds."

He was peering at the inspector over the top of his reading glasses, and Davenport shifted impatiently in his chair, anxious to leave.

"Inspector, why don't I see how the ministry would like to handle this matter; it may be more delicate than it appears. It shouldn't take more than an hour at most. You haven't left anything out, odd details that might be useful to the minister, perhaps?"

"Can't think of any, sir," said Davenport, rising from his chair. "We're not rushing to investigate this one, sir. We have our hands full, as you can imagine, what with the students back."

"Yes, Inspector, we all have our hands full, but I thank you for your report, most commendable, as always. And please make sure the lab is properly secured, as per my instructions."

The vice-chancellor turned, a move of dismissal designed to let the inspector know he was the busier of the two men and that university affairs were more important than police work. Davenport, familiar with the gesture, let himself out.

When the door had closed, Professor Goodhart moved swiftly back to his desk. Inspector Davenport could easily dismiss the theft of a handful of seeds, but Goodhart knew better. These could be Professor Scott's apomixis seeds, possibly some of the most valuable seeds in the world, seeds, he knew, that were priced by his future employer, Panrustica, at tens of millions of dollars, which probably meant billions. Goodhart shuddered at the thought.

He picked up the phone and pushed the button for the School of Botany. When the operator answered—she took her time, he thought—he asked for the professor. Professor Scott had not been in all day: in fact, he had not been seen since last Friday and the only person in the museum's laboratories was a senior researcher named Karen Lichfield. The vice-chancellor asked to be put through to her.

"Ms. Lichfield, this is the vice-chancellor speaking. I am bothering you—and I apologize for that—but I am calling about last night's break-in, as you might have imagined. I cannot find Professor Scott. Have you any idea where he is?"

He was using his most official, lordly tone.

Scott had not been around since Friday, she said. That was not so unusual, she was starting to explain when the vice-chancellor interrupted.

"Who was working directly with Professor Scott on apomixis?"

"A Russian researcher, Tanya Petrovskaya."

"Put me through to her, would you, Ms. Lichfield?"

"I'm sorry, sir, I can't. She hasn't been in since Friday either. I called her at home but there was no reply."

"Ms. Lichfield, kindly tell members of staff not to talk to the press or to anyone, including family members, about the break-in." Goodhart's voice became measurably sharper as he delivered his orders.

Karen Lichfield showed her willingness to help.

"Yes, sir," she said, and again, "Yes, sir."

"And if you find out where the professor is, give me a call at my rooms in Balliol."

Then he rang off and called Scott's home in North Oxford. There was no reply. He called Inspector Davenport's office and asked him to send a squad car to the professor's house in Squitchey Lane. Fifteen minutes later, at 3:45 p.m., a police sergeant called back. There was no reply to a ring at the professor's front door. The police had been round the back of the house into the garden, where the next-door neighbor, an elderly woman, had introduced herself as Miss Richards. She said she believed the professor was off on one of his rambles or cycling tours. She had seen the milk bottles on his doorstep that morning and had taken them into her house, as she usually did when he was away.

The vice-chancellor looked at his watch, wondering how long he could keep the ministry waiting, when Ms. Bridgland knocked on his door. She was holding a copy of the *Oxford Chronicle* and reading to him the story in the Stop Press, "Burglary at Oxford Museum."

"Dammit," Professor Goodhart exclaimed. He knew that he could not delay telling the ministry a moment longer.

Three

he new Minister of Agriculture and Fisheries, Aneurin Williams, alerted by the vice-chancellor's call,
was in his office early on Tuesday morning, thumbing
through the Arthur Hemmings file. His ministry, fondly known as
Ag & Fish, was housed in one of Whitehall's drafty neoclassical relics, reflecting a distant time when Britain's food production was
more closely linked to its colonies. Oil portraits of Britain's great
botanists and plant breeders peered down from oak-paneled walls.
The minister's office was as big as a ballroom, with heavy glass
chandeliers and Oriental rugs—bigger than the Bethesda Chapel in
Merthyr Tydfyl was how the minister's personal aide, Merrill Davies, described it.

In all criminal investigations with potential to disrupt the nation's food supply, it was the minister's prerogative to choose his
personal agent from the Office of Food Security, a clandestine service of the British government whose exploits were never made

public until many years after the event, if at all. The theft of seeds from the School of Botany had been given top priority at the ministry, and agent Arthur Hemmings was at the top of the list.

"Best possible man for the job," Davies had told his boss without hesitation.

"First-rate qualifications. Detailed knowledge of Scott's seed research. Excellent background. Father was a physicist in our atomic bomb project. A first-rate scientist and a good detective. Hemmings has worked for OFS as a forensic biologist for twenty years—on everything from wine scandals to biological weapons. A full and successful life in the service of his country, Minister."

Scanning Arthur Hemmings's long list of scientific qualifications, his languages—French and Russian and some German—his excellent work on Soviet agriculture during the last years of the Cold War, his reputation as a fast worker, Williams could not disagree. The minister was especially impressed by the results of Hemmings's last physical exam, six months ago, that had concluded he was in excellent shape for fifty-two.

"Don't want any sluggards on this job," Williams muttered to himself.

Only a few entries gave the minister pause—prolonged bouts of drinking at Oxford and then again at the University of Colorado; a failed marriage to an American as a graduate student; a short-fused temper, a trait that seemed to be growing with age; uncertain politics in the seventies.

One entry stopped Williams from reading on: "1972–4 marched in aid of CFMAG."

"What the hell was that?" Williams asked.

"I believe it was the Committee for Freedom in Mozambique, Angola and Guinea," replied Davies, proud of his knowledge of such matters, including this long-defunct group. "You know, Minister, get the Portuguese colonists out of Africa, that sort of thing."

"Yes, I heard that he was a marcher," Williams said, scornfully. "I don't want any bloody radicals on my watch."

"He's no Tory, but he's no radical either," said Davies. "Independent, you could say, sometimes fiercely so. He needs a licensed driver, but don't worry, Minister. I'm it."

"And somebody has to explain the importance of this bloody apomixis that Scott was working on," Williams said. "Why the hell can't scientists use terms everybody can all understand?"

"Again, Minister, the best person for that is Hemmings. He knows the science."

"To hell with the science, Davies, what's the threat? The economics. The politics."

"Well, Minister, they call it the race to find a supergene that controls asexual reproduction in plants, known as *apomixis*. Whoever finds the gene, or group of genes, and patents it, controls world food production. It's sort of that simple." Here Davies paused to let the idea register.

"It would revolutionize crop breeding, drastically cut the costs of seed production, and open up breeding of à la carte plants that could produce pharmaceuticals, plastics, or any raw materials, not just food. Companies like Panrustica are willing to pay handsomely for exclusive rights to university research, as you know. Apomixis research in American colleges is already being funded by one of Panrustica's rivals."

He paused again to let the minister catch up.

"To agribusiness it's the ticket to the future—but only if they can patent the research. Agribusiness executives are terrified that if they don't own the apomixis supergene through a patent, they will lose their opportunity to control the entire food chain."

He paused again as the minister's scowl deepened.

"They fear a competitor or a liberal professor like Scott will try and put the invention into a 'patent commons' where everyone can share it, improve it, and use it, free of charge, like open-source software. Scott's plan offers farmers freedom from the domination of the seed companies. It moves capital from suits to serfs, instead of serfs to suits. Politically, the West is also worried Russia or China will get there first."

"Nicely put, Davies. I think I get it. You're assuming the seeds stolen from the museum contained the supergene, is that it?"

"It's possible; we're not sure. That's where Hemmings comes in, Minister."

"OK. OK. We need your friend to help us," Williams grunted as he went back to reading the file.

Merrill Davies looked out the window and down onto Whitehall, where the morning rush hour was in full cry. In two decades since leaving rural Wales, Merrill had never got used to the rush hour, and to miss it, he came to work shortly after dawn and left after a couple of pints in the George V. Since he was a bachelor, these hours were easy to keep and had become a habit, a good habit that had brought with it a good reputation at the ministry. Ag & Fish ministers he had served, and Williams was the fifth, thought it was his devotion to them personally. He had never told anyone, not even his friend, Arthur Hemmings, the real reason. Now this new Minister Williams was arriving early and leaving late, just like him, and Merrill found it unsettling. His carefully carved-out space had been invaded, and it had already threatened to sour his relationship with his new boss, at least in his own mind. He had not taken to Williams in any case. The man had a reputation as a sly operator, spreading his considerable charm only when votes or careers, mostly his own, were at stake.

As Merrill waited for his boss's decision, the only sound in the office was the minister's grunting. He did not ask any more questions. Merrill knew Arthur would get the job—there was really no one else with so many of the necessary qualifications—and he was looking forward to working closely with his unpredictable but wise old friend.

After a few minutes, Williams cleared his throat.

"Bring in Hemmings, then," he barked, more a voice of resignation than satisfaction, Merrill noted. Arthur had only met Williams once and had instantly disliked him. "Beware the black-haired Celt," Arthur had said to Merrill, who took it as a compliment to himself. Williams was black-haired and sleek—in contrast to Merrill, whose unruly thicket of red hair always made him look slightly underdressed, even for Ag & Fish. There would be more than the usual friction between Arthur and the minister in the days ahead, Merrill feared.

Four

Each morning before breakfast, in all but the very worst weather, Arthur Hemmings could be found jogging through the Royal Botanic Gardens at Kew, on the outskirts of London. He adjusted his route by season, sometimes by species, to catch Kew's full-tended splendor. In the spring, the azalea and the bamboo gardens offered their calm as Arthur tried to unravel the problems—puzzles really—sent him from the Ministry of Ag & Fish. The path along the Thames, past the seventeenth-century Dutch House and into the bee garden, drew him in full summer, its delphiniums and dahlias, the lavender, irises, and snapdragons reminding him of growing up in the Oxfordshire countryside alongside his mother's magnificent herbaceous borders. As the summer wore on, he often switched to Capability Brown's Walk, and in winter, he preferred a trail that wound around the Corsican pine and the monkey puzzle, a tree that could always make him smile, its curling branches and spiked leaves mimicking the botanical confusion he so often found in his bosses at the ministry.

No matter which way he went, Arthur would always end up at the Palm House, the centerpiece of Kew, the greatest greenhouse in the world. He knew its vital statistics by heart—363 feet long, 100 feet wide, and 66 feet high, a monumental reminder of the successes of Victorian horticulture. Under its elegant glass roof were some of the world's most valuable plants and most exotic flowers collected from the distant lands of the British Empire, and beyond. Arthur knew most of them by name, the Latin name, and entertained visiting colleagues and impressed women friends with tales of the celebrated plant hunters who had collected them.

On this Tuesday morning, the sun was at last peering through the gray clouds that had covered Britain for most of April and the temperature was already in the seventies. Arthur felt his lungs clear and the tightness in his shoulders ease as his body reached its comfortable stride through the bamboo garden. A quick five miles, he thought, no more, enough to earn the pleasant hours of reading in Kew's herbarium that he had planned for the rest of the day. On his last lap, Arthur paused outside the Palm House to admire a late-blooming forsythia. As he bent forward, inspecting the bright, mustard yellow flowers, his cell phone rang, a simple urgent bell, no Beatles, no "Für Elise."

"Arthur," the male voice said, a few notes higher than normal. "It's Merrill."

Arthur knew perfectly well, of course, from the number, but Merrill's phone manners were old-fashioned, as were many things Arthur liked about him. His friend wore tweeds in the winter, cream linen suits in summer, and only white shirts and red ties.

"Sorry to interrupt your morning constitutional, boyo, but something's come up. It's about Alastair Scott."

"Take a breath, Merrill," Arthur instructed his breathless colleague, as he did at the beginning of most of these phone calls from the minister's aide.

"There's been a break-in at the Oxford museum, you know, the botany lab where the seeds are kept, and no one can find Scott." Merrill was now talking even faster, afraid of losing Arthur's attention.

"Scott's been absent for a couple of days and we thought he was on one of his rambles. But he seems to have gone missing."

"Gone missing?"

"That's what I said." Merrill was sounding even more frantic as he reached the climax of his story. "Scott didn't turn up for work. The *Oxford Chronicle* has a big story. The pressure is on."

Merrill took a quick, much-needed breath.

"Seeds were taken from the depository. Don't know if any slides are missing or cultivars or DNA sequences. Everything's been cordoned off with yellow tape."

"Yellow tape," said Arthur, emphasizing each word and staring at the forsythia.

"And one more thing," Merrill sputtered, the words now coming faster than ever. "The Russian researcher, you know, the one working with Scott, Tanya whatsername. She's gone AWOL too—hasn't been in the office since Scott disappeared on Friday. At the ministry they suspect they've done a bunk, run off together, the two of them. Our codgers are imagining that they've gone to Moscow, something to do with Scott's past. Socialist, Cold War, all movie plots if you ask me. The media haven't picked up the Russian connection yet, but it's only a matter of time."

"*Alors, la guerre froide continue,*" Arthur said, stretching his legs and taking one forlorn last look around Kew's comforting landscape.

"Arthur, bloody pay attention, will you. It's madness here. More meetings. The first one at nine with the minister. He'll want you there to explain the importance of Scott's research. You'd better get a move on."

As Arthur hung up, he reached for a sprig of the yellow forsythia. Against every code of behavior in the Kew guidebook—and his own—he carefully but firmly broke the stem away from the bush and headed indoors. The sprig would pay for his day lost, spent explaining the sex lives of plants instead of watching them get on with it here in Kew. He would barely have time for his breakfast, toast and marmalade, thick-cut, and a cup of Earl Grey tea, that his five miles had earned him.

Five

The *Oxford Chronicle,* circulation 38,371 at the height of the tourist season, had never had so much publicity in all its seventy-four years of modest existence—and all, apparently, for a few bags of stolen seeds. As far as anyone could remember, and there were two people on the staff slightly older than the newspaper, no one had ever asked that the front page be sent to a minister of the Crown, and certainly not to anyone of importance abroad. But this Tuesday morning, as the staff arrived for work, the phone was ringing insistently with calls from London, from Europe, and even all the way from Washington, D.C.

First on the line was a Mrs. Winchester from Zurich. She was personal secretary to one of Britain's most powerful industrialists, Sir Wilfred Owen, as she announced to the operator in a forced upper-class English accent clearly intended to intimidate. Sir Wilfred, Mrs. Winchester emphasized, was chairman of the world's largest life sciences company, Panrustica, plc.

She requested, or rather demanded, an immediate fax of the Monday *Chronicle*'s Stop Press items and any subsequent articles about the break-in at the museum or the disappearance of Professor Scott. She also wanted biographical details of the professor and even a biography of Fred Barton, chief feature writer, whose byline was appearing on the morning's stories declaring the professor a missing person.

The newspaper's telephone operator took down the requests without mentioning that in Britain, Sir Wilfred Owen was a familiar figure, one of the best known in British industry. The public knew him simply as "Freddie," but the operator was too polite to make the point to Mrs. Winchester and simply sent the faxes. Then she stuck a note on Fred Barton's computer screen that read, "Mrs. Winchester of Panrustica has her knickers in a twist over your Scott story and the stolen seeds."

When Sir Freddie arrived at his Zurich headquarters, promptly at 8 a.m., as usual, Mrs. Winchester was waiting for him, clutching the faxes from the *Chronicle*. She could see that Sir Freddie was not his usual collected self. Even his tie, always immaculately tied, seemed to be lopsided, and the gray silk handkerchief in the breast pocket of his suit jacket was strangely absent. He had apparently dressed in a hurry.

"I thought you'd like to see everything about the burglary and Scott in print, Sir Freddie," said Mrs. Winchester, handing him the latest wire story about the museum and the professor's disappearance.

"Yes, yes, of course. Most thoughtful of you."

Sir Freddie took the copies, balanced his half-moon reading glasses on his nose, and settled back into his desk chair. He was a very old-style chairman for such a very modern company. Unlike so many younger chief executives, he knew a thing or two about the simple power of good manners. Many said his outward calm and pleasant ways—what his detractors called an oily charm—had been the secret to his rapid climb to the chairman's suite and one of the main reasons he was still there, apparently unassailable, at the age of sixty-eight.

In more than two decades with Sir Freddie, Mrs. Winchester had rarely seen the chairman so off point. He was bending over the copies on his desk and grumbling to himself, like a gardener surveying the damage from a violent summer storm.

"This has been very useful, Mrs. Winchester, thank you. You'd better find Eikel. He is supposed to have lunch with the vice-chancellor in Oxford today."

"He's been waiting in his office since seven this morning, Sir Freddie."

"Good, then send him up, Mrs. Winchester. He's leaving for London in half an hour. Then tell the plane to come back for me this afternoon."

"Yes, sir."

Mrs. Winchester wanted to suggest that he might like to phone Lady Owen and let her know of his unexpected arrival in London, but she knew better with Sir Freddie in this mood. She moved swiftly to the door and closed it silently behind her.

She had been gone only a few seconds when Richard Eikel, smooth and perfectly dressed as always, came in. Eikel was the company's top patent attorney, the best attorney any life science company could wish for. He could write a patent application as effortlessly as a postcard to his mother, and he had acquired prize biological patents from under the noses of other attorneys still puzzling over the invention's full potential. The commercial world had admired Sir Freddie's swift capture of Eikel; a company like Panrustica was only as good as its patents, and its patents were only as good as its patent strategist.

Sir Freddie got up from his desk and greeted him.

"You seem to have stirred things up a bit, Richard. Well done. How long will it take to analyze the seeds?"

"Twenty-four hours. At our labs in London."

"Before the Dandelion Crisis Group meeting at the embassy?"

"Yes, but we must assume Minister Williams and his team will be reporting on their own findings by then. Our results will simply be confirmation."

"Then what?"

"Then, Mr. Chairman, we will know precisely what Scott has achieved. But already there are complications. We were unable to recover the lab notebooks or DNA sequences. They were simply missing. Scott, as you have read, is also missing. So, I hear, is his Russian assistant. This could mean that Scott has his own plans for patenting the material. If that is the case, we have a serious problem."

"Can't the vice-chancellor help? You're seeing him at lunch, right?"

"Yes, in Oxford. He doesn't come on the payroll until next month and he'll be rather occupied until then. But don't worry, Mr. Chairman, Professor Scott is low-hanging fruit. He won't be a problem."

"Well, keep me informed, Richard. And good luck."

As Eikel turned to leave, Sir Freddie asked, "Oh, what about the girl, Lichfield, the researcher at the museum?"

"She did well. She'll be taking a few days off. Then, if all goes well, she'll be joining us."

"Excellent."

"Thank you, Mr. Chairman."

Sir Freddie went back to his desk and buzzed Mrs. Winchester for coffee and the papers. She had circled a story about a Greenpeace protest against Panrustica in Zurich yesterday. The banner said, "Panrustica Enslaves Us All." Sir Freddie took a sip of Mrs. Winchester's excellent coffee. "They're finally on the right track," he muttered to himself, smiling in satisfaction.

Six

In his tiny kitchen at Kew, Arthur Hemmings surveyed the dishes from last night's pesto and groaned. If he left for the ministry in half an hour, he would not be late for the meeting, as he so often was. There was time for tea, but the dishes would have to wait.

Like his Kew Gardens colleagues, Arthur lived in the former workers' cottages—compact, two-up-two-down, sandy-brick Georgian buildings, on the edge of Kew Green. In today's real estate market they would have been sold at the higher end, but there was never any chance of that.

For Arthur, the cottage was a perfect fit. A comfortable living room downstairs with a fireplace provided a retreat from people in authority, like ministers and vice-chancellors. French windows opened into a small, walled garden, which Arthur had turned into a patio. A rock garden at the back nourished his desire for rare plants. Arthur was particularly proud of his trilliums, prized cousins of the lily family, only found in the wild in North America and Japan. He also grew several species of alpine plants, a few of them quite rare. When he traveled, Eva Szilard, from the Kew library, always watched over the rock garden as though it were her own, sending him email bulletins about the health of individual plants, like updates on family members.

The kitchen stretched into a small dining room, spacious enough for Arthur's periodic cooking fevers to entertain Merrill Davies from Ag & Fish, or the occasional woman friend. Those evenings had been too occasional of late, Arthur noted to himself, as he dialed Eva Szilard's number to see if she would be at home if he had to go away on the Oxford museum case.

"Good morning, Arthur," she said breezily. Her voice was always the same, bright and attentive, whatever the hour. "The ministry sending you on another mission?"

"How do you know that?" Arthur asked, a slight irritation in his voice.

"Merrill has been on already. He wanted to know the last time you went to Russia."

"Did he, indeed, the cheeky sod, and why, pray, did he not ask me?"

"How would I know, Arthur? Perhaps he thought you might not have the date exactly in your mind so early in the morning, and I have it here in the file. You know how the new minister likes to be precise."

"I can tell you the date, precisely," said Arthur. "It was September 2001, the twelfth."

"So, he could have asked you," said Eva, laughing gently.

"And what else did my dear Welsh friend want to know . . . from my file . . . behind my back?"

"Don't be paranoid, Arthur," said Eva. "These are routine questions, always examined before you go on a mission. Merrill even asked whether your expenses were up to date."

"And what did you tell him?"

"I said they were."

"Are they?"

She snorted. "What do you think?"

"Eva, you are wonderful, the most—"

"Save it, Arthur, and let me know how the meeting goes. If they send you away, the answer is yes, I will be here to water the plants—and attend to anything else you might require." She hung up.

Arthur was peeved and didn't mind letting Eva know. She was not just the person who watered his rock plants when he was away, she was really at the center of his world, his anchor in his double life as a Kew researcher and an agent for OFS. As far as the other researchers in the herbarium knew, Eva was the librarian: that was her job description against her name on the wall on the third floor. And Arthur, officially, was a specialist in the origin of cultivated staples—food crops like wheat, corn, oats, barley, rice, potatoes, and cassava. But a year after joining Kew, he was approached by the director to work on classified botanical material—something he did not realize existed beyond the world of biopoisons. Officially, he was still paid by Ag & Fish, still at the minister's beck and call, but when the higher echelons needed him, he worked under instructions from Britain's secret services.

OFS had a proud heritage. It had engaged in agricultural espionage during Hitler's rise to power in the thirties. After the war, its agents had performed brilliantly, bringing home to Kew the larger share of the coveted German seed bank of cultivated plants. Arthur did not think of himself as a special agent, and certainly not as a spy. But as Agent Hemmings he had worked undercover in several parts of the world. The work had always been challenging and often risky, none of it possible, he would be the first to admit, without Eva.

She had come to England, aged two, from Budapest with her

parents as a refugee after the '56 uprising in Hungary. Her father was an economist who started working for the Foreign Office, where his assessments of the Eastern bloc economies were highly valued. Eva, who had always been interested in plants, became a part of the Kew staff. When Arthur joined OFS, Eva entered his secret world, becoming his personal researcher, fixer, factotum, and trusted friend, his first line of protection from the minister and other government officials.

Arthur took his large cup of tea up to the bathroom and, as he looked at himself in the shaving mirror, saw the face of a man much younger than his fifty-two years, a face only slightly flushed now after his run through Kew Gardens. The doctor had said with care and attention he would live to be a hundred. He still had good strong features, a firm neck, few facial lines, only a slight shading under the eyes, which were still a clear blue except, occasionally, on Sunday mornings. His hairline had not moved in twenty years and the hair itself, once blond, had turned the color of unburnished brass, longish, wavy, and respectably out of control. He had never spent more than twenty pounds on a haircut, and his favorite barber in Kew, a recently arrived Uzbek, did the job for fifteen pounds, wash included. Otherwise, he rarely brushed his hair with anything more durable than his fingers.

To a very few people very high up in the scientific branch of the British civil service, Arthur was regarded as one of the government's most valuable assets. The new minister of agriculture would have been churlish to resist this face of experience, adventure, and, yes, endurance, he thought, and chuckled as he lathered his chin. After the shave he wiped his face with a hot damp towel, poured the cold tea down the drain, and wondered what the new mission would entail—a trip to Oxford, at least, his old university, and in May, one of the best months of a botanist's year.

★   ★   ★

As had become his custom recently, Arthur took a small detour to the tube station, round the back wall of Kew, hoping to catch a glimpse of Sydney Rodgers tending her front garden. Sydney was an American, a New Englander who had gone to Harvard and become a rice and maize specialist. She had been working in the Kew labs for six months. She was slim and athletic, with a welcoming smile and thick brown hair, the kind expected in vitamin-enriched American women, and if she had been working in some other place, not at Kew, he would have tried to lure her back to his cottage long ago. He had taken Sydney to dinner several times, but always to a restaurant, keeping his distance. He had a rule against relationships with Kew staffers, and also with Americans, since his wife, Tracy Oliphant of Toledo, Ohio, had elected to abandon him and return home all those years ago. There were women in his life, often ones earnestly put forward by his friend Merrill, often from among the other patrons at the Green Dragon on Kew Green. They rarely lasted more than a few weeks.

Sydney sometimes joined him on his morning run around the gardens, an event that always quickened Arthur's pace, a workout that also reminded him, in the end, that she was impossibly younger—by twenty good years. He regarded her as a welcome, youthful addition to Kew's aging population and was looking forward to seeing her again. Merrill, to whom Arthur had confessed his attraction after a few pints one night, told him that having a fling with a junior researcher was probably healthy for him, even expected, at his age. Otherwise the staff would think he was "running out of puff," as Merrill had put it, mercilessly. Not having enough "puff" would reduce his chances of finding a mate in the recesses of the herbarium and possibly even affect his career, Merrill had warned.

"In any case, a person like you, in his fifties, who spends a lot of time with plants, needs some outside assistance—shall we say—to get the blood flowing," Merrill had counseled. "You need to kick-start that big heart before it seizes up on you, boyo." In his own clumsy way, Arthur knew, Merrill was showing that he cared.

As Arthur approached Sydney's cottage, she was in her front garden, on her knees, digging furiously into the soil with a trowel. She wore a loose blue denim overall that showed more than enough of her breasts to keep Arthur's heart from seizing up.

"Hi, Sydney, great day," he managed, as he paused at her garden fence. "Can't stop. Late for a bloody meeting at Ag & Fish. Dinner this week?"

"You said Wednesday."

"I did, that's right, Wednesday, right, wonderful." And he was gone.

Good specimen for early fifties, Sydney thought, sizing up Arthur's disappearing body as she might analyze a variety of her other living passions—*Oryza rufipogon,* the wild ancestor of rice, or *Zea mays,* the maize plant. Good genes, she calculated, as she refocused on her seedlings. Sturdy physique, magnificent head of hair, cute butt—must have been athletic when young.

As Arthur was waiting for the tube, his cell phone rang. It was Merrill in a panic.

"Better get a move on, boyo. Scott's disappearance is now official," he heard before a train arrived and Merrill's voice evaporated.

Seven

On that crisp May morning, a thin layer of fog hovered over the upper reaches of the River Thames, thickening obstinately on Cumnor Hill and obscuring the oaks and beeches of Whytham Wood. In a few minutes, Captain Wilford knew, the sun would burn off the fog and bake the riverbank, releasing the intoxicating odor of drying mud and reeds, the smell he had eagerly awaited since the end of last summer.

Captain Wilford was the keeper of Queen's Lock and had been controlling this short stretch of the Thames, a few miles north of Oxford, for almost twenty years. He considered it one of the best jobs in the land, after the service, of course. Easy, it was, and steady. A little lonely in the winter perhaps, but still a good job for a navy man, retired.

The short blast of a horn that morning set him in motion. It was the approved signal from boaters who needed him to open the river's next reach. He would remember that it was shortly before nine o'clock, late morning by his standards, when he began to turn the wheel. Sluice gates that had kept river traffic moving for more than a century slowly began to open, the chain links clanking rhythmically as each engaged its cog.

Inside the lock, a modest, two-berth cabin cruiser rocked gently. Not one of those fancy Thames River crafts, Captain Wilford noted with approval. Not a brashly decorated canal boat, trumpeting the new owner's gaudy tastes. This one was named *Daffodil,* a name he approved of, a proper boat's name to go with its sensible white plastic hull, the bright yellow awning over the cockpit and its very proper-looking owners, an elderly couple from London. They were steadying their boat properly, Wilford considered, as he thought about the tourists now preparing plans to summer on the Thames without the first lesson in boating etiquette or how to maneuver. Not these two; he smiled down at them as they prepared *Daffodil* for the rush of water into the damp concrete channel around them, lifting their boat to the next level.

The couple had positioned themselves expertly—one at the bow, one at the stern. *Daffodil* was the first boat through the lock that morning, and Captain Wilford continued turning the wheel effortlessly. He had logged more than two thousand craft of various sort coming up or down the river last year, and the number was increasing each year as more boaters discovered this peaceful route through the English countryside. Each time he filled or emptied the lock, raising or dropping the level of the water by five feet, he would make seventy turns of the wheel, thirty-five for each of the two sluice gates.

From her post on the bow, the wife was holding *Daffodil* by hanging onto the chains running down the lock wall. The husband, wearing his white boating cap with a gold anchor embroidered above the peak, was astern at the wheel holding onto the shore with a wooden boat hook. As the water cascaded into the lock, *Daffodil* started to rise slowly, too slowly, Captain Wilford noted with a slight frown. After all his years at the wheel, he knew the lock's rhythm like his own breathing, and just as he realized that he needed to stop the wheel and check the gears or the gates, the wife began to scream, a high-pitched scream that echoed with increasing urgency throughout the well of the lock.

"He's staring at me," she yelled. "Oh, God, he's looking straight at me." Her voice had risen to such a pitch that even the sheep in the nearby meadow stood still, alert to a human alarm.

The husband had rushed to the bow of *Daffodil,* where his wife had slumped in horror on the deck. His swift, unsteady movement had made the boat rock precipitously. Captain Wilford cupped his hands and shouted at the couple to keep calm. A lamb had probably fallen into the river, he figured, and clogged a sluice gate. It was not unknown at this time of the year.

As Captain Wilford moved toward the couple, readying an explanation of the stupidity of young sheep and the dangers of moving about in the boat when the gates were open, he turned to see the sluice from the couple's vantage point. He gasped. Not a lamb, not this time. Instead, caught in the gate were the head and shoulders of a man, one arm through the opening, the other apparently stuck on the other side. His face was blue, his mouth open, and his eyes bulging, clouded over like those of a long-dead fish. One eye was now staring straight at the wife and her fully rattled husband. The water was still moving through the sluice, but the opening was not big enough for the man's body.

"He's stuck," yelled the husband, loudly stating the obvious. Badly shaken, he was trying to be helpful.

"Hang on, hang on," cried Captain Wilford. "Stay where you are. I'm going to close the first gate." He rushed back to turn the wheel shut as fast as the old mechanism would allow. Then he came over to get a better look at the corpse trapped on his watch and in his own quiet stretch of the river.

In his years of naval service, Captain Wilford had seen men drown in terrible circumstances, but even he was sickened at the sight of such a grotesque figure wedged under the iron gates of the sluice, one arm extended as though crying out for the help that had not come. The water was rising and would soon obscure the body, but for a long moment, Captain Wilford and the husband simply stared at that ghastly face.

"Hold still, hold still," said Captain Wilford, bending down onto the lock side and putting his hand firmly and comfortingly onto the husband's shoulder. "In a minute the water will be high enough for you to come ashore. I'm going to call the police. You hang on to your wife."

A few minutes later, police sirens and a fire engine could be heard wailing across the meadow. Before Captain Wilford could get the couple safely in his keeper's cottage and fortified by a cup of strong tea, two frogmen with oxygen bottles had already started diving on each side of the lock gates, trying to free their lifeless quarry. The man was only partly dressed; his shirt was torn, stained in brown and green from the river. A leather belt still held his trousers in place. The shoes and socks, if there had been any, were gone, leaving feet that seemed strangely small and white compared to a body so discolored from its rough passage down the river.

By the time the firemen had laid the body out on the bank and covered it gently with a blanket, Fred Barton, of the *Oxford Chronicle,* had arrived. Barton prided himself on being first in the Oxford area, first on the scene, at the very least. As he began writing notes, a *Chronicle* photographer began taking pictures. The photographer asked for the blanket to be removed—for one more shot of the man's face.

"Enough," scowled a police officer, waving him away.

It was only a matter of time, the photographer and Barton knew, before television trucks and then the London media would be on the scene.

"One of those city hacks is bound to call him the Scholar Gypsy," Barton scowled.

"The what?" asked the photographer, cocking his head at his partner.

"Scholar Gypsy, matey, it's a poem by Matthew Arnold, written up there on Cumnor Hill, about an Oxford scholar who disappeared one day and went off to join the Gypsies. Then his ghost haunted the hills and meadows. One of my dear colleagues is bound to write that the scholar has been found."

"So you think this is the professor, then?" asked the photographer.

"'Course it is," said Fred without hesitation. "Strong circumstantial evidence, very strong. As good as Thoreau's trout in the milk." Fred was known for having definite opinions about everything on his patch, and for quoting writers that his colleagues had never heard of.

They watched the police string yellow tape around the lock and seal the body into a plastic bag. The body, clearly of an elderly man, had no wounds that Barton could see. He wondered how long it had been in the water, how far it might have traveled with the current downstream—questions that could not be answered now.

"When was that scholar poem written, then?"

"Middle of the nineteenth century," Barton answered the photographer as he wondered how to make his own allusion to Arnold's scholar for tomorrow's story.

Eight

On the way into London, Arthur's tube train was delayed at Acton Town for what seemed like an age to anyone in a hurry. With only two minutes to go until the meeting, Arthur, still tying his tie, jogged into the ministry, flashed his pass at the guard, and bounded up the marble staircase to the second floor, two steps at a time.

Each time he entered this cavernous building, Arthur quickly developed a high degree of irritability that required an enormous effort to overcome. He believed that the building should be uninhabited, a museum, a memorial to times past when the British Ministry of Agriculture was, in effect, the overlord of world agriculture. It should contain statues and portraits instead of people, and relics from the Golden Age of Botany in glass cases instead of desktop computers. That was an image he could stomach, even admire. But here there were real live workers, thousands of them, scurrying up and down dimly lit, carpeted corridors or sitting silently, unseen, at outdated,

overlarge consoles on giant, glass-topped mahogany desks. The
people he met in this building, even the youngsters and the recently
hired uniformed security staff, seemed to be instantly affected by its
past, adopting its grand demeanor in a way that was as inappropriate
to the modern world of the life sciences as brass microscopes on a
laboratory bench. Each time he climbed the staircase, he vowed never
to return, and if it had not been for the one shining exception to this
suffocating collection of humanity—namely, his funny and delight-
ful ally, Merrill Davies—he might have seriously considered keeping
his promise.

There were a few other bright spots, he had to admit. OFS meetings were always held in Room 208. At one end was a king-size paint-
ing of his botanical hero Sir Joseph Banks, longtime president of the
Royal Society and one of the greatest plant hunters of the eighteenth
century. Banks had been a moving force behind the development of
Kew Gardens; Arthur, when OFS meetings went beyond their use-
fulness, as they so often did, would respectfully touch his forelock to
the great botanist and think of the grander visions that had preoccu-
pied Banks in a different time. At the other end of the room was an
equally oversized portrait of John Tradescant the Younger, the royal
gardener to Charles I and another of botany's stars.

As Arthur entered Room 208 this morning, trying not to show
that he was breathing hard, Merrill Davies was already seated at the
middle of the conference table.

"Saw Sydney. Blood's up," Arthur whispered in Merrill's ear.

"You're going to need all the blood you can muster, boyo," Merrill whispered back. "The body of a man fitting Scott's description
was found drowned in the Thames near Oxford a few minutes ago.
Place is in turmoil. You would think we were fighting the Cold War
all over again."

"Drowned?" exclaimed Arthur.

"Like a rat," said Merrill, "stuck in the sluice gates of a bloody
lock."

Arthur moved swiftly to his appointed chair, which was always at the end of the table. Around the table sat a strange group of men, no women except for secretaries in this narrow club. Arthur recognized the regular MI5 man, the humorless Reggie Featherstone in his pin-stripe suit; his counterpart Collins from the CIA, also in a pinstripe; and J. B. Foster, a smart but anxious Yankee from upstate New York who represented the U.S. Department of Agriculture's Research Agency. There was the usual array of deskbound clerks from Ag & Fish and a few unfamiliar faces, most of them unseasonably pale from the long hours the new minister expected of his staff.

Williams strode in carrying the large red leather ministerial folder, which looked ominous even when empty, which it often was, according to Merrill. The minister preferred the spoken word. There were no formalities, which Arthur realized he missed somehow.

"Bring us up to date, Merrill," Williams barked, then leaned back in his chair to listen. The American diplomat, J. B. Foster, opened his yellow legal pad and began writing furiously.

Arthur sat back in his uncomfortable utility chair knowing that he would enjoy the next few minutes, at least. Merrill's lyrical Welsh voice could make a report of a drowning, or a murder, or whatever had befallen the unfortunate professor, seem pleasing to the ear. Even the old carbuncle from MI5 showed the barest of smiles at the prospect of a Merrill Davies summation.

The body of a man matching the physical description of Alastair Scott had just been recovered from the Thames, Merrill began. Apparently, he had drowned. There were no marks on his body. An autopsy was under way. Then Merrill recounted the break-in at the museum and Scott's work at Oxford. He had been at the university for more than thirty years and had led the botany department into the biotech age. He had invented the SCAM process, Merrill said, slowing his delivery for a scientific explanation. SCAM was a biochemical acronym for a biotech lab technique that made it easier for scientists to track alien genes when they were inserted into plants. Scott's invention had put Oxford, and Britain for that matter, on the front line of biotech research. The importance of the SCAM process to Oxford gave Scott unprecedented leverage with the university, and he had—uniquely—negotiated an agreement that he and he alone would own his intellectual property. Since those days—ten years ago—Scott had worked on several genetically modified food plants—maize and soybeans. Recently his laboratory had produced a GM tomato that lasted longer on the shelf. It tasted like cardboard and was never marketed to the general public.

Merrill paused and Arthur, guessing what was coming next, admired his friend's theatrical timing.

"Professor Scott's preoccupation for the last several years had been *apomixis,* by which a few plants indulge in," and Merrill paused again, *"virgin birth."*

Faces around the table finally reacted—a frown, a few grins, even a low laugh from the end of the room. Featherstone of MI5 raised his index finger and simply said, "Explain."

"Hemmings is science," barked Williams.

There was one more thing, Merrill continued. On the same day that Professor Scott went missing, a researcher in his laboratory, a young Russian woman from the St. Petersburg Botanical Garden, had also disappeared. Her name was Tanya Petrovskaya. She also had not been home since Friday, the last day anyone saw Scott.

Merrill sat back, his job done. Arthur wanted to applaud, but he restrained himself, instead giving Merrill a quick, approving smile.

Around the table, the older members stirred at the mention of Russia. Even the MI5 and the CIA representatives drew out their notebooks.

Minister Williams then turned to Arthur.

"As short as possible, Hemmings," the minister barked. "We have a press conference at eleven."

"Essentially, apomixis is, as Merrill says, virgin birth," Arthur began, stressing the words *virgin* and *birth,* as Merrill had done. "The word *apomixis* is from the Greek *apo,* with the short *a,* meaning 'without,' and *mixis,* meaning 'mingling.' In plants capable of apo-mixis, the egg, or the ovule, produces the seed on its own, without any help from the male pollen. The result is a clone of the mother plant. There are three different forms of this asexual reproduction—diplospory, apospory, and adventitious embryogenesis."

"Stop," yelled Williams. "No one has a clue what you're talking about. Tell them why this is so bloody important—in English, Mr. Hemmings."

"Certainly, Minister," said Arthur, winking at Merrill.

"Most plants, including the major crop plants, reproduce sexu-ally, like humans; the male part, the pollen, fertilizes the egg, or ovule, to produce the seed. This means that each new generation can be slightly different from its parents, just as in human repro-duction. It's a nightmare for plant breeders who dream of fixing the most desirable combination of genes in their prize varieties of staple crops—wheat, corn, and rice—year after year. Apomixis is their an-swer, or would be. Plants that produce seed asexually produce clones of themselves and retain their best characteristics.

"You've all heard of the success of hybrid maize and its tremen-dous yields. The problem is that the extraordinary 'hybrid vigor'—the unusually high yield—only lasts for one planting because the genes are jumbled up again during sexual production of the seed. If maize were apomictic, or asexual, the hybrid vigor would be perpetuated."

"I can just about follow that," said Williams.

"The other problem," Arthur continued, "is that apomixis occurs in only about ten percent of the four hundred families of flowering plants, including several wildflowers like dandelions, but in only a handful of food plants—blackberries, mangos, and lemons. Staples—corn, wheat, rice, and barley—still require the egg to be fertilized by the pollen to produce the seed. Breeders have been searching for de-cades for the supergene that controls apomixis in plants that clone themselves, but so far they haven't found it."

Arthur paused, looking at Merrill, who nodded his approval.

"There is a furious international scientific race with plant breeders from America, Britain, Russia, Australia, India—and probably China—all trying to identify this supergene so they can patent it. Billions of dollars are at stake.

"If breeders can make crop plants that clone themselves, agriculture can move into new areas of production, not simply food but biofuels, medicines, plastics, and other key raw materials, which are cheaper to produce in a maize plant that clones itself than in a factory."

The members mumbled to each other and then fell silent. The minister folded his arms to signal that Arthur's time was up. Featherstone of MI5 raised his index finger again.

"How close was Scott?"

"Don't know," said Arthur, "without examining his lab. Britain and the United States are ahead of the others, as far as we can find out, but the Russians might not be far behind and the Chinese are advancing rapidly. Two prominent Russian researchers who left after the fall of communism worked for six months in the West, one in America and the other, the missing Russian researcher mentioned by Merrill, with Professor Scott."

"OK, OK, we all get it," interrupted Williams. "There's a race—which we need to win, or at least get a place at the table. But what are we to tell the media about Scott's research? Seeds were stolen. Were they important seeds, basic to his research, *Western* research?"

"We simply don't know," said Arthur. "Until we do, perhaps you could talk about the professor's tomato research. It's already quite well known by the science correspondents—and even appreciated by a few."

Williams shook his head.

"The media dogs will want more than a bloody tomato for lunch," he snarled, rolling his wedding ring around his finger, a gesture Merrill had quickly learned was his signal to end the meeting. Arthur knew it too.

"I was going to say, Minister, that I think we should mention Scott's apomixis research. It's bound to come out. We don't have to pose it as a secret race where Britain leads America or whatever—just something theoretical that would be nice if it happened sometime in the future, say twenty years from now. We should probably also mention his Russian researcher. Otherwise it will look like a cover-up."

Williams had heard enough. The meeting was over.

"Thank you, Hemmings. Davies and I are going next door to draft a statement. Make yourself available, please, for the next fifteen minutes."

Arthur had apparently passed muster. Another day, he told himself, when he had managed to hold on to the best job in the civil service. He went downstairs to the library and flicked through the latest farming journals, glad to be out of the meeting, away from the condescending gaze of MI5, who tended to dismiss OFS as a soft appendage barely worth acknowledgment. Even Scotland Yard sniffed at OFS, referring to them as the hanging fern boys. He didn't care. Merrill's urgency always made him feel wanted. He only hoped that this mission would not keep him from enjoying the English summer.

Suddenly Merrill's voice was booming through the library.

"Arthur, where the hell are you?"

"Here in the African section."

Merrill was red-faced and agitated.

"Williams says you're to go to Oxford immediately," Merrill now whispered hoarsely, his library manners barely intact.

"*Alors,*" Arthur said with a smile, gathering his satchel, "*peut-être, mon vieux, la guerre froide* is not so *finie* after all."

"Just go to Oxford," Merrill huffed, "and bloody call when you get there."

Nine

Arthur Hemmings arrived at Oxford by the fast train from London a few minutes after midday. Whenever he came through this premier stop on the Midlands line, he was reminded, briefly but painfully, of the comings and goings of his youth, and even now, his stomach tightened at the earliest and most persistent memories. At the beginning of every school term, from the age of eight onwards, his mother would deposit him on platform 3 with his large brown suitcase, so large he could hardly lift it. From there, he would catch the branch line train to Swanton, which was the stop before Bletchley. At Marsh Gibbon and Poundon, twenty minutes down the track, his school friend Acton would join him, with his own large suitcase. At Swanton, they would lug their belongings across a meadow to Tordell School for Boys, which was run with Spartan orderliness by the Rev. Kevin Farrell and his wife, Maureen. In those days, this ritual was called character-forming, and despite the unhappiness it caused a small boy, Arthur had always told himself that his dominant gene for independence had been well nurtured by such an experience.

There had been jollier times, of course. During his Oxford student days, the train had taken them to London for expeditions to the West End, drunken evenings in pubs, sessions at jazz clubs, and experimental love with the easy girls of Soho. By then, Arthur's carefully molded British character, adventurous, resourceful, and robust, was well formed.

Today, at the start of another mission for Ag & Fish, he felt a little older but not that much older, frankly. For a civil servant he had lived an unusually fast, exciting life that had kept him youthful and had stoked an irrepressible curiosity, first encouraged, he admitted, by the passionate educators at the Rev. Farrell's disciplined establishment. Forty years later, that same curiosity was about to set him on one of the strangest paths he had taken in all his time at the Office of Food Security.

Arthur decided that a bicycle would suit his purposes admirably in Oxford, where parking a car had become impossible for all but the rich or well connected. At the station's bicycle rental office he selected a gleaming black Ridgeback upright ten-speed and set off at an easy clip for Balliol College, where he planned to drop in on the vice-chancellor, Simon Goodhart. He was instantly pleased with his choice of transport, perfect on a day like this, a golden day, filled with the promise of summer. Arthur liked to pedal fast, but speed was not as easily attained in Oxford as it used to be in his day, with thousands more students and so many more traffic lights. At Balliol, he locked his bicycle into the rack outside the college beside a row of students' older models.

He had deliberately not given the vice-chancellor warning of his arrival. The descriptions of Professor Goodhart—clever, efficient, pompous, lofty, an establishment man at ease with his important office—suggested to Arthur that dropping by, rather than making an appointment in these stressful times, was likely to be more profitable. In the anteroom of Professor Goodhart's rooms, Arthur found his secretary, Ms. Bridgland, head down, madly shuffling papers on her desk and punching numbers into the telephone pad.

"This is the vice-chancellor's office, could I speak to Inspector Davenport, please, it's extremely urgent?" she said, brushing a wisp of brown hair from her face. Either she failed to realize that Arthur was there or maybe, he thought, she was deliberately ignoring him.

The person at the other end of the line apparently told her that Inspector Davenport was not available.

"Kindly leave a message to say that the vice-chancellor needs to speak to him urgently, extremely urgently," she said, a full panic in her voice. Then she put the phone down, looked across the room, and, with a start, saw Arthur.

"What can I do for you?" she demanded, in an official, decidedly unfriendly voice.

Arthur said he had come from the ministry, apologized for not calling ahead, and wondered if Professor Goodhart could spare a few moments.

"Oh, yes, the ministry . . . ," Ms. Bridgland said, moving swiftly to block access to the vice-chancellor's door. "The professor is extremely busy, as you can imagine, Mr. Hemmings, and he has an important luncheon, but I'll ask him . . . if you can wait here, please." She went into Goodhart's room, closing the door behind her.

Arthur moved quickly to her desk, where he had spotted an appointments diary. He saw that the vice-chancellor's lunch was at 1:15 p.m.—in half an hour—at the Randolph Hotel, royal suite, with Richard Eikel. The only Richard Eikel that Arthur knew was the legendary American biotech patent attorney, formerly of Transgene, now employed by Panrustica. He had never met Eikel, but with Scott dead and the research deal with Panrustica apparently going through, Eikel and the vice-chancellor would have a lot to talk about, he imagined, maybe even to celebrate. Ms. Bridgland reemerged, this time quite composed.

"The vice-chancellor will see you," she announced in a voice now softer and far more accommodating.

The vice-chancellor was sitting at his desk and rose to shake Arthur's hand, an unexpectedly timid handshake for a man supposed to be on top of things, Arthur noted. He apologized again for not making an appointment, saying that everyone at the ministry had been in a bit of a rush this morning.

"Yes, yes," said Goodhart. "Rushed, yes, very rushed, here, especially this morning."

Arthur explained that he was a Kew Gardens researcher and had come to Oxford, for the ministry, to assess the scientific impact, such as it might be, of the theft of the seeds from the museum. He was seeking the vice-chancellor's permission to visit the Botany School lab and the Lower Witton Experimental Farm.

"Of course, of course, no problem whatsoever," said Goodhart. "Please feel free to visit whichever university facility you wish. I'd be glad if you would keep me informed of the results of your inquiries. I will be making my own report to the minister, of course."

"Anyone in particular I should speak with at the museum?" asked Arthur.

"A Ms. Lichfield, er, Karen Lichfield, one of Scott's researchers, is receiving calls," said Goodhart. "I don't know her personally, but she seems to be efficient and willing. I told her, and all the staff, not to speak with anyone, but she can speak with you, of course."

Obviously, the vice-chancellor was not in a talkative mood, and knowing about his luncheon engagement, Arthur imagined that any second the man would ask him to leave, so he fired a few quick questions.

"The body is definitely Scott's, in your view?"

"Oh, yes, it seems so, I'm afraid," said Goodhart, without elaboration. "The autopsy will take a while, of course."

"Any clues as to what happened?" Arthur asked.

"The police have no clues at the moment, no," said Goodhart.

"Is Inspector Davenport in charge of the police inquiry?" Arthur asked.

"Yes, yes, he is in charge," replied the vice-chancellor, looking surprised at the mention of Davenport's name. "You know him?'

"No, actually, I don't, I just heard your secretary trying to get through to him."

"Oh, yes, of course," said Goodhart.

"The seeds, Vice-chancellor, do we know which seeds were taken—ones from Russia, perhaps?"

"Yes, er, no . . . ," stammered Goodhart. "We really won't know until the staff has had a chance to take an inventory. But it's possible they were seeds from Russia, yes."

"And Tanya Petrovskaya, any news of her?"

"Ah, you know about her, of course. No, no news of her at all. Strange business. Can't believe it, really. But there it is."

Arthur realized he had already overstayed his welcome.

"Anyone else in town I should see while I'm here? Am I likely to bump into any corporate visitors, wondering what's happened to the apomixis research?" he asked, hoping for a last bite.

"No, I don't know of any," replied Goodhart, "but if I think of anyone, I'll get in touch, of course." He paused. "You're staying at the Randolph?"

"Hardly, on a civil servant's expenses," Arthur said, giving a little chuckle. "No, I always stay at the Rose and Crown, off Longwall."

"Nice place, very convenient," said Goodhart, appearing relieved.

"But I thought I might lunch at the Randolph; someone told me the food has got much better," Arthur added, not giving up.

"Oh, I wouldn't if I were you," snapped Goodhart. "Whoever

told you that about the Randolph's food was mistaken. The food is as dull as it ever was. I advise the Rose and Crown for lunch, jolly good salads, good value. And now I really must press on, Mr. Hemmings, if you'll excuse me."

The vice-chancellor moved from behind his desk for the first time and gently but firmly led Arthur to the door.

"I hope you have a successful day, and please tell the minister we are coping as best we can—so far."

In the anteroom, Ms. Bridgland was no longer at her desk. As he walked out of the college, across the quad, Arthur wondered why Professor Goodhart had lied about his lunch with Richard Eikel at the Randolph. It was awkward, coming on the day Scott's body had been found, but it would all come out in the end. The vice-chancellor was clearly in a flap and not coping very well.

Instead of unlocking his bike and riding to his hotel, Arthur walked round the corner to the Randolph, but he didn't go inside. He crossed the road and climbed the steps of the Ashmolean, where he could mingle with the lunchtime visitors and watch the front of the hotel. At 1:15 precisely, the vice-chancellor walked into the lobby. Arthur waited a minute, crossed the road, and went into the hotel. He picked up the house phone and asked for Richard Eikel. An American male voice answered. "Eikel."

Arthur asked to speak to the vice-chancellor. Eikel said that Professor Goodhart was on his way up; he could wait or call back in a few minutes.

Arthur hung up. He walked back to Balliol, unlocked his bike, and rode the couple of hundred yards to the Rose and Crown.

Ten

Richard Eikel greeted Professor Goodhart on the threshold of the Randolph's royal suite with a rare smile.

"Good to see you again, Simon," Eikel said, letting the vice-chancellor know that they were now on first-name terms in their new relationship.

"I'm just enchanted with these rooms," Eikel said, showing off the suite, the most expensive set of hotel rooms in Oxford. "Of course, you've been here many times."

Actually, Professor Goodhart had not been in the royal suite since it had been spruced up to mark the three-hundredth anniversary of Charles II's visit to Oxford following the restoration of the monarchy. Normally, Goodhart would have bluffed an answer in keeping with his status; after all, a vice-chancellor would be expected to be a regular visitor to the suite, greeting VIPs, but Richard Eikel was one of those men to whom telling a lie, even a small one, seemed unwise.

It was not just his commanding height—he was a good four inches taller than the vice-chancellor—it was his small black eyes and the prosecutorial stare, guaranteed to make anyone feel vulnerable and instantly compliant.

"I suppose I should have been here, given the number of important people I know who have stayed here, but I simply haven't," Goodhart admitted.

"Well, Simon, it's not the Peninsula in Hong Kong or the Bristol in Paris, both of which grand institutions you will be getting to know soon enough as a board member of Panrustica. Let me show you around."

The vice-chancellor respectfully followed Eikel as the American strolled through the suite, peering at the cracked oil paintings, the small library, a few of the books having apparently weathered several real readers, and pausing appreciatively at the well-stocked cocktail bar in the lounge.

"A drink before lunch?"

"I don't as a rule."

"Nor do I, but we have something to celebrate, don't we? I have champagne on ice," Eikel offered.

"That would be most acceptable," said Goodhart, beginning to feel slightly uncomfortable, a feeling of already being manipulated by this clever attorney.

"What I really like is the piano," said Eikel, running a long pianist's finger across the shiny black top of the baby grand squeezed into the bay window. "Do you play?"

"A little," said Goodhart, "like every English schoolchild of my generation and class, middle class."

"You know, Simon, when all this is over and I have reached that place where I can look back and celebrate Panrustica's new role as the leader of a world agricultural revolution, maybe I'll learn the piano. In my life so far, there has been so little time for extras, even family, not that there's much family anymore."

He paused, letting the vice-chancellor know he was about to impart a confidence.

"My father came to America from Germany as a child after the war and grew up in New Orleans, where he met my mother in high school. They both went into real estate. Together, they spent every dime they earned to boost my status by sending me first to Groton, then Harvard. I grew up with privileged rich kids. They patronized me, but I beat the best of them in class as well as on the squash and tennis courts."

He looked at Goodhart and smiled. "What about you? Private schools and Oxford, I take it."

"Yes, my father was a country solicitor, just north of here, not rich, but comfortable. I took the obvious route, to Oxford and one of the most popular subjects, history."

Eikel suggested they move into the small dining room, where lunch had been laid, two plates of cold salmon and salad, a small pot each of black caviar, and a bottle of champagne in an ice bucket.

"Do sit down, Simon," Eikel insisted, offering him one of two antique chairs at the table, chairs for people much shorter than Eikel.

"To your appointment to the board," Eikel said, raising his filled glass.

Goodhart touched Eikel's glass with his own and took a long draft.

"You have brought the contract?"

Goodhart reached into the inside breast pocket of his suit jacket, took out the papers Eikel had sent him, and handed them over.

"Duly signed," he said.

"Excellent. Then in that case we can spend this hour on other matters. I have been looking forward to this meeting. It's a chance to get to know each other better. Tell me, Simon, how do you feel, a distinguished historian like yourself about to join a multinational life science company? Are you prepared, Simon?"

"Historian of science," Goodhart said, emphasizing the word

science. "Never been so ready to leave Oxford, frankly, Richard. I've needed a change for a long time. I'm bored. My colleagues here die early, in their minds, I mean."

"And speaking of such matters," said Eikel, balancing a lump of caviar on a piece of black bread, "I'm sorry to hear about your Professor Scott. Are we to assume that he took his own life?"

"I really don't know. He was under a lot of strain, but he was also on the verge of a great discovery. It's hard for me to think that he would suddenly decide to abandon his research."

Goodhart told him all he knew—about the break-in, about the stolen seeds, important seeds from Russia, apparently—and asserted confidently that Scott's body would be officially identified later that afternoon.

"More than that, I don't know. Most unfortunate events, most awkward, for everyone," said Goodhart, wondering whether Scott's death would affect Panrustica's offer of research dollars to the School of Botany.

Eikel wiped his mouth with a napkin and pushed the salmon plate gently to one side, signaling that he had already had enough to eat and more important matters should now be considered.

"I think Scott's death should have no effect on our offer," Eikel said emphatically.

"Of course, between us," Eikel continued, lowering his voice, "you could say this has come at a propitious moment for our proposal to fund Oxford science research. I would not want anything to slow us down. You don't know of anything like that, do you, Simon?"

Goodhart said he did not—except that the identity, and the motive, of the museum thieves was still a mystery. There was also the question of a patent for Scott's work.

"You know, of course, that Scott intended to patent his research in such a way that it would be available to everyone, through a protected commons, I think they call it, but you'll know more about that than I do."

"Yes, I know about that, and that is what concerns me about the theft of the seeds. If Scott had found the supergene for apomixis, and if he planned to patent it himself, he would need the seeds to file a patent. Do we know which seeds were taken?"

"I only know what the police have told me. According to a researcher at the botany lab, the seeds taken were Russian seeds. They were coded SP for St. Petersburg and NS for Novosibirsk. I don't know if they were important."

"Oh, I think you can be sure they were important," Eikel said. "One day, I'll tell you how I know." Then he dropped the topic and quickly moved on.

"Let's talk about the future," said Eikel, suggesting they move to the more comfortable chairs even though Goodhart had barely taken a mouthful of lunch. Eikel picked up the bottle of champagne and a bottle of Perrier as Goodhart followed him into the lounge. Eikel sat back in his chair and took a cigar out of a box on the coffee table.

"You don't touch them, I remember," said Eikel, as he lit the cigar with his gold Dunhill.

"No, thanks," said Goodhart, trying not to show his discomfort as Eikel blew out a mouthful.

"I may not have properly explained how much identifying the genes of apomixis has become part of my life, my secret challenge," Eikel began, topping up Goodhart's glass but not his own.

"It has been in my sights since I engineered the merger between British Imperial Chemicals and Transgene to form Panrustica. You see, Simon, for a long time I have understood the full potential of apomixis, far better than my colleagues, much better than Sir Freddie or even the hard-nosed politicians in the Bush administration.

"Controlling research about this strange natural phenomenon has become an obsession of mine. It's my Manhattan Project, if you like.

"I have employed all my skills and resources as a patent lawyer to research the science and assess the geopolitical implications. I have used my Harvard credentials to interview America's leading plant geneticists. The CIA has given me classified briefings on the state of foreign research into apomixis, not only in Russia but also in China. What I have learned, Simon, has merely fed my obsession."

Goodhart liked what he was hearing: he appreciated a man with an obsession. Eikel was turning him into a confidant.

"Politicians think it's a race with the Russians, against the rebirth of Russian agriculture," continued Eikel. "They see their task as preventing the Kremlin from getting the secret and using it to spread their influence, and reap new profits, in Asia and Africa. But they haven't paid enough attention to China."

As he poured himself a Perrier and dropped in a slice of lemon, Eikel recited statistics about Chinese agriculture that he had learned by heart, primarily for his own satisfaction, but also to impress people like Goodhart.

"Simon, just think about this. To keep pace with increased population, Asia needs to more than double its cereal production over the next fifty years—and do it on the same land or on land less arable than that currently in production. Breeding hybrid seeds is one answer, a reality that has already been demonstrated by the use of hybrid rice in China. In the eighties, China increased its rice production by twenty-two percent while actually decreasing the area planted by more than five million acres. New hybrid lines could increase production by another thirty to fifty percent—but developing these new varieties could be achieved with apomictic plants in half the time and at greatly reduced cost.

"For me, Simon, apomixis has never been some dusty discovery in an unknown greenhouse, like it has been to some people, including our chairman, Sir Freddie. Its control through a patent would be worth billions of dollars. Billions, annually, Simon. You only have to think of biopharming, growing drugs in genetically modified corn. I pioneered this technique at Transgene—despite green protests—and we are continuing the program at Panrustica. It's cheaper than producing drugs in factories. And it would be vastly cheaper with apo-mixis. Essential drugs needed by Africans could be supplied at a cost they could afford."

As Goodhart listened to Eikel's recitation, he began to picture himself making a similar speech on the company's behalf in distant places where his restricted life had never taken him, Nairobi, Delhi, Beijing, and Singapore. But his speech would be better, ringing with historical references, more rounded than this American lawyer's. The more Eikel talked, the more Goodhart warmed to the prospect of working for Panrustica. Even Eikel's cigar seemed less irritating.

"I have elaborate plans to achieve this goal," Eikel continued. "Panrustica has already secured exclusive rights to the U.S. Agriculture Department's research on apomixis. In Britain, as you know, we have the support of the government and especially Williams, the new minister of agriculture."

He paused, staring at Goodhart.

"And now, Simon, I am going to tell you something that must not go beyond this royal suite.

"One of Scott's researchers, a Karen Lichfield, has come to the notice of our CIA. She's brilliant. Does great work. You may know she works on plant viruses and fungi, toxins that can be fatal to humans at extremely low doses, a hundredth of a milligram per kilogram of bodyweight. Karen is way ahead of our researchers because Scott had a line into the Russian research and material through Tanya Petrovskaya."

"I didn't know," said Goodhart.

"The CIA is worried that terrorists will get hold of these toxins and viruses and use them to disrupt food supplies and spread epidemics. You may not have heard of black Sigatoka, an airborne fungus that devastates banana trees. Or *Striga,* a parasitic weed found in Africa. More than a hundred million Africans lose some or all of their crops to *Striga.* This parasite inserts a sort of underground hypodermic needle into the roots of corn and sorghum, sucking off water and nutrients and killing the plant.

"In her work, Karen has identified new strains of these fungi and viruses and is looking for ways of making crop plants resistant to them. Breeding crop plants resistant to such plagues would be much quicker, and cheaper, once the apomictic supergene has been identified. Defensive traits can be bred in new varieties in a year or two, instead of twelve, and fixed for all future generations."

"What are you saying exactly, Richard, from the company's point of view?"

"The CIA is willing to pay a lot of money for this research. It's a black project, from their secret budget. They would like to buy Ms. Lichfield's research, and her expertise, but of course, she will never go along with that, at least not directly. Nor would any self-respecting researcher. But Panrustica can hire her and then the company can make an arrangement with the agency. I met her at a fungal toxin conference in Geneva and offered her a job in Panrustica's R & D—at a huge salary, for her—but still she wasn't interested, at least not then. Loyalty to Scott, or something. The connection is not completely dead. She has been very useful in other ways, though, keeping us abreast of the apomixis research. With Scott's death, she might be ready to change her mind. She is coming to see me this afternoon, when I will repeat the offer. Make it more attractive. I don't know whether she will accept. Simon, as your first act for the company, I need you to talk to her, make the case. Delicately, of course. You know what I mean."

"Of course," said Goodhart, wondering how he could possibly be more persuasive than this slick attorney. "I spoke with her only yesterday. I have a good excuse to bring her into my office for a chat, about the Scott business."

"Excellent," said Eikel, rising out of his chair.

Goodhart understood that Eikel had declared the lunch was over.

"Of course, we'll meet again very soon. And, Simon, I'm delighted to have you in the company. Delighted."

As Eikel walked Goodhart to the elevator, the vice-chancellor said, "There is one thing I didn't mention that might interest you. Williams, the new minister, has sent down his own agent to investigate the Scott case, Arthur Hemmings, from Kew Gardens. He is said to be good, very good. He is staying at the Rose and Crown, off Longwall."

"That's good information," said Eikel, as he ushered the vice-chancellor into the elevator. "Very good information. I look forward to meeting Mr. Hemmings."

Eleven

For Arthur, the Rose and Crown ranked as the best bed-and-breakfast he had found anywhere, inexpensive, comfortable, and central. The inn had only four bedrooms carved out of an Elizabethan black-beamed, whitewashed house with sloping floors and slanting windows. It was well hidden from the tourists at the end of a cobbled passage off Longwall Street—no sign outside. To Arthur, avoiding tourists was a bigger attraction than a bath and toilet en suite. He also acknowledged that staying there was a pleasant diversion, allowing him to recall his undergraduate days, since the rooms felt remarkably like his own small digs as a student, over a quarter of a century ago.

After checking into his favorite room, overlooking the passage where he could keep an eye on his bike padlocked to the lamppost, Arthur set off for the Oxford museum on the shortest route, from Parks Road, past Wadham College and the gardens of St. John's. Suddenly there it was, the great Venetian Gothic stone edifice Tennyson once described as "perfectly indecent," a judgment Arthur had taken to mean something exciting and seductive, like a new mistress. Even now, he thought of the building as pleasantly decadent with its grand façade and glass roof.

Several cars were parked in the little lot between the museum and the science library. He stored his bike in the rack, snapped the padlock around the front wheel, and headed for the main entrance, where a uniformed policeman stood guard. Arthur had two official passes, one from Kew Gardens and the other from the ministry. He flashed the one from Ag & Fish and the policeman made way.

Inside the museum, statues of Galileo, Newton, and Darwin stood on marble piers, surrounded by skeletons of dinosaurs, rows of glass cabinets displaying fossils, stuffed birds, butterflies, and giant moths. As a student Arthur had spent many pleasant hours poring over the exhibits and reading in the library. Now he was surprised at the excessive use of yellow police tape. It zigzagged across the hall, and was even wrapped around the slender cast-iron columns supporting the glass roof. Yellow chalk marked the path of the intruders across the main hall, and more tape barred the way to the laboratory upstairs.

At the lab, a second policeman looked at his pass and then let him through.

"You won't mind if I accompany you, sir, just orders," said the constable, respectfully.

"Not at all," said Arthur. "Let me know if I'm touching something I shouldn't."

"Don't worry, sir, the print boys have done their work. Only place off limits is the poison lab behind the door with the red light on, sir."

"How did they break in?" Arthur asked, as he eyed the sign warning about deadly plant toxins.

"Well, as I understand it, sir, the service door downstairs was open and so was this big old door. Inside job is what they're saying, sir, but I'm sure you know that."

"Yes, so I heard."

The constable showed Arthur Professor Scott's office, the broken pane of glass in the door and the safe that had contained the stolen seeds. The seeds had been in white bags, the constable said, like the bags in the mahogany filing cabinets. He pulled out a drawer to show Arthur. Each drawer was marked with a coded label. Standard practice in botany labs, Arthur noted. The stolen seeds had been coded with the letters NS and SP, the constable said.

"For Russian cities, so they say, sir," volunteered the constable, but he did not attempt to explain further.

Nothing else seemed to be out of place inside the lab. Of course, appearances could be deceptive and no more so probably than in an Oxford professor's lair.

"Some materials—the desktop—were taken for analysis, I assume," said Arthur, more for want of something to say to the constable than expecting an answer.

"Couldn't say, sir," said the constable. "This is my first time on duty."

"Did Professor Scott have another office?"

"Couldn't say, sir, sorry."

"No other staff here? The vice-chancellor mentioned a Dr. Lichfield?"

"Yes, sir, she's in the biohazard lab right now. Experiments can't wait, apparently. Frankly, I'd rather not know about such things. If you'd like to speak to her, we can call her on the intercom."

"If you wouldn't mind, Constable."

The policeman moved to the intercom outside the poison lab. He pressed the button and a woman's voice answered promptly.

"Lichfield."

"It's the constable here, miss. A Mr. Hemmings to see you from the ministry."

"I'll be right out, Constable."

The red light above the lab door went out and Karen Lichfield emerged in her white lab coat, a petite, earnest-looking woman in her late twenties or early thirties, Arthur judged, with straight dark hair pulled back to the nape of her neck. Her face, a little pale for the time of year, was camouflaged by a pair of bold tortoiseshell glasses with thick lenses. He guessed she had probably spent too many youthful hours looking through a microscope.

Arthur introduced himself and offered his hand, which she shook awkwardly with her left hand. On the back of her right hand he noticed two Band-Aids.

"Nothing serious, I hope," Arthur said, pointing to the bandage.

"No, no, just a piece of broken glass," she said, a sudden flush on her face.

"You ought to see a doctor with all these poisons around, just in case," advised Arthur.

"Thank you, but it's fine, really," she insisted.

She offered him a stool by a lab bench, rather reluctantly, Arthur felt. She seemed overly nervous and he sensed that his time with her would be short, like his time with the vice-chancellor. He gave his condolences for Professor Scott, and at the mention of his name, she turned her gaze away, in a deliberate gesture apparently intended to make him aware how upset she was. She sat on the edge of a stool beside him and asked the policeman if he could wait outside while they had a chat. When the constable had gone, she let out a long sigh.

"The professor was a lovely man," she said, quietly. "Can't believe it, really—that he finally gave up."

"You think he committed suicide?"

"Well, they said that there were no marks on his body."

"But when you say 'gave up,' what do you mean?" asked Arthur. She looked away again.

"Everyone knew about the pressure from the university to accept corporate funds. He told us himself. He was so against it. You could see it was wearing him down because he seemed to be losing ground every day. We were terribly short of funds and in need of new equipment—new microscopes, especially. Look around, Mr. Hemmings," she said, pointing to the laboratory's odd collection of instruments. Then she straightened herself, as if preparing for an important announcement.

"If you want to know the truth, I am surprised he lasted this long, though don't say I said so."

Arthur nodded his agreement. She seemed in need of his reassurance.

"Of course, I don't mean I thought he was going to kill himself, but I thought he might resign. It would have been easier, that way . . . and probably would have ended what they were doing to him."

"Doing to him?"

"The threats."

"What threats?"

She looked at him for a moment as though he ought to have known what she meant.

"Oh, Mr. Hemmings, you mustn't get me started," she said finally, shaking her head and looking down at the floor, as if the burden of her knowledge was almost too much to bear. "You know I'm not really supposed to be saying anything to anybody without the vice-chancellor's permission."

Then she stared down at her hands. The left one was clasped tightly, too tightly, around the hem of her lab coat. The right one, with the bandage, was resting on the coat.

Arthur nodded again and quickly changed the subject, asking about her work and the other researchers.

There were a dozen in the lab, she said, and her own specialty was mycotoxins, fungus toxins. Arthur knew about fungus-produced toxins on food crops and the deadly epidemics they had caused in the Middle Ages.

"You mean trichothecenes from *Fusarium*, like T2," he said, using the chemical shorthand for the most toxic poison of the group.

"Yes, exactly," said Karen. "There was a well-documented outbreak in the Soviet Union at the end of World War Two when thousands died. Recently, the Russians discovered a new mutant fungus that produces a more potent toxin. They named it T3. The Russians are probably the world's leading experts. We're trying to breed wheat resistant to the fungus."

Arthur knew about T2, perhaps more than she did. As part of his official job at Kew, he had discussed this group of toxins with J. B. Foster, the agronomist at the American embassy, because the Americans had accused the Soviets of using it as a chemical warfare agent in Southeast Asia. He knew the Americans were worried about terrorists using the new mutant, T3.

"Your work is presumably classified, given the military application, not to mention the terrorist threat," Arthur ventured, wondering if she had a security clearance.

"No, what I do is not classified," she said, quite emphatically. "There is a classified application of *Fusarium* toxin, of course, but I don't have anything to do with the military, Mr. Hemmings. And I don't want to, either."

Arthur wondered aloud whether she had come across J. B. Foster, from the American embassy. "He's in the embassy's agriculture section and knows a lot about mycotoxins, T2 in particular."

She had met J. B. Foster when he came down to see Professor Scott a few weeks ago.

"He wanted to know all about our apomixis research but Scott refused to talk to him. The professor could be very stubborn. I was in the lab, so we had a chat, yes—about trichothecenes—and also about our work on other plant toxins, such as abrin from *Abrus precatorius* and the toxin from aconite. I'm sure you know more than I do about them, Mr. Hemmings. Foster was fascinated and wanted samples to send to Washington. Of course, I was not allowed to give him the trichothecenes, that was our top-drawer research, but I did give him some *Abrus* seeds. They were from Thailand, the only ones we have right now. He wanted to compare them with ones from Florida, he said."

Arthur knew about these poisons, found in the wild and sometimes a bother to livestock, but he realized that this hard-nosed mouse of a woman was not giving much away, not without the boss's permission.

Gently, he began to ask her about her own life. After her PhD she had wanted to work in America on the USDA's apomixis project, but she had been offered a UK government grant to work with Scott's lab. She had worked for a while on Scott's apomixis project, but a Russian researcher had come to work in the lab and had brought materials from St. Petersburg. Professor Scott had been very generous to the young Russian woman, Karen said, giving her the top research position. Arthur sensed a little rivalry there, but Karen quickly explained they were friends, confidants even. Karen had become interested in mycotoxins, and Tanya had brought the *Fusarium* materials she was working on.

"You mean Tanya Petrovskaya?"

"Yes." She looked up, startled. "You already know about her."

"I know that she is missing, apparently," said Arthur.

"Well, we can't find her, that's true," she said. Karen paused and then brightened.

"There's a remarkable story about her, if you'd like to hear it."

Arthur said he would, and Karen seemed to relax.

"Tanya's great-great-grandfather had actually known Mendel," Karen said. *"Mendel,"* she said again for emphasis. "Can you believe that?"

Mendel had apparently invited her great-great-grandfather Ivan, who was a botanist in St. Petersburg, to visit him in Brunn, just before Mendel died. Ivan was the only one of Mendel's contemporaries to acknowledge the abbot's work.

Arthur had a faint memory of this episode, but he did not interrupt as Karen continued what could be a very Russian story—as much family lore as scientific history, he guessed.

"I have no idea whether it's true," Karen said, "because, frankly, I instinctively don't trust some Russians, if you know what I mean. But that's what she told me."

She paused again.

"You know what I'm talking about, of course," Karen said sternly, rather too sternly for Arthur's liking.

"Certainly," said Arthur, shaking himself back to the present. "Poor Mendel. When he bred hawkweed and dandelions, he could not obtain the same variety ratios in the next generation as he got from his peas. In those days, they didn't understand anything about apomixis."

"Exactly," Karen nodded, apparently satisfied he was following her, and then she continued.

Ivan had taken the samples back to St. Petersburg and was working on them when he died around the turn of the century. Then came the Great War, the Revolution of 1917, Stalin's purges, and World War Two. Tanya's family had lost someone in each terrible disaster, and somewhere along the way, Ivan's papers disappeared. But after the war his work on the curious behavior of hawkweed and dandelions was resumed at the St. Petersburg Botanical Gardens, possibly even with some of Mendel's original seeds. Tanya herself became a botanist, a molecular biologist, and secured a job in the gardens to work on apomixis. That was how she got to Oxford.

"That is a truly amazing story," agreed Arthur, still wondering, like Karen, how much of any seductive Slavic tale was actually true.

"I think I'm the only person who knows the story, apart from Professor Scott, of course," Karen added. "Maybe Matt Raskin knows."

"Matt Raskin?"

"Yes, he used to work here—on the apomixis project. Then he went back to America."

Arthur would have liked to hear more about Tanya's story, but he was eager to learn what, if anything, Karen knew of the current state of the apomixis project.

"Scott and Tanya had been very secretive recently, like a couple of old Stalinists," she said. "They *were* old Stalinists, in my view. They still called St. Petersburg Leningrad. They took home everything each night—notebooks, slides, DNA sequences, all except the seeds."

"DNA sequences. What sequences? You mean of the backcrossed progeny?"

"I really don't know. I was just guessing that there must have been some," she answered rapidly, as though she had said something she regretted.

"But the seeds were left here? The ones from St. Petersburg and Novosibirsk?"

"I shouldn't really say," said Karen, suddenly flustered, like someone who had her own seductive story to tell but couldn't tell it.

"I'd better not say any more now. I'd rather have the explicit permission of the vice-chancellor, if you don't mind, Mr. Hemmings."

She looked at her watch. "In any case, I have an appointment to keep in town."

"Well, maybe we can discuss your work in more detail," Arthur said. "I'm in Oxford until tomorrow afternoon. Perhaps you could ask the vice-chancellor's permission?"

"Yes, yes, that would be better," she said, obviously relieved that the interview was over.

"I'm sorry I can't say more. Sorry," she said, folding her arms across her lab coat to emphasize the door to her secrets, whatever they were, was firmly closed, at least for now.

Arthur gave her one of his Kew business cards, adding the phone number of the Rose and Crown. She promised to be in touch as soon as possible. He told her that he was going to Lower Witton to see the experimental plants.

"I'm envious; it's lovely on a day like this. I would like to go with you, but unfortunately, I can't," she said. "I hope you have a profitable afternoon."

Arthur walked down the stone steps to the exhibition hall and the service door exit. He strolled once more through the exhibits on the ground floor. The museum was pleasantly stuck in the mid-nineteenth century, the years of Darwin, still proudly displaying its original collection, with very little added and not much subtracted, except now, in the depository, where a few bags of seeds, possibly some of the most sought-after seeds in the world, had been stolen. Outside in the lot, Arthur retrieved his bicycle and walked it across the road into an alleyway that gave him a good view of the service door entrance. He propped his bike against the wall and waited for Karen Lichfield to come out of the museum.

Twelve

rthur did not have to wait long. A few minutes later, Karen emerged from the service door carrying a small backpack. Arthur moved down the passageway to avoid being seen as she went to the bike rack, unlocked her bicycle, and rode off toward the city center, wobbling a little, Arthur noted with surprise, for such a self-possessed young woman. He followed her, riding at a discreet distance. At a curbside mailbox she stopped to mail a package and then pedaled, briskly, into St. Giles, past the Martyrs' Memorial, and into Beaumont Street. She put her bike into the rack outside the Ashmolean Museum, locked it, and walked across the road, pausing to buy a copy of the *Oxford Chronicle* from the newsstand before she went into the Randolph Hotel. Arthur propped his bike against the wall of the Ashmolean and followed her. In the hotel lobby, she was waiting with other guests to go up in the elevator. Two cars arrived one after the other and she switched at the last minute to the second car, going up on her own.

Arthur stayed in the lobby, out of her sight, until the elevator had started its upward journey. The car went directly to the penthouse, Eikel's royal suite.

Arthur felt betrayed, annoyed really because he had been too soft with her, but he resisted the temptation to call Eikel on the house phone. A confrontation would not be productive at this stage. He left the hotel and headed north. The Banbury Road was in full flower—herbaceous borders still boasting a few bluebells, the forsythia giving way to prunus, bridal wreath, and lilac. The red brick Victorian mansions radiated the wealth and learning of the academic families for whom they had been built more than a century ago. Now they were divided into flats and offices. No modern university professor could afford to live in such splendor.

The road was so familiar to Arthur—he had cycled along it almost daily as a student—that it was like going home. He pedaled as fast as the traffic would allow, thinking of Tanya Petrovskaya's great-great-grandfather Ivan, and how cleverly Karen Lichfield had used the story as a diversion, to avoid answering more questions about the apomixis research. She had let slip the matter of DNA sequences, though, that suggested Scott was preparing a patent application.

He was wondering what she was doing in Eikel's suite and what task she might be performing for Panrustica when he found himself turning his bike into Squitchey Lane, a short, peaceful street of mostly postwar houses, lined with flowering cherry trees. He could see a police car about halfway down the street, presumably at Scott's house. Arthur had always imagined Squitchey Lane to be filled with maiden aunts, retired sea captains, and grannies. As if on cue, an elderly resident tending her garden raised a trowel to acknowledge his arrival. He waved back and stopped his bike outside her house.

"What's going on?" he asked, on the off chance she might have seen something.

"Haven't you heard?" said the old woman, surprised at his question. "That's the professor's house, the one who drowned in Queen's Lock. Nice man, only lost his wife a couple of years ago. And now this."

Arthur readied himself for a full report on the neighborhood.

"The police have been here all day," the woman continued, "and yesterday afternoon . . ."—she lowered her voice in confidence—"I saw the vice-chancellor himself drop by the house. I know his face from television. Very distinguished-looking man."

"What time was that?" asked Arthur.

"About four o'clock. He just drove up, looked in the windows, knocked on Miss Richards's door, the next house over, and then drove off. And that's not all. Some strange cars have been parked in this street for the last two weeks."

"Well, I must be on my way," Arthur said. "I'm going to do the same thing myself, take a peep."

"Wait a minute, you haven't asked about Miss Richards," she said, crossly.

"No, no, so I haven't. Should I have done?"

"Yes, I happen to know that she's been after the professor for years," she said, her eyes widening and a mischievous grin lighting up her face. "Oh, yes, dear me, yes, I know all about that. But you'll not find her at home now. She's a crafty one; she knows when to lie low."

"Well, as I said, I must be going," said Arthur, remounting his bicycle and thinking how he really disliked aging busybodies, like this old woman.

"Good luck, young man—if you can get past the coppers," she called after him, waving her trowel.

Two police cars were parked outside Scott's house, which was cordoned off with more yellow tape. It was an uninspiring brick house with a gray slate roof and a garden at the back. It had a slightly ragged appearance: the bushes had not been trimmed for a while and the green paint on the garage was peeling.

As Arthur propped his bike against the fence outside, a constable approached.

"Sorry, sir, I have to ask you to move on unless you live in the street."

"I'm from the ministry," said Arthur, showing his pass. The constable checked it, both sides.

"Yes, sir, of course, sir. You can put your bike over by the garage. Wasn't expecting a boffin to arrive on a bike."

"Haven't heard that word for a while," Arthur remarked, smiling.

"I'm older than you, sir," said the constable. "We always called technical people like yourself boffins in my day."

"Yes, well, bikes are good for boffins." Arthur smiled, pleased at his little joke. "It gets them exercise."

"Yes, sir, of course." The constable grinned. "I'll keep an eye on it, sir."

"Oh, by the way," said Arthur, "you haven't noticed any unusual activity in the street, spectators in parked cars, have you?"

"No, sir, you're the first, as far as I know, and I've been here since dawn."

"Thank you, Constable."

Arthur walked up the short gravel driveway. The front door was open. Two plainclothes officers were having a cup of tea in the kitchen. A copy of the *Oxford Chronicle* was on the table.

"Afternoon, Hemmings, Ag & Fish. I was on my way to Lower Witton and thought I'd just drop in to see how things were going."

"Afternoon, Mr. Hemmings. They said you might be coming. Nothing new, sir—except the Russian woman is still missing, of course. We don't know anything more about her. Would you like a cup, sir? No milk, I'm afraid."

Arthur declined. "Yes, curious business. Mind if I take a look around?"

"Help yourself, sir. And you can touch what you like. The print boys have already been through."

There was a large living room looking out onto the garden at the back, with its splash of green lawn, a fully grown cherry tree, a herbaceous border, a stone birdbath, and two wooden garden benches, all enclosed by a privet hedge. Standard equipment for this part of suburbia. Scott had made part of the living room into his study, and it was lined with books. The filing cabinet was empty; so were the desk drawers. There were no computers or CDs. Family snaps, if there had been any, were gone. The police had wasted no time in collecting evidence—all of it, apparently. Nice place to work, thought Arthur, as he moved instinctively toward the bookcases crammed with volumes, mostly scientific, but including some popularizers of science, such as Matt Ridley's *Genome,* Colin Tudge's *Impact of the Gene,* and *Food, Inc.,* which, Arthur knew, had a chapter about agriculture and corporate patents. He ran his eye across the shelves. There were rather ordinary sets of Shakespeare, the Waverley novels, Dickens, and Kipling, none of them showing signs of recent use.

There was an extensive poetry section, mainly early twentieth century—Joyce, Sassoon, Brooke, Grenfell, and three copies of the *Oxford Book of English Verse.* Arthur guessed such a collection could be found in any Oxford professor's home except, perhaps, for one of the copies of *English Verse,* the 1939 edition, a smaller, almost pocket-sized volume bound in red leather and printed on India paper. Arthur knew the little book well; it was edited by Sir Arthur Quiller-Couch. He gently pulled it out of the bookcase. He had one like it but had not seen it in someone else's house for many years. The inscription caught his eye. "To the Scholar, from the Gypsy. Together we will knock down Preferment's door." It was signed with the initials "M. R." There was no date. Was this a present from a lover or a maiden aunt? A student, perhaps? Karen had mentioned an American named Matt Raskin.

He held the little book in his hands and ran his finger down the spine.

"Don't make them like that, these days," he sighed quietly. The phrase "Preferment's door," Arthur knew, was from Matthew Arnold's "Scholar Gypsy." It had been required reading at his school. He copied the inscription into his notebook and recited the poem from his youth.

> The story of the Oxford Scholar poor,
> Of pregnant parts and quick inventive brain,
> Who, tired of knocking at Preferment's door,
> One summer morn forsook
> His friends and went to learn the Gypsy-lore.

This inscription might lead nowhere, but he felt lucky to have found a tidbit of evidence. Before leaving the house, he went upstairs. The big bedroom, presumably Scott's, seemed virtually untouched. The double bed was made up, and there were plenty of clothes—well-worn tweed jackets and several pairs of unpressed corduroy trousers. No surprises.

The policemen called from downstairs. "We're about to lock up, sir, new shift coming. Do you need any more time?"

"No, thanks, I'm fine," Arthur called back, coming down the stairs. "Anything new?"

"Nothing, sir. You didn't take any property—for evidence, like—did you?"

"No," said Arthur, "seems the important stuff has already gone. Thanks again."

He walked back down the drive, retrieved his bike, and nodded a goodbye to the constable outside. He was about to ride off, lost in a pleasing haze of Matthew Arnold's verse, when he realized he had forgotten to ask about the neighbor, Miss Richards. Her house next door looked all locked up.

"Do you know if the neighbor is at home—Miss Richards, is it?"

"No, sir," answered the constable, "she left for a few days—to avoid the fuss, I believe."

"Any idea where?"

"I believe I heard Lyme Regis, sir, to be with her sister, but couldn't swear to it."

Arthur thanked the constable and mounted his bike, thinking of Miss Richards and her story about the milk bottles. It would be unusual for someone who had milk delivered to the door to run out, he thought, and yet the policemen said there was no milk for the tea. Instead of setting off north again to his next appointment, Arthur returned to the old woman up the street. He could see her eyeing him as he rode up.

"Find out anything?" she asked. "You must be some kind of official to be allowed inside. What do you do?"

Arthur ignored the question and asked his own.

"I just wondered . . . ," he began.

"Yes, young man, what do you want?"

"Who delivers the milk around here?"

"What a funny question. Mr. Greenwood, of course. He's been doing it for years. I can remember when his father came with a horse and cart. He kept the horse in a field up by the roundabout. We used to feed it rotten apples."

"Mr. Greenwood?"

"Yes. Now it's his son. He drives a milk van from Smith's Dairy. He comes every morning except weekends, but the milk is not as good as it used to be. What do you want to know all this for?"

"I wanted to check that the professor's milk delivery had been stopped."

"Stopped? He hasn't been having milk delivered since his wife died two years ago. What did you say your line of work was, young man?"

"Estate agent," said Arthur quickly, and as he turned his bike to go, the old woman was saying, "Ooh, you didn't waste any time, did you? How much do you think the professor's house is worth, then?"

Arthur didn't answer. He just waved a goodbye.

Thirteen

The village of Lower Witton (population 203) was Arthur's next stop, and he was looking forward to the ride, about twenty minutes, through Wolvercote and round by the Trout, past the ruins of the nunnery where Henry II wooed Fair Rosamund. He rode down to the canal, sitting back in the saddle and breathing in the heavy scents of early summer—a potpourri of apple blossom, riverbank and cow parsley. At the bridge he stopped, pushing the bike across when a car horn blared behind him. As he pulled smartly to the side, the car, a garish lime green Fiat Punto, sped past, uncomfortably close. He shook his fist at the little bug as it disappeared over the crest of the bridge. Too early for a drunk, he guessed; a tourist, perhaps, or a reporter. On the other side of the bridge, he rode on to Lower Witton.

The experimental farm was there even in his day at Oxford. The undergraduates grew their own vegetables and a few exotic plants of questionable origin. The patch had come under firmer control and expanded considerably since then, he had heard.

As he cycled through the village, he noticed the green Fiat parked at the top of the lane leading to the farm. There was no one inside. He stopped his bike beside the car and saw a road map open on the front seat. He peered through the window and saw Lower Witton circled in red. He took out his camera and took a shot of the car with its license plate showing, and the map on the front seat. Then he cycled down the lane to the farm.

Arthur was relieved to see a police car and no media; they had not yet had their fill of Queen's Lock across the meadow, where he could see the the TV vans, antennae fully extended. The white wooden sign outside the farm read, "University of Oxford, Experimental Farm. Private, Keep Out by Order of the Ministry of Agriculture and Fisheries." He was taking a snap, just for the record, when a uniformed constable got out of the police car. Arthur introduced himself and showed his Ag & Fish pass.

"We've been expecting you, sir," the constable said. "There's no research staff here, I'm afraid, but the farm manager, Mr. Hendon, will take care of you. He's in the second cottage on the right."

The farm consisted of half a dozen small cottages and several large greenhouses. Mr. Hendon emerged from one of the cottages wearing a dirty brown dairyman's coat.

"Afternoon, Mr. Hemmings. They told me to look after you. No one else here right now but I can show you the greenhouse. I suppose that's what you're here for."

"Yes, routine stuff, really," said Arthur. "A few samples, perhaps."

"We grow anything from pampas grass to pineapples, and a lot of fancy stuff in between like bok choy, and ah-ru-gla." He struggled with the pronunciation. "Too bitter, if you ask me. We also grow tobacco plants, and I've got my eye on them."

Arthur glanced at his watch. Almost five o'clock. He wanted to be well clear before the media convoy arrived.

"I would like a tour of number six," Arthur said. "If it's no trouble."

"No trouble at all," said Mr. Hendon. "That's the one they all want to see. But only officials like you can go inside. This greenhouse is the cream of the crop. Newfangled everything inside, temperature and humidity gauges, dials and computers. Then there's the grenade-proof glass, special locks, video cameras. We've even got closed-circuit TV covering the parking lot outside, but it's so well hidden, those damned greens still don't know they're on film. Nor do the people coming to the Badger in Lower Witton. They'd freak out, if they knew. Those greens are always tossing something at us from the road, mostly cowpats. This glass is three-quarters of an inch thick. Cost a fortune, they say. And your ministry, Mr. Hemmings," he nodded at Arthur, "they paid for it all. I'll wait outside this time if you don't mind; there's a lot of pollen from those grasses and I seem to get more allergic as time goes by."

Arthur nodded and went inside. Mr. Hendon had described the greenhouse well. It was brimming with dials and temperature gauges, TV monitors and water hoses that spurted a fine mist, like a rain forest. This was where he would find the plants that were worth, so far, a break-in and a suicide, or a murder.

Arthur moved swiftly through the rows of maize plants, conscious that he was being filmed. Some of the plants had already grown to maturity, more than six feet high and with good-sized cobs. They were all tagged on the stem. One row started with the letters NS. He assumed that these were maize plants crossed with apomictic wild grass from Novosibirsk. The next row of maize was coded LG. There was no SP for St. Petersburg, as he had expected. Then he remembered what Karen had told him: Scott and Tanya still called St. Petersburg Leningrad. LG must mean plants crossed with apomictic grasses from St. Petersburg, probably the most important plants.

Using a penknife from his satchel, Arthur carefully scraped a sample of the yellow kernels off the LG cobs and then snipped the tassels, letting each cutting drop into separate plastic specimen bags that he folded neatly and marked with a felt-tipped pen. Then, clearing away the potting soil, he clipped the LG maize root tips as far from the stem as possible. The root sections would make the best slides for the chromosome count, the vital evidence of Scott's progress. He repeated the process with a healthy-looking NS-coded maize plant.

When he had enough specimens, he carefully closed the satchel and took photos of the plants. As he moved outside into the sun, he felt more like a thief than an official envoy from the ministry, but Mr. Hendon did not seem to have paid him any attention. He was smoking a cigarette.

"Didn't see your tobacco plants, Mr. Hendon," Arthur said, trying to keep the conversation away from his important discovery.

"They're in number three. You want to have a look?"

"Sure," said Arthur, although he hadn't smoked a cigarette in thirty years.

Mr. Hendon proudly showed off a row of tobacco plants with big green leaves, tinged with yellow at the edges.

"Looks as though they're about ready for drying," Arthur said.

"Any day now," said Mr. Hendon. "I hang them in the attic of my cottage. Wonderful sweet smell fills the house. Lasts through the winter."

"Where do the plants come from?"

"Sãn Paulo, Brazil," said Mr. Hendon, proudly. "Here's the tag code SP. Ms. Tanya, the Russian—I like her, by the way—she always lets me have some tobacco and she told me they came from Brazil. High nicotine. Has a good kick to it, mind you. If you want to try some, Mr. Hemmings, I've got a tin in the cottage from last year."

"Not just now, thank you," said Arthur. "But I'd like to look at the closed-circuit TV before I go. Just to see myself on television, of course."

"No problem," said Hendon as he led Arthur into a cottage by the main gate. Inside was a control room with TV monitors, one for Greenhouse 6, and a second for the parking lot.

"If you want to look at a day, you just punch in the date and then it's activated by movement, mostly cars arriving for opening time at the Badger. They use this as a spillover car park. Most days there's nothing going on and you get through a day in no time," Hendon advised. "Never bother with the thing myself unless there's been a demo . . . Give a shout when you're through."

Arthur sat down at the Greenhouse 6 monitor and punched in the day's date. There he was, taking cuttings and putting them into his satchel. He looked as he had felt, like a thief. It was clear that you couldn't do much in the greenhouse without being on camera. Hiding behind a large plant didn't work because the cameras took all angles.

Then he punched in the same date for the parking lot camera. It had a limited view, mostly the lot itself. Around midday cars started arriving; most people walked back in the direction of Lower Witton, going to the pub, Arthur assumed. The picture was not bad for this kind of camera, Arthur noted.

As Mr. Hendon walked him to the gate, Arthur asked about security.

"I assume you're under instructions not to let the media into Greenhouse six," Arthur said, seeking reassurance that the plants, and the codes, would be protected.

Hendon nodded. "Don't you worry, sir. Like I said, no one gets into number six, except officials like you."

As Arthur walked his bike down the lane from the farm, he heard the sound of cars coming across the meadow. The media had evidently finished at Queen's Lock and were heading for the farm. Instead of going back to Lower Witton, he took a rough track across the fields in the opposite direction, toward the river.

★   ★   ★

The meadows of Godstow in May were glorious to both the trained
and untrained eye, Arthur noted as he surveyed the fields and hedge-
rows around him. The riverbank was bursting with new plant life,
tufts of luminescent green grasses and long, slender reeds. He
reached the river's edge where the stripling Thames of Arnold's
poem was in full flood. The water was less than a foot below the
bank. A swimmer could just roll in. Perhaps this was where Scott had
drowned, he thought, as he lay down in the grass and took out his
notebook to review the day.

He was now satisfied he had solved the riddle of the plant codes,
thanks to Karen Lichfield. LG was St. Petersburg. But that meant
the seeds stolen by the museum intruders included one set of corn
kernels crossed with apomictic grasses from Novosibirsk, and then
tobacco seeds from Brazil. The wrong swag. But the thieves would
quickly discover their mistake. Corn kernels are big and yellow; tobacco seeds are tiny. Karen had definitely not divulged all she knew,
and this woman apparently had some kind of relationship with Richard Eikel. He was looking forward to seeing her again.

Arthur's musings were suddenly halted by the sound of voices on
the opposite bank. As he sat up, he saw two fishermen, ridiculously
overdressed as fishermen tended to be, in camouflage jackets filled
with pockets, green waders, and green baseball caps with flies hooked
into them. He wondered what on earth they thought they might
catch in old Father Thames that would be worth the gear they wore.
If they had seen him, they didn't react. They disappeared around a
bend in the river.

If he rode back to Lower Witton, Arthur figured, he could have
a pint at the Badger—for nostalgia only, of course—before going to
the science library to look up Matt Raskin's thesis. He took the path
around the back of the village—to avoid the media. The green Fiat
was still parked at the top of the lane leading to the farm.

Fourteen

The Badger was the only pub in Lower Witton. The sign above the door read, "Serving Oxfordshire Ale since 1642," the year the Civil War started. Arthur wondered if there had been a connection; the pub looked sturdy and royalist and was built of local limestone, weathered gray. Above the gabled entrance swung the hand-painted sign of a badger peering through bulrushes on a riverbank.

Arthur propped his bike against the wall and stood back from the entrance to drink in the memories the pub evoked, most of them pleasant. The Badger had been a pit stop on the Oxford biochemistry department's pub crawl in the 1970s—number five, as he recalled, after the Trout, the Lamb and Flag, the Red Lion, and the Swan. He shuddered to think about it, now, drinking all that beer and driving home.

Inside, he found the same scuffed flagstones on the floor, the inglenook fireplace and the high-backed wooden pews, blackened by the wood smoke of so many winter nights. The tiny bar had added a few unfortunate neon signs advertising spirits and Continental aperitifs, but the place had not been remodeled, like most English country pubs. There was no jukebox, or game machine.

The bar was empty except for a shortish, tubby man, balding, with thick, black horn-rimmed spectacles, khaki pants, and a matching khaki shirt with a row of pens clipped into a breast pocket. On the bar in front of him was a reporter's dog-eared ringed notebook. The man was ordering a drink.

"Bloody zoo out there now, Bill," he said to the barman. "TV crews falling all over themselves and mad as hell because they won't let them film in the greenhouse where the miracle plants are supposed to be."

"Fearsome Bob will keep them at bay," said the barman as he poured the man a pint.

"You mean Hendon," said the man.

"Yeah, Hendon."

The barman asked Arthur what he would like to drink. He said a pint of bitter, but he was not sure which brand.

"Brakspear's is what you want, matey, best in the county," said the man at the bar.

"Brakspear's it is then," said Arthur, amused by this brassy reporter who seemed to have a lot of knowledge about the drowning of Professor Scott.

The reporter extended his hand with his visiting card.

"Fred Barton, *Oxford Chronicle.*"

Arthur smiled. Under Barton's name was printed "Chief Feature Writer. The County Is My Beat."

"Arthur Hemmings, Kew Gardens," Arthur said, taking Barton's extended hand and then regretting that he had so readily identified himself. He was supposed to be quietly sleuthing for the ministry, not having a pint with the local press. But curiosity had got the better of him. Fred Barton had broken the story about the museum in the morning paper and he seemed to have the place so buttoned down that while his colleagues were out in the meadows recording Professor Scott's demise, he had time for a pint.

"Come from London, then?" he asked.

"Yes, I'm here to check the science," said Arthur guardedly, hoping that the word *science* would give him an out, should he need one.

Barton brightened. "Just the very man I need to talk to."

"Bill, I'm buying. Put Dr. Hemmings's pint on the slate."

"No, that's not necessary," Arthur protested, but the deal was already struck. A pint of beer for information about miracle plants.

"Seriously, Doctor," Barton said, "can you spare a few minutes? I think I understand about virgin birth in plants, or apomixis, or however you pronounce it, and I get the bit about fixing genes for future generations, but what exactly was Scott doing to accomplish this? By the way, Bill here thinks apomixis is a disease that rabbits get."

"Excuse me, I know what myxomatosis is," growled the barman, as he pulled Arthur's pint.

"Happy to be assistance, no names, of course," said Arthur.

"Shall we sit out in the garden so as not to disturb the activities of the landlord with our highfalutin talk?" Barton suggested.

"Be my guest, *Doctor* Barton," the barman said to his reporter friend as he handed over Arthur's beer.

They sat at one of the wooden picnic tables outside in the walled garden. To Arthur's relief they were alone.

"So, what have you learned from the police blotter today?" he asked, anxious to lead the conversation.

"Nothing, yet." Barton shook his head. "Too early for an autopsy. The TV lads will stir it up a bit, but everyone is tight-lipped. The museum's still not saying anything. You must know more than I do, Doctor."

"Oh, I'm strictly science," Arthur lied. It was a habit after so long and he didn't think twice about it.

"Well, in this neck of the woods, there's nothing," said Barton. "They've locked up the house in Squitchey Lane. Miss Richards, the next-door neighbor, has gone on hols, or so they say. She sounds a little off, if you want to know what I think. Bob Hendon is playing guard dog at the farm. And of course, they've found the body, *the* body, obviously."

"So you think the body in the lock was definitely Scott's?" Arthur asked, just checking what was out there.

"Gotta be, hasn't it? Only question is, was it murder or suicide? I don't believe any of this crap about fleeing to Russia. I knew the professor. Interviewed Scott once over the Panrustica affair. Talk about depressed. Morose. Hard to think of him taking a trip to Brighton, let alone Russia. Ever meet him?"

"No, never knew the man," Arthur fudged. He had met Scott at Kew lectures but had not known him even as well as Barton, apparently.

"He was brilliant, of course, like they say: he invented that SCAM process. And all his students loved him—or used to until his wife died. They held big parties in the summer in the museum. I went once. Smashing place to have a party, among the dinosaurs, the fossil fishes, and the stuffed birds. They've even got a duckbill platypus in there."

"A dodo, I think you mean."

"Dodo, whatever. But they say Scott never recovered from the loss of his wife. She died a few years ago of cancer. And after that they said his heart just wasn't in it, so to speak."

Fred Barton took several gulps of his bitter.

"And then there's the vice-chancellor, Simon Goodhart, trying to make all the researchers take American corporate dollars. Made himself very unpopular, he has. Something strange about him. When I profiled him—you know he's leaving at the end of this term—he sounded like a shill for Panrustica. He went on about how important the funds were for Oxford. I thought it was over the top, so I left a lot of it out. He went mad, complained to the *Chronicle*'s editor. So I did a bit of digging with his neighbors. They'd heard a rumor he's put his house up for sale and is moving to Switzerland. There's talk he might even do this before the end of this term. How does he do all this on a professor's salary? And he can't have saved much because he sent his kids—all five girls—to private schools. Anyway, what I'm saying is that something is not quite right there."

Barton, now on a roll, was talking and drinking fast. His pint was almost gone.

"Scott was way past retirement, seventy-odd. Now they say he was working on this stuff of great importance to the future of the world. So, Doctor, tell me about this, er, apomixis, however you pronounce it."

"I use the short *a,* as in the original Greek," said Arthur, smiling. "Would you like the long or the short history?"

"Oh, come on, Doctor, I work for the *Oxford Chronicle,* the font of human knowledge, guardian of the public interest, a literary tour de force. We are a serious newspaper, don't you know? Short version will do fine." Barton laughed. "But to tell you the truth, this story has really got to me. I'm locked in. I'll buy you supper. Bill serves excellent pies."

Arthur looked at his watch. It was six thirty. He had nothing else planned that evening—except to put the samples from Greenhouse 6 on a train to London. And he was warming to Fred Barton, who was fetching two supper plates.

"If it's basic science you want, I can give it to you. You could get it from any number of scientific papers."

"Yeah, but I'd have to find them, and then read them. It's quicker this way." He opened his notebook, adjusted his spectacles, and leaned in to listen.

Arthur went through his explanation of apomixis and the international race to identify the genes. Fred scribbled furiously and still wanted more.

"Imagine you're an alpine grass, or even a Canadian dandelion," Arthur suggested. "You have to deal with incredibly harsh winters, unchanging and brutal. Well, if you get your genetics all in order to adapt to those conditions, imagine how frustrated you would be to see all that fine tuning of your genes just frittered away, all because of sex. When plants—or people—have sex, there is no telling what the progeny will be like. But with apomixis, it's seeds without sex, and your progeny are just like you, clones of yourself. So these dandelions kept the mix right, generation after generation. Now, imagine if you could apply apomixis to complex crop plants, like maize and wheat. Once you've bred the perfect plant, it stays perfect, forever."

Fred laughed. "I like it, Doctor, sex with yourself. I'll try and get it in my story."

The garden was filling up. Arthur was becoming a little uneasy about being overheard; after all, the only topic at the bar that night would be the finding of a body in the Thames. He didn't want to become the source of apomixis information for the entire pub.

"So, the big question." Barton was now speaking so softly that Arthur could hardly hear him. "Had the professor successfully bred an economically viable apomictic maize plant? One that would grow in, say, Kansas?"

Arthur shook his head. "That's the key question and I won't know the answer until we've done some tests—and then I probably won't be able to tell you."

"Well, thanks, Doctor, got to go, deadline's approaching," Barton said as he gathered his gear to leave.

Before they parted, Arthur asked Fred whether he had any contacts among the staff at the museum.

"I do, of course," said Fred. "But they won't talk to me at the moment. There's a gag order. There's a young researcher named Karen Lichfield." He flipped back the pages of his reporter's notebook and gave Arthur her phone number. "Karen is a very serious, straight girl."

"And one more thing," Arthur said. "Does the *Chronicle* have pictures of Scott and his workers?"

"Of course, Doctor. I'll leave word with the picture desk. We also have pix of those summer parties at the museum. There's probably one of Karen Lichfield—and Tanya, the beautiful Russian. Beautiful she is, too. Come to the office anytime; it's in the Botley Road, you can't miss it. Can I give you a lift into town?"

"No, thanks, I have a bicycle."

"Of course, excuse me, botanical gardens and bicycles, I forgot. Come on, Doctor, I'll give you a lift. Mine's a convertible. The bike can go on the luggage rack."

Fred Barton drove an old TR3 two-seater, British racing green, somewhat faded.

Arthur lifted his bike onto the rack and fastened it with a bungee cord next to several fishing rods. As they left Lower Witton Arthur noticed that the lime green Fiat he had seen outside the pub was following them, a respectable distance behind. He didn't mention it to Fred.

"I've lived with my Triumph for twenty years," said Fred as he gunned the car's four cylinders. "Most people of my age are married with kids. I have my car."

"How old are you?" Arthur figured Barton could be his own age, or twenty years his junior. There was something ageless about this rounded man.

"Forty-three. Same age as my car."

Arthur wanted to tell Fred about his own obsession with old sports cars, but he saved it for another day.

"You missed out that you're a fisherman," said Arthur.

"True. My beloved Triumph is my wife and fishing is my mistress. I know the Thames round here—all the good pools and the decent stretches. And I've won many cups."

"So, would you fish around Queen's Lock at this time of year?

"Only if I wanted to get caught by the bailiff. Come on, Doctor. The season doesn't open till June 1. And there's a three hundred pound fine awaiting anyone who's caught. In season there are pike, perch, and roach. Upstream of the lock, the water is sluggish—until the lock starts operating for the summer season. Opening the locks is like changing the bathwater. The fish come alive."

"So, if I were to say to you that today I saw two fishermen, all decked out in their gear, on the towpath upstream of Queen's Lock, between the lock and Bablockhythe, what would you say to that?"

Fred didn't hesitate. "I'd say they were actors on a film shoot."

Fred dropped Arthur at the top of Longwall, and as Arthur was lifting his bike out of the car, he saw the lime green Fiat stop a hundred yards up the road. Arthur would get Eva to check on the car. His priority now was to send the Witton farm specimens to London on the eleven o'clock train. He had suggested to Merrill that Sydney could do the analysis, given her expertise in maize. Merrill had resisted at first because she had no security clearance. He wanted Arthur to do it—keep it in the OFS family. But Arthur had pressed him: speed was the issue and Merrill had agreed.

In his room at the Rose and Crown, he carefully transferred the cuttings to a cardboard box provided by the friendly receptionist. Fifteen minutes later he was at the station putting the box on the train. Then he called Sydney, apologizing for the late hour. The samples would be at Paddington shortly after midnight, on the slow train. The guard's name was Evans. He had been told it was for Ag & Fish.

"How exciting," said Sydney. "Thanks for getting me involved." She promised to call in the morning.

As he was putting the padlock onto his bike outside the Rose and Crown, the receptionist said he had a phone call. It was Karen Lichfield.

"Mr. Hemmings, Mr. Hemmings, is that you?" She sounded agitated, even more so than when he had interviewed her in the lab. "I was just calling to say I have spoken with the vice-chancellor and I can meet you at his office tomorrow at midday."

"That's excellent," Arthur said. "Are you all right?"

But the line had already gone dead.

Arthur dialed the number back. A female voice said, "Randolph Hotel. Good evening."

Arthur asked to speak with Ms. Lichfield.

"Is she a guest, sir?"

"No, she just called me on this number."

"This is the main hotel number, sir. I am sorry I can't help you."

Arthur hung up. Karen Lichfield had apparently been with Richard Eikel all evening.

Fifteen

he sleep had been good, a four-star sleep, much like the one promised by the brochure on his bedside table, and Arthur resisted its sudden interruption by the urgent knocking at his door.

"Mr. Hemmings, Mr. Hemmings, your early morning call. Not so early, I'm sorry," a woman's voice apologized, then paused. The knocking began again.

"You awake there, Mr. Hemmings?"

The woman from the front desk was not merely rousing him, as promised, but seemingly making sure that he hadn't skipped out or even expired peacefully in this lovely cocoon of a bedroom. He squinted at his watch. Nine o'clock.

"I'm awake, my dear," he called out. "Thank you."

Another half hour would have been nice. An hour even. Arthur often had difficulty fitting his six-foot-two frame onto the standard hotel bed, but the beds at the Rose and Crown were surprisingly

long, especially for such small, antiquated rooms. The mattresses
were soft and overstuffed, much like the ones he remembered as a
student when sleep was easier and seemed to make more of a dif-
ference.

The sun streamed into the cobbled passageway outside his
bedroom window, signaling another fine day. The ministry and
duty and Merrill called—or they soon would be calling. It would
be a long day, he knew. He made the extra effort required to extract himself from his bed, shook his head, and scrubbed his hands
across tired eyes. He sat up, slowly, stood just as slowly, removed
his white T-shirt, his preferred sleepwear, and stretched, running
his hands easily across the low ceiling of the room. Out of his duffel bag he pulled a green cotton shirt and khaki pants—the same
outfit as yesterday's, only clean. He chose one of several pairs of
black socks, wool and nylon mix, his socks of choice since the day,
many years ago, when he had determined how much of his life
could be wasted matching different styles and colors. Completing
the outfit was a pair of brown leather loafers, one of several in his
closet at the cottage, brushed but not exactly polished.

He checked that his cell phone was off, wrapped a towel around
his waist, grabbed his shaving kit, and made his way to the bathroom
down the hall. It was a small room, the air a little damp from the last
user.

The large, ancient white tub was too tempting, so he ran a
bath. The steam off the hot water cleared his head as he shaved,
looking into a portable mirror balanced on the soap rack. It was
one of those unforgiving mirrors with a magnifying circle, and as
he moved his chin closer, he bared his teeth into the glass, good-
looking teeth for an Englishman in midlife, he reckoned, a set
of teeth that would compare favorably with any floss-obsessed
American of similar vintage.

★   ★   ★

Downstairs, the paper was waiting on the front desk, its headline blaring, "Professor's Body Found in Thames." Fred Barton's confident prediction of the identification of the body ran beside a grotesque picture of the drowned man being hauled from Queen's Lock by frogmen.

Arthur ordered toast and his neat Earl Grey and squeezed into a bentwood chair at a table with a floral tablecloth, his kind of place. He felt like letting out a low, contented purr. Breakfast was definitely the best meal of the day.

Inside the paper there was another picture of Scott in his hiking gear. Evidently, the *Chronicle* had an album of such shots, and he was looking forward to seeing them.

Barton's story said that it had taken only a few minutes for frogmen to release the body and bring it to the surface. This operation was described in full color, details of which Arthur could have done without this early in the morning.

In a separate story on the front page, headlined "Moscow Plot to Steal Western Science?" Fred revealed the disappearance of the Russian researcher. According to an anonymous caller to the *Chronicle*'s offices, Tanya Petrovskaya had not been seen by her colleagues since Friday, the last day Professor Scott was seen at the museum. There was no comment from the vice-chancellor's office. He guessed Fred Barton had talked to Karen Lichfield.

Barton gave what Arthur thought was a pretty good thumbnail sketch of apomixis, better than he had expected after their brief conversation. A spokesman for the vice-chancellor's office would neither confirm nor deny Ms. Petrovskaya's disappearance. Ag & Fish had also refused comment. At his press conference, Minister Williams had made no mention of the Russian researcher. And he would only say that Professor Scott was working on new ways of understanding reproduction in plants, which, of course, was true, as far as it went.

"Bloody Taffies," he mumbled about Williams and his friend, Merrill Davies. "Couldn't run a cheese shop in Caerphilly."

Arthur stopped reading. It was all too upsetting this early in a perfect morning.

As Arthur contemplated a pleasant and easy bike ride to the *Chronicle* to pick up the photographs, the receptionist called him to the phone. It was Merrill.

"Arthur, what the hell is wrong with you and cell phones? Why don't you leave the damn thing on? You're missing all the action," Merrill sputtered. "The body's been officially identified as Scott's. I've emailed the prepared ministry statement. Look it over and let me know. Williams wants it put out within the hour."

Arthur could not bring himself to say anything in reply. In this mode Merrill was best left alone. He put down the receiver and returned to the dining room to finish his tea.

He fired up his laptop, logged onto the broadband, and pulled down the ministry's email.

"The Ministry of Agriculture and Fisheries is deeply saddened by the drowning in the Thames of the distinguished Oxford University don Professor Alastair Scott. For many years, Professor Scott has been a leader of Britain's publicly funded research into agriculture biotechnology. He was the inventor of the SCAM process, a laboratory tool widely used in biotechnology. At the time of his death, Professor Scott was researching reproduction in cultivated plants. He was a world authority on the natural phenomenon known as apomixis, by which plants reproduce asexually. Throughout his prestigious career Professor Scott was funded from time to time by government grants, and part of the funding for the apomixis project was provided from the Ministry's National Science Awards Fund. The project will continue, but Professor Scott's leadership will be sorely missed."

Arthur called Merrill back.

"Seems fine, too much sex maybe, but fine."

"Thank you, Arthur, I'm sure the minister will appreciate your input. Where will you be today?"

"In Oxford and then with you at the first, and let's hope only, international session of the Dandelion Crisis Group at the U.S. embassy. That should be a gripper. Cheer up, my dear boy, you now have a body, officially."

Sixteen

The *Chronicle's new offices* in Botley Road looked like a warehouse that the owner had bought on the cheap. Shortly after ten o'clock, as Arthur approached on his bicycle, he recalled the old office, a converted cinema on Walton Street, close to the colleges. He had once visited a reporter hacking away at his typewriter in the cinema's box office. Arthur had been seeking publicity for a student anti-Vietnam rally. Now, in the newspaper's brand-new headquarters, he walked to the photo desk at the end of a smoke-free, open-plan room of cheap carpets and clicking computers.

Fred Barton had arranged everything, as promised. The receptionist had Arthur's name, and she directed him to the picture library. Fred was out on the story, she explained. Two large envelopes of black-and-white pictures were waiting for him. One was marked "Oxford Experimental Farm." The other, fatter packet was marked "Scott, Professor Alastair and Oxford Museum—mug shots, museum summer party, 2002."

The pictures were exactly what Arthur needed—shots of the "miracle plant" greenhouse, but only from the outside, and several photos of Scott with his students gathered around the dinosaurs at the museum. Arthur quickly flipped through the pictures, with captions naming the participants. One showed Scott, with his wife, Jane, Karen Lichfield, and Tanya Petrovskaya. Fred Barton was right, the Russian was a beauty, tall, blond, and willowy, with big eyes and a broad smile. Another print showed Scott with a shorter young man with dark curly hair and glasses. The caption read "Professor with senior researcher, American Matt Raskin." He ordered copies of them all.

"Popular, this professor, isn't he?" said the young female assistant. "Poor man, fancy coming to an end like that. Kids, you expect to drown. They're always falling in the river. But a professor? Doesn't make any sense."

"None at all," said Arthur. "Popular, you said?"

"I copied these same pictures for a customer yesterday, an American, and today I had another call from the American embassy in London. Wanted copies as well."

"Cowboys," Arthur muttered.

"Sorry, what was that?"

"Nothing," said Arthur. "Did you say someone else besides the American embassy wanted copies?"

"Yes sir." The assistant was proud to tell all she knew, down to the last morsel. The American embassy had said never mind the cost and was sending a man down from London, but another Yank got here before them. Like they were queuing up."

"Didn't leave his name by any chance, the other, er, Yank?"

"No, sir, he didn't. Paid in cash. And gave me a nice tip, although don't say anything about that. We're not supposed to accept tips. Seemed in an awful hurry. These Yanks been coming out of the blue, like the U.S. Cavalry. Not like you, with connections to Fred."

"Couldn't describe the other Yank, could you?" asked Arthur, probing gently.

"Well . . . he was medium height, stocky, fair hair, and dressed like an American, you know, jeans, T-shirt, baseball cap. Funny why they wear those things. IQ deflaters, my hubby calls them. But he had a nice aftershave." She thought for a moment. "Like spiced soap."

The copies were ready in a few minutes. Arthur put them in his backpack and rode his bike back into town, thinking how much he did not like following in the tracks of these Americans—whoever they were.

The next stop was a quick one, the university's science library, around the corner from the museum. A young librarian—not exactly the librarian type, Arthur reflected, as he eyed her overly brief cotton tank top—quickly found the list of Scott's PhD students, plus the abstracts of their theses for the last five years. There were eleven candidates, including Matt Raskin, whose thesis had been on the origins of apomixis. He put the list in his backpack and pedaled back to the Rose and Crown, weaving among students pouring out of a lecture.

He was about to set out for Balliol and his appointment with the vice-chancellor when Ms. Bridgland called the inn. She still sounded flustered.

"Professor Goodhart regrets that he must cancel your meeting," she said. "Unfortunately, Dr. Lichfield has been taken ill," she added, in a tone about as flat as could be. She certainly was not inviting a discussion.

But Arthur immediately asked what was wrong.

"She has a stomachache," said Ms. Bridgland, again without elaboration.

"Is she at home?" asked Arthur, thinking that he had her telephone number from Fred Barton.

"No," said Ms. Bridgland, adding, reluctantly, "she's had to go to the hospital."

"Which one?" asked Arthur.

"The JR."

"The JR?"

"The John Radcliffe."

"Thank you, thank you very much, Ms. Bridgland, you've been most helpful," Arthur said, barely suppressing his irritation with her deliberately uncooperative manner.

He called a taxi and twenty minutes later he arrived at the JR's emergency room to find three police cars outside. He showed his ministry card to an officer at the door and said he had come to meet Inspector Davenport.

"It's urgent," he told the officer.

The officer escorted Arthur inside. Davenport was in earnest conversation with the doctor who had treated Karen. Arthur waited and then introduced himself, quickly explaining his reason for being in Oxford, his meeting with the vice-chancellor, and the fact that he had interviewed Karen yesterday and discussed the plant poisons she had been working on. He thought he might be able to help with the diagnosis.

"I'm afraid you're too late," Davenport said. "She died an hour ago."

"Anaphylactic shock associated with a severe decrease in blood pressure," said the doctor.

"Not unusual for mycotoxin poisoning," said Arthur, surprised at his own coolness.

"Mycotoxin?" asked Davenport, looking puzzled.

"Yes, she was working with a new strain of *Fusarium* fungus that produced a trichothecene toxin said to be ten times more toxic than the normal T2 strain. The Russians discovered it. Dr. Lichfield had some in her laboratory."

"I've not heard of that," said the doctor.

"Nor me," added Davenport, turning to his aide. "Make sure that lab remains sealed and close her residence." Then he asked Arthur, "Perhaps you can help us out."

"The technical staff at Kew know a lot about mycotoxins, and I'm sure they would be amenable," said Arthur, "if they had the right samples."

"What would they need?" asked Davenport.

"Blood, for sure, and tissue. I would expect there will be lesions in the liver and kidneys, but that would take time, obviously. I think time is of the essence here, isn't it, Inspector?"

"We can give you a blood sample immediately," the doctor volunteered. "They would have been taken when she was admitted earlier this morning. It's not usual practice to hand these out," he said, looking at the inspector.

Davenport nodded his assent. "We're in uncharted territory. We need all the help we can get."

The doctor obviously felt the same way and looked relieved that the ministry was now involved in the postmortem.

"The nurse will assist you," the doctor said to Arthur. "You could help us with making a positive identification." Arthur followed the nurse out the room.

She led the way to the morgue, where Karen's body had already been taken. She lay under a white sheet, which covered everything but her head. Her mouth was open and distorted. Death must have come suddenly, Arthur guessed. He had seen the effects of anaphylactic shock before.

Arthur made his positive identification, and the mortician went to a table with the nurse to write on an official form. When their backs were turned, Arthur lifted the sheet on Karen's right side. He wanted to see her right hand. The back of the hand was still covered with a Band-Aid, which he swiftly peeled back and placed in his handkerchief, putting the handkerchief into his coat pocket. He replaced the sheet cover just as the mortician was calling him to the table.

"If you'll just sign this release form for the blood, Mr. Hemmings, the nurse is locating the sample. The blood was drawn immediately after she was admitted shortly after ten this morning."

As the mortician drew the sheet over Karen's head, Arthur noticed how short she was. He had not remembered that. He drew in a deep breath, touched her foot beneath the sheet, and found himself saying, "Goodbye, Karen."

The nurse came back with a refrigerated pack and handed it to him, volunteering to take him back to Inspector Davenport. "I have to go back into Oxford immediately, I'm afraid. I need a taxi, thank you. Could you give the inspector my phone numbers?" Arthur wrote in his cell phone number and handed her a card.

At the Rose and Crown Merrill Davies had called several times. Reluctantly, Arthur punched in his number.

"Where the hell are you?" Merrill demanded, with his customary urgency.

"I'm at my hotel, Merrill, where you called."

"I just wanted to make certain you are going to be at this meeting at the embassy. Sir Freddie is flying in from Zurich and the minister will be there, of course. You will be required to give a preliminary analysis of Scott's research. Do you have anything to say?"

"What is this?" asked Arthur, knowing that he sounded irritated. He was frustrated. Events were spiraling around him and he was being called back to London. He didn't mean to be taking it out on Merrill.

"Just asking, boyo, no offense."

"The answer is probably yes. I will probably have something to say about the analysis," Arthur managed, coolly. "I sent samples to

Sydney last night on the train and she should have a few results by now."

"Excellent. Turn your bloody cell phone on, will you?"

"I will also have something to say about Karen Lichfield, one of Professor Scott's researchers, who was taken to the hospital this morning, apparently suffering from fungal toxin poisoning, and has since died," Arthur said, as calmly as possible.

"What the hell are you talking about? Karen who?"

"Why don't you call your pal the vice-chancellor?" Arthur shot back and closed the phone.

He went back to his room. Merrill was in a tizzy. Nothing new about that. It happened every time the minister harassed him. This would pass. If he knew what Arthur knew, he would have to be mildly sedated. Maybe not so mildly. Arthur delved into his satchel for a plastic specimen bag, carefully unfolded his handkerchief, and placed the Band-Aid in the bag, sealed it, and put it in the refrigerated pouch with the blood sample. Then he went to the bathroom and scrubbed his hands.

What he had just done was not only illegal—tampering with a dead body in the morgue—but against all the hygiene rules for handling suspected poisons. However, it was the only way of finding out quickly what he desperately needed to know. What had caused the inflammation on the back of Karen's hand and could it have caused her death? Pus from the wound had leaked onto the Band-Aid. He would test it for trichothecenes. If it was the new Russian strain, it had to have come from her lab. If not, it could have come from any number of sources.

Merrill's urgency about the Dandelion meeting gave him only a few minutes to talk to Eva Szilard at Kew, but he indulged her—for a moment. She always liked a little gossip before they got on to business. Today she asked Arthur about Oxford and the preparations for

Eights Week. He described the place for her, buzzing with students, and how wonderful it would be, he thought, to return as a don.

"Oh, come on, Arthur, you always say that when you go to Oxford. You'd hate it, let's face it. So, what do you want?"

He asked if she could do a check on Matt Raskin. Secondly, he needed the latest research papers—especially anything in Russian—on mycotoxins produced by the fungus *Fusarium,* also known as T2. The T stands for *trichothecene,* he told her, and she asked him to spell it.

"Yes, Arthur, you are getting quite involved, aren't you?"

Eva said he'd not missed much at Kew—except that an American had been in the library. He had wanted to know about a nineteenth-century Russian biologist named Ivan Petrovsky.

"The library had one paper, a dissertation in German done in 1874," she said. He had taken a copy of it.

Arthur froze. "Did he give his name?"

"He did, in the visitors' book, and I can't read the signature, all loops and squiggles, almost as though he didn't want anyone to know. He gave his address as twenty-four Grosvenor Square."

"That's the bloody American embassy. What did he look like?" asked Arthur, impatiently.

"I'm sorry, Arthur, I never saw him, and the guards have changed. Of course, I will try and find out."

What the hell was someone from the American embassy doing looking up Tanya's great-great-grandfather's thesis—in *German*? Arthur was thinking. And how did this person know about Petrovsky and Mendel? He suddenly felt badly outnumbered, and he absent-mindedly closed his cell phone.

"Arthur," Eva was asking, "are you still there?"

Seventeen

Arthur hurriedly packed his bag and raced for the railroad station, weaving his bicycle in and out of the traffic. The Ridgeback had been an effortless ride. There was a line at the station's rental office, and since the bike was on his credit card, he just propped it against their sign. The train was not crowded and he chose a seat by the window, on the east side to avoid the afternoon sun. He flipped open his cell phone and called Sydney.

"The initial analysis of the seed samples is great for Scott," she announced. "It looks as though they have moved the maize-*Tripsacum* ratio considerably in favor of maize, way beyond previous research. But I've only done a few. I need more time."

"Take your time," said Arthur. "Let's get it right. I'm on the train on the way to a meeting at the embassy. I should be back in time for dinner. If you'd like, come to my place. Hemmings's spaghetti, the best north of Bologna."

If he had to endure the Dandelion crowd, the promise of a pleasant dinner would help.

"Lovely," she said. "I wasn't expecting you, with all this new stuff about Scott, but thanks."

Cheered at the prospect, he started to ask her if she had ever known an American microbiologist named Matt Raskin at Harvard, but she had already rung off. It could wait, at least until dinner.

As he settled into his seat, Arthur thought of Karen Lichfield. In her normal lab analysis she could have been exposed to a mild dose of the trichothecenes: that sort of thing happened all the time. A glass test tube containing the toxin in solution could have broken. Even so, death had come unusually fast. She was apparently hyperallergic. He would put Eva in charge of having the hospital samples analyzed and not mention it to Merrill, not yet. They might not reveal anything. Minister Williams would have a fit if he knew his investigator was spending time on what could turn out to be a simple laboratory accident.

Arthur took his reading glasses out of their plastic case and looked more closely at the photographs of the museum party. A few arty shots of Scott talking to people were set against the background of a dinosaur's massive knee bone. In others, students were peering through the dinosaur's rib cage. They were obviously having a good time, appearing in silly poses. In some scenes even Scott himself seemed to be at ease; in one shot, with Tanya Petrovskaya, he was smiling. That was almost a year ago.

Matt Raskin looked overly serious—except for one picture of him with Tanya. They had their arms around each other. The intense, bespectacled face of Karen Lichfield seemed to be in the background, mostly, if at all.

There were several pictures taken from outside the museum showing off its enormously long frontage. A recent one, the Sunday before the break-in according to the date stamped on the back, had been shot from across the road on the Keble College side and showed cars parked under the cherry trees on Parks Road. Several cars were parked at an angle into the curb, showing their license plates. He would ask Eva to check them, just in case. The party pictures were useful for the identification of Matt and Tanya, should he ever catch up with them.

In London, he had half an hour to spare before the Dandelion meeting, so he took a cab to Marble Arch and walked down Park Lane toward the United States embassy, a hulk of concrete and white marble on the west side of Grosvenor Square. Park Lane and the square always reminded him of the anti-Vietnam demonstrations he had joined in as a student. Somewhere in the State Department's archives, maybe in the bowels of the embassy itself, his face could be seen, no doubt, on the film taken by the embassy guards from the roof. Back then, it was possible to get close enough to the embassy to launch a well-aimed egg. Now the main building was cut off from the square by concrete barricades, as a protection against real terrorist attacks.

As he negotiated a path through the fortifications, the armed guards, and the metal detectors, Arthur was dreading the meeting but quite looking forward to seeing the "Gooseberry"—the nickname given to J. B. Foster by the Ag & Fish crowd. Foster, they thought, was like the unwanted third person on a date. Arthur had encountered this American several times. J. B. was a regular visitor to Kew Gardens, dropping into Arthur's office in the herbarium for a coffee and chat always, it seemed, when Arthur was excruciatingly busy with other things. But Arthur had always found J. B. courteous and well-informed about the latest botanical research, and they had passed many pleasant lunches in the Orangery dining room discussing the resistance of food grains to insects and fungus.

J. B. had been appointed during the Clinton administra-

tion, and in those first years, peaceful years, it was a rare day
when he received a cable from Washington, he had told Arthur,
and an even rarer one when he was expected to reply. His colleagues joked that he was very large man—about 250 pounds,
Arthur guessed—with a very small job. The fallow period came
to an abrupt end with the Bush administration's pursuit of apomixis. J. B. had suddenly acquired his own personal secretary
and an assistant. From a minor functionary in the agricultural
section of the United States embassy in London, J. B. had suddenly become a major player in transatlantic relations. Now he
had a brand-new office, a new desk—a broad, gleaming wooden
desk with a shiny glass top—and a swift promotion from plain
"agronomist" to head of the European section of the United
States Agricultural Research Agency, a move which Arthur could
still not quite believe. The fast lane was not a place where J. B.
Foster really belonged, even he would be the first to admit. J. B.
talked of moving back to New York and taking up a university
job, or moving into industry, just for the pay. But recently, and to
his surprise, Arthur had noticed that J. B. quite relished his new-
found responsibilities.

Several weeks before Scott's death, J. B. had confided in Arthur that he had started receiving cables from ARA headquarters in
Washington, with the new code name "Dandelion." He had been
ordered to make contact with Scott's lab and had gone down to
Oxford. The CIA minder, named Collins, had insisted on accom-
panying him, and they had interviewed Scott. They had a pleasant tour of the Oxford museum and of Scott's laboratory, but the
professor was not forthcoming. They learned absolutely nothing
about his research. At times, the professor had been openly hostile
and J. B. had concluded that he was overwrought. "Unstable" was
the word he used, Arthur recalled. J. B. had also been shocked at
the lack of security at the museum. "Just a big old oak door from
King Arthur's court" was how the American had put it.

After the abortive trip to Oxford, another Dandelion cable informed Foster that he would be receiving a second assistant whose job was to find out more about Scott's research than he had been able to learn.

That afternoon, Arthur was the first Dandelion outsider to arrive at the embassy. The door to J. B.'s new, large office proclaimed his new status in large gold letters. "J. B. Foster, ARA Administrator, Europe."

"Nice shingle," said Arthur.

"It's only velcroed on," snapped J. B.

Arthur found his American friend unusually ruffled.

"This is terrible about Scott," J. B. said. "Poor man, we heard that he was depressed. I know he was under a lot of pressure. And I definitely thought he looked sick when I saw him in Oxford a couple of weeks ago. But suicide?"

"Well, we don't know much yet," said Arthur. "You look harassed; tell me what's bothering you. Maybe I can help."

"A minute, I have one minute," said J. B., dropping into an armchair.

He told Arthur that on Monday, when Scott was reported missing, he had sent his two new assistants to Oxford to snoop around and had lost touch with them.

"These people are morons, Arthur, morons."

They had taken seriously his suggestion that they go fishing in the upper reaches of the Thames, where he thought Scott might be found. They had been arrested and charged with fishing out of season. J. B. was worried that the incident would be reported in the media and cause more trouble.

Arthur laughed. "I think I know all about your so-called fishermen," he said, relieved that he seemed to have solved one of the mysteries of his Oxford trip. "I saw them on the riverbank. Then they followed me around on my bike in a ghastly lime green car. Not exactly undercover. At one point they almost ran me over. They were in a lime green car, weren't they?"

J. B. apologized. The embassy car he had given them was lime green.

"It used to be mine," he said. "But I've been upgraded. I told them to find you, if they could, and follow you. Apparently they did."

Arthur told him not to worry about the arrests. The river wardens came under Ag & Fish, and Merrill would file the incident away out of the *Chronicle*'s reach.

"By the way, did you meet Karen Lichfield in Scott's lab when you went to the museum?" Arthur asked.

"Yes, mycotoxin researcher. Nice girl. Knows a lot. We had a nice chat. Working on T3, the Russian strain. Collins asked her for a sample and she refused. She said it came under a new antiterrorism act."

"She died this morning, anaphylactic shock."

"You're kidding. Something from her lab?"

"No one knows."

"The hazards of those biolabs are never fully appreciated. People never take the proper precautions."

"And speaking of the activities of your countrymen," said Arthur, "do you know anything about the visit of an embassy official to the Kew library, this week?"

J. B. said he knew nothing about it.

"I don't think my assistants would be able find their way around your library," J. B. said, gloomily. "It could have been one of the services. Washington is still convinced that Tanya Petrovskaya has skipped to Moscow and is preparing to file a patent on behalf of the Russian state. The pressure is on to find her." J. B. paused.

"You know they're going to tell you to go to St. Petersburg," J. B.

said, eyeing Arthur for signs of resistance. "You're the one with the contacts on the Neva."

Arthur nodded. He had already assumed that Williams would want him to go to Russia and had thought what a waste of effort that would be.

"And what am I supposed to do in St. Petersburg when I find Ms. Petrovskaya? Drug her, kidnap her under the cover of a giant Siberian spruce in the St. Petersburg Botanical Gardens, and whisk her back to England in a cigarette boat, clutching her precious cargo of wild grass seedlings?"

"That would do," J. B. chuckled, "Double-O."

Arthur suddenly wished he had missed the train from Oxford. J. B. Foster, whether he liked it or not, was now a team player in Washington's overheated game with its code words and its meetings and its undercover agents dressed up as fishermen. Unless Arthur could find an exit, he was sure that he was about to be dispatched on a labor of Sisyphus to St. Petersburg.

As he was weighing his options, J. B.'s secretary came into the office with an official cable for her boss.

"Jesus Christ." The American diplomat slapped his hand to his forehead and let out a squeal.

He passed the cable to Arthur. It was from U.S. Agriculture Secretary Brown and read, "The President wanted you to know he appreciates all you are doing to resolve this crisis. Good luck."

"We are supposed to believe that George W. Bush knows about apomixis?" asked Arthur, looking pained.

J. B. grimaced. "No, of course, he doesn't. He might have been persuaded that it was a weapon of mass destruction," he said, giving Arthur a big grin.

"Brown does think, like the rest of our crowd, that if we don't get the patent before the Russians, or the Chinese, the secret will be in the hands of the bad guys, and American farmers will lose out.

Brown is a self-important prick. But his cable is also a threat that if I don't succeed, I'm outta here."

Arthur looked puzzled. He had not heard J. B. speak in such terms about his bosses.

"Hey, I get paid to translate this crap," said J. B., a comment which left Arthur none the wiser.

Eighteen

The Dandelion conference room could have been in any agency of the U.S. government, anywhere. A large round table took up most of the space in a room with no windows, gray carpet, white walls, color photos of past presidents, and a slightly larger one of George W. Bush. Two large flags on brass stands stood sentry in the corner, the Stars and Stripes and the flag of the U.S. Department of Agriculture with sheaves of corn and wheat in yellow and green.

"So, J. B., you got your own flag at last," observed Arthur as he scanned the table for his name card.

J. B. gave him a dirty look but squashed a comment as the door opened. In filed the other members of the group—the Ag & Fish minister Williams, Merrill Davies, Sir Wilfred Owen with Richard Eikel, Collins of the CIA, his MI5 minder Reggie Featherstone, plus assorted gray and anonymous note takers.

Arthur knew Collins and Featherstone from OFS meetings, and

he had seen Sir Freddie on television, even met him once at Ag &
Fish. But this was the first time he had met Richard Eikel. Arthur
forced a smile for the official handshake. Eikel was very tall, even
taller than Arthur. When Eikel was introduced, he didn't smile. His
small black eyes showed no emotion. The effect was the opposite of
that made by Sir Freddie, with his easy bonhomie. Arthur wanted to
ask Eikel, "How was your evening with the late Dr. Lichfield?" but
he restrained himself.

Opening the meeting, J. B. Foster asked Minister Williams to report on the latest development at the museum and the sudden death
of Karen Lichfield, apparently from T2 poisoning. Arthur noticed
that Eikel did not move a muscle, barely an eyelid. When J. B. mentioned that Karen had worked on a new potent strain of the *Fusarium*
toxin discovered by the Russians and known as T3, Arthur was staring at Eikel, but there was still no reaction.

"We know about T2," volunteered the CIA's Collins. "The Soviets used it against the Hmong in Laos."

Lying bastard, Arthur muttered under his breath. But it was not
his position to confront Collins on his own turf.

"Another pointer to Moscow," said Williams, who quickly turned
the subject back to apomixis and asked Arthur for a report.

Arthur said a preliminary analysis of Scott's research seemed to
indicate he had indeed identified the apomixis supergene. He then
advised the group now listening so intently to his every syllable that
the museum thieves, whoever they were, had missed the most important seeds, the ones coded LG.

Eikel was again expressionless, only reacting when Arthur reported, without emotion on purpose, that he had found LG plants
at the Experimental Farm and had started to analyze them. Their
maize-*Tripsacum* chromosome ratios were higher for maize than any
previous results, including the patent taken out by the USDA.

"Enough to convince a patent examiner?" demanded Eikel, giving Arthur a full-bore stare.

"More than enough, I would say," Arthur replied, glaring back at the American, adding, "especially with the low standards of the U.S. Patent Office."

"But are the chromosome ratios higher than thirty to nine, maize to *Tripsacum?*" insisted Eikel.

The other faces in the room looked blank. Arthur was impressed. This corporate lawyer had certainly done his homework.

"I'm aware that those are the ratios claimed by the U.S. patent on the Novosibirsk samples," Arthur said, briskly. "The answer is yes, Scott's are higher for maize."

"What assays are you using—FISH or FACE?" Eikel asked, his questions rapid and dispassionate.

"Both, of course," Arthur answered, curtly.

Now Eikel was showing off, and Arthur smiled at him, to make sure Eikel understood. Arthur explained to the group that there were several ways of staining the chromosomes in order to count them under the microscope, and Eikel had just mentioned the lab acronyms for two of the most recent tests. He assured the group that Kew analysts knew what they were doing. There would be no mistakes, no false positives.

Eikel kept probing. "And what about DNA sequences? Did you find any sequences?"

"No, I found no sequences and I understand that none were found in Scott's hard drive," said Arthur.

"So, this could be a simple improvement in the ratio without any discovery of the locus of the genes on the genome that actually govern apomixis?" asked Eikel.

It could be, Arthur nodded, feeling that he needed to explain what Eikel was saying to the rest of the group. A patent on Scott's work could have two critical components. The first was to have improved the maize-*Tripsacum* ratio in favor of maize and, therefore, to have created a plant that was capable of cloning itself with some regularity. The second part of the invention was to have identified the supergenes that governed apomixis and to have located them on the *Tripsacum* genome. The second claim was the more important one because it would give other researchers the ability to transfer the apomixis genes to other crops. The information would be contained in DNA sequences, a string of letters of the genetic code, usually stored on computer disks. He had not found any.

"Let's not get too technical," interrupted Williams. "We know there's a race to patent this stuff; the question is who's winning it?" No one volunteered an answer.

To change the subject, Arthur asked if anyone knew anything about Petrovskaya's background—family or otherwise—in St. Petersburg. They shook their heads, including Eikel. Another lie for sure, Arthur thought, now assuming that one of Eikel's minions must have been at the library at Kew searching for Tanya's great-great-grandfather's thesis, but he decided not to pursue it. Not yet.

"How long would it take to draw up a patent application, assuming someone has the necessary data and seed samples?" asked Collins of the CIA.

"A week, maybe a few days if you're in a hurry."

Collins's question prompted one from Featherstone. It was a ritual: if CIA asked a question, MI5 followed up. Featherstone asked where such a patent might be filed.

The obvious place would be Zurich, Arthur explained, at the World Patent Organization. Until now, the patent would have been filed at the European Patent Office in Munich, but those patents had applied only to Europe. Since patent reform, patents filed at the WPO were now international patents having legal force in all countries.

Minister Williams held up both his hands in despair.

"Wait. This is way too technical. I'm interested in whether the Russians or the Chinese have stolen this stuff and are about to get ahead of us. What we are saying, aren't we, is that Professor Scott and whatever her name is, the Baltic beauty, were sitting on research results which could bring to a close a century-and-a-half-old mystery of one of the great curiosities of the plant kingdom, namely, virgin birth. In doing so, they could possess the tools to revolutionize farming and control world food supplies.

"And," he said, his voice steadily rising, "of the two brilliant scientists who did this work, in Britain, at our famed Oxford University—at the expense of my ministry, the public purse—one is dead, drowned in the Thames, how or why we don't know, and the other, a Russian researcher, is missing, possibly delivering this jewel of British science to the Kremlin, as we speak. Is that right?"

"That's certainly one version," said Arthur, "on the evidence adduced so far."

"Bloody hell," Williams boomed.

There was silence in the room. Eikel asked to be excused and walked out taking his cell phone out of his pocket. No one had any solace to offer the minister, or suggestions as to how to cope with the PR mess the British government now faced.

Richard Eikel came back into the room and moved briefly into a huddle with Sir Freddie, from which the Panrustica chairman emerged, saying, "Would you excuse us, gentlemen? We have some calls to make." He raised his hand, more a goodbye salute than a wave.

Williams turned to Arthur and told him to "get his ass to St. Petersburg and find the Russian woman." Merrill was told to tell the media there was nothing new—and "to watch that bugger Barton on the *Chronicle*." The meeting was over and the stellar participants were already on to the next item in their busy schedules.

Arthur asked to use J. B.'s office phone—just to get himself out of the room. In the corridor, Sir Freddie and Eikel were talking heatedly. He was too far away to hear what they were saying, but they parted like guilty schoolboys as Arthur approached. He definitely heard Eikel say, "Zurich immediately."

In J. B.'s office, Arthur called Sydney at the Kew labs and told her he was on his way home.

"How's it going?" he asked, a question more about the work than about her, he realized.

"Even better," said Sydney. "Why don't you come here and you can see for yourself." She sounded like a kid trying not to ruin a surprise.

"Be there in half an hour."

He hung up as Collins entered the office.

"I just wondered, any news of the autopsy, Arthur?"

"Sorry, Collins, can't help you," Arthur said and took the elevator to the street. Let him find out for himself, Arthur thought, as he happily breathed in some London air.

As he was walking to the tube station—the quickest route to Kew in the rush hour—he called Eva at the Kew library.

"Any news on Matt Raskin?"

In her most professional and calm voice, Eva said, "He lives in Zurich and works as a patent attorney."

Arthur imagined her beaming with satisfaction at the other end of the phone.

"Does he indeed?" said Arthur. "Book me on the first flight in the morning, SWISS, please. No word to the folks upstairs. They think I'm going to Russia."

"Consider it done. Raskin's biog will be at your cottage."

"And could you call Marc Haber in Zurich and ask him if he can find out anything about a Tanya Petrovskaya arriving in Zurich from London."

"I already did, Arthur; I knew you'd want to make contact. I have a number for him."

"You are—" Arthur began.

"Save it, Arthur. Just bring me some chocolate liqueurs—cherry brandy."

"Consider it done," he said, feeling that he was catching up with the Americans, at last.

Nineteen

In the reflected light of the microscope, Sydney watched as Arthur's fingers, steady as a surgeon's, moved the slides first one way, then another, adjusting the mirror to provide a high beam directly into the nucleus of the cell.

On each slide he saw the familiar maize and *Tripsacum* chromosomes, marked by the staining agent. He counted the chromosomes for each and wrote down the number with a felt-tipped pen on the pad of graph paper beside the microscope.

"*Zea* thirty-five."

"Now for *Tripsacum.*"

Arthur changed the slide and started counting again. He reached three and then stopped.

"Beautiful," said Arthur, excited. "They did it. The average ratio is thirty-five to three."

"Yes, they did do it." Sydney beamed, proud of being the first scientist outside Scott's laboratory to recognize this botanical revolution.

"How many slides do we have?" Arthur asked.

"I've been through about a couple of dozen made from the material sent from Oxford. They all give the same ratios."

"That's enough to file a patent with the WPO. But what about the DNA sequences from the backcrossed progeny? They'll also be needed for the patent. Who has them? Let's get some dinner." A quick dinner, regrettably, he thought.

As they walked back through the gardens, Sydney tucked her arm into Arthur's.

"I have to confess," she said, "I'm just a bit overwhelmed. I've never witnessed a scientific discovery. And certainly nothing like this. And I've never been this close to a mysterious death, or murder, or whatever. Did you actually see the body?"

"No, thank God. A ghastly sight, judging from the pictures."

"Who could have done it?"

"I don't know. Maybe it was suicide. They'll take their time over the autopsy, no doubt. The only relative is an estranged sister living in Australia. And she has already said she wants nothing to do with it."

Arthur paused.

"But you don't know the latest," he said. Then he told Sydney about Karen Lichfield. Sydney moved closer to him.

"What are you getting into, Arthur?"

"I don't know anymore, I simply don't know," he said.

The gates onto Kew Green were shut. Arthur used his electronic pass.

"Let's have a quick one in the Dragon. We should toast the professor, at least."

"And Tanya, don't forget Tanya," Sydney said.

"And Karen Lichfield."

"Yes, and her too."

"Merrill will probably be there," said Arthur, for once not relishing the thought. He needed a break from the ministry's hysteria.

They were barely through the door of the public bar when Arthur spotted Merrill, in his summer office attire of a cream linen suit, white shirt, and red tie. Merrill came barreling toward them through the evening drinkers.

"Watch out," he warned Sydney. "Here he comes." He loved it when Merrill was on point—red hair flying.

"What the hell are you doing here, boyo? You're supposed to be in Russia." Then he saw Sydney. "Oh, I see. Nice to meet you again, Ms. Rodgers."

"Before you get too excited, Merrill, Ms. Rodgers and I have been in the lab, and we thought you'd like to be kept up to date with our results of the samples from Lower Witton. We knew we'd find you here." Arthur gave him the bad-boy smile.

"Don't be disrespectful, Arthur. Of course I want to know. Come and join me—that is, if I'm not interrupting."

When they reached his table, Merrill was reading the latest copy of the *Oxford Chronicle* over a mixed grill with an extra portion of black pudding, his Green Dragon favorite. The banner headline read, "Body in Thames Prof. Scott—Official." The story was by Fred Barton. The second lead, also by Fred, was "Scott Researcher Fatally Poisoned." It mentioned that Karen had been working on fungus toxins.

"The *Chronicle* has the scoops again," Arthur observed.

"But what's all this about the Russians using T2 or T3 or whatever as a chemical weapon?" Merrill asked.

"That was a charge made during the first Reagan administration—that the Soviets had sprayed T2 toxin on the Hmong tribesmen in Laos. It was said to come down from planes as a yellow rain, but it was never proven and a Harvard biochemist made a brilliant case for the yellow rain being bee feces."

"Bee shit?" cried Merrill, dropping his beer glass to the table. "You're kidding me."

"No, I'm not, and that's what I believe it was, actually. Bees keep their hives clean. When they shit, they fly away from the hive, and it comes down like yellow droplets of pollen—digested pollen grains that can be contaminated with fungus spores.

"Recently," Arthur continued, "the Russians discovered a mutant strain of *Fusarium* fungus, known as T3, that produces a poison ten times more potent. Karen Lichfield was working on it, trying to find a wheat resistant to the fungus. The CIA is worried the poison could be used by terrorists. It could also be used as a murder weapon, of course."

"So, you think someone murdered Karen Lichfield because she knew too much, or whatever?" asked Merrill.

"I didn't say that."

"Bloody Russians," said Merrill, taking a long draft of his beer. "So what's the latest from the hot labs of Kew?"

Arthur turned to Sydney. "Why don't you tell him?"

Sydney explained that they had found consistent chromosome ratios of thirty-five maize to three *Tripsacum*. This confirmed the preliminary analysis reported to the Dandelion Group.

"Scott created the golden goose, found the motherlode, whatever cliché you want to use. The best the Americans had ever done was thirty to nine. Whether one or several genes are involved in apomixis is still an open question."

"I get that bit now," said Merrill, impatiently. "But what do we think Ms. Petrovskaya has taken to St. Petersburg, or wherever she has gone?"

"We assume she has the same seeds and root samples we have," said Arthur. "In addition, she may have the DNA sequences from the backcrossed plants—the full kit that would allow her to apply for a patent claiming to have invented apomictic crops, and not just maize."

Merrill raised his eyebrows. "Backcrossed?"

"The crossing of a hybrid back to the original parent generation," said Arthur.

"Bloody Russians. I bet they stole the seeds," said Merrill. "I bet they killed Scott . . . and Miss Lichfield . . . and bloody Tanya is selling it all to Putin, right now, just like the minister said."

"But we do not know she went to Russia," Arthur said as firmly as he could. "Let's drink to Alastair Scott and Tanya Petrovskaya, inventors of apomictic maize. Whatever happens now, they are headed for the history books."

"And the whole world is going to be eating cornflakes made in bloody Moscow," added Merrill, gloomily.

"Merrill, will you stop it," snapped Arthur.

"Boyo, this means your trip to St. Petersburg is even more important than we thought. Those fucking Russians. They come over here, use our labs and all our high-tech equipment, and then they break into the lab and steal the result. First they stole our A-bomb secrets—from our own Klaus fucking Fuchs and then the frigging Rosenbergs. Now the Russians are supposed to be our friends and they nick our food secrets. Then they poison one of our research assistants. Jesus!"

Arthur wasn't listening.

"OK, OK," said Merrill. "I assume your flight is at dawn."

"Predawn," said Arthur, showing his irritation. Actually he had no idea which plane Eva had booked him on. "And Merrill, no calls, OK? All requests go through Eva until further notice."

"OK, boyo." Merrill looked crushed.

Normally, Arthur would have confided in Merrill when he was so brazenly disobeying orders—like going to Zurich instead of St. Petersburg—but this time was different. He felt he could not trust his friend, in his present mood, to keep this secret from his boss.

Sydney said she had to go home too, and Merrill eyed them suspiciously as they stood to leave. Outside the pub, Sydney said, "Dinner's off, isn't it? You need to pack. Let's do it when you come back."

Arthur had been looking forward to the evening, but he knew she was right. It wasn't the packing—a laptop and a change of clothes—so much as the phone calls he had to make. He needed to be alone, but it was hard to leave her.

"You know something, Sydney, Kew Gardens needs more people like you. No, not just Kew Gardens. The world needs more people like you—smart, honest, funny, hardworking, independent, sensible people. That's what the world needs more of."

"Thanks, Dr. Hemmings, but is that really how you see me?"

"That's one view." He smiled, his best and most seductive smile. Merrill had once told Arthur that this smile could fell women like saplings in a high wind.

"And what do you know about my funny gene, pray?" She was smiling back at him, a wide-open sexy smile from her own seductive arsenal.

"Let's put it this way. An experienced breeder can usually tell a lot about the genotype from the phenotype, the outside hints at what's inside."

She looked him in the eye, shook her hair, and chuckled.

"Bloody Brits. But thanks for letting me in on the discovery, Doctor. It's been truly amazing. Good luck—wherever it is you're really going."

She gave him a peck on the cheek and walked off into the night, still smiling.

He watched her disappear across the common. He thought she might turn around and wave, but she kept going. Her walk had a spring in it: on some people it looked silly; on Sydney it was sexy, swishing her thick brown hair. He shook his own shaggy head and turned for his cottage. Enough romance for one evening. He had work to do.

As Arthur opened his front door, he almost tripped on the white envelope that Eva Szilard had put through the letter box. Inside were Matt Raskin's résumé and the research papers he had asked for on

Fusarium toxins, including a recent paper in Russian and toxicology studies on *Abrus* and aconite. Eva had added some touches of her own to Raskin's biography. Such additions were her trademark, and they were often more useful than the stuff he'd asked for.

Born in New York City, April 28, 1975. Only child. Father and mother academics at Columbia University. Father biologist, mother historian. Supporters of the antiwar movement during Vietnam. Lifelong Democrats. Father died last year. Mother continues to work at Columbia. Raskin went to Duke for his first degree—"an American hodgepodge," as Eva put it, of biological sciences—but he won a place at Harvard to study biotech agriculture under Professor Kaplan, one of the best in the business. But after a term, he found Kaplan too "detailed." Wanting to spread his wings, he applied for a summer program at Oxford.

At the time, Scott was running a series of seminars on apomixis—the hot topic for PhD botany students—and there was a chance for a full doctorate. Scott apparently liked Raskin, and the youth's summer work took him to the labs at the Lower Witton Experimental Farm, where he worked with Scott for two years cross-breeding maize with *Tripsacum*. Scott's team had made steady but not spectacular progress at raising the maize-*Tripsacum* chromosome ratio.

Raskin left Oxford with a PhD, returned to Harvard to add a law degree, and became a patent attorney in Zurich, where he had been ever since. His specialty was biotech patents. U.S. citizen. Unmarried. Eva had included his home address and phone number.

Arthur smiled. "Beautiful," he said to himself as he read on.

Marc Haber, of Zurich Interpol, had returned her call and left his home and office numbers. He had information. Arthur's plane to Zurich was at 7:15 a.m. Ticket at the airport. She would water the rock plants. "The high-low in Zurich today was 68–57. Zurich has had a late spring. Take a light sweater for the evenings," she advised.

Eva, amazing Eva, Arthur sighed. He left her a billet-doux on the kitchen table and two requests. First, could she get the biohazard lab at Kew to test Karen's blood and Band-Aid samples for trichothecenes? Harry Torrens would be his first choice for the job. He should be told that the Band-Aid had covered a human skin lesion, thought to contain T2. The samples were in an ice pouch in his fridge. Second, would she get the Kew photo lab to blow up the *Chronicle* picture of the cars in front of the museum on the day of the break-in, and if the license plates were visible, find the owners? He penned a "P.S. Please ignore the mess."

He called Fred Barton, who was still in the *Chronicle*'s office, and offered his sympathy for his friend Karen. Fred sounded very low. He was writing her obit for the next day's paper. The police were analyzing objects from Karen's flat. The vice-chancellor had stopped the hospital from issuing any details about her death. Arthur said he would be away for a couple of days and would get in touch on Saturday.

"That's the day of Scott's funeral, just been announced, at Magdalen Chapel."

"See you there," said Arthur.

Then he dialed the number Eva had given him for Haber.

"Marc, Arthur here. You probably know what I'm calling about . . . "

"Yes, yes. What a mess. You were right, as always. She's here, your Russian. I won't go into details on the phone. When are you coming?"

"First thing in the morning."

"Call me when you get in. You'd better hurry. The Americans are ahead of you. *À bientôt.*"

Twenty

Arthur spent the flight to Zurich reading about mycotoxins. The Russian report was the most interesting, as he had expected. The new variant of *Fusarium,* T3, had been found on moldy wheat in the Orenburg district, north of the Caspian Sea. Russian researchers were working on antidotes and also genetically engineered wheat that could resist attacks by *Fusarium* fungus—exactly what Karen Lichfield had been doing.

Arthur put his head back against the seat and thought about the possibilities. Tanya could have brought samples of T3 with her, as Karen Lichfield had said. When the Russian work became more widely known, the secret services would warn about terrorists' use of the new toxin, maybe even suggesting a Kremlin link, one more reason why Arthur's freelance detour to Zurich would send Williams into a full-court rage. He knew he had to move fast.

When he arrived at the Zurich airport shortly after nine o'clock, there were urgent messages from Eva. She picked up before the first ring of his cell phone.

"Merrill is frantic and wants to talk to you."

"Tell him I'm in St. Petersburg, out of range," Arthur said.

"But that's a lie, Arthur."

"A white lie, Eva."

"Yes, sir," said Eva.

"Sorry, I didn't mean to bark. I'm finally in the right place, thanks to you, but I've got a lot of catching up to do."

He hailed a taxi, slung his duffel bag on the seat beside him, and told the driver to go Lindenhofstrasse. He had not been to the Interpol office for several years, but he remembered that the building looked like an ordinary town house. The wine scandal that had brought Arthur and Marc Haber together had attracted a lot of publicity and launched Haber's career. Back then Haber was a lieutenant. Now he was an inspector, working on customs fraud and money laundering, and close to retirement. Arthur was looking forward to seeing him again.

The town house was unmarked and shabbier than he remembered it, at least from outside. The building itself was not a secret, of course. There was even a bar named Interpol a few doors up the street, with photographs of deceased agents on the walls. Haber met Arthur coming out of the elevator on the fourth floor. He was a jolly man and rotund, to put it gently. He still had the mischievous eye and a small mustache, a contrivance to resemble Hercule Poirot, so Arthur believed, although Haber always took some joy in making fun of the Belgians.

Haber had put on weight, rather a lot of weight, and Arthur was sure the Swiss policeman was looking at him with a similarly critical eye, discerning a slightly saggier version of the trim youth of almost thirty years ago.

He gave Arthur a bear hug.

"*Ça va, mon vieux?* You're looking splendid."

"And so are you, Marc. You've been living well," he teased.

Haber laughed, brushing a large hand across gray hair, smoothed back. "You seem to have found a few good restaurants yourself. Shall we go and have a drink? Or would you prefer to talk here? I have some excellent brandy."

"Here is better, I think," said Arthur. "One of your famous schnapps would go down well before lunch."

Haber's office featured the dreary utility furniture of any policeman's quarters—with one exception. There was a prominent drinks cabinet, with about a dozen wine bottles in a sturdy metal rack and a formidable selection of schnapps.

"So, my friend, you are chasing Russians again," said Haber, raising his glass in a toast and trying to look comfortable in his angular office chair.

Arthur told the story of Scott's death and why he was interested in meeting up with Tanya Petrovskaya. By Arthur's reckoning, the final stage of a race to patent the apomixis research had to be going on here, somewhere in sleepy Zurich. He did not go into unnecessary details. He did not mention Matt Raskin. That could come later.

"Well, the Americans are ahead of you, as I told you," Haber said, sifting through a pile of papers on his desk. "We have had several phone calls over the past few days from the offices of a New York law firm asking for any details on your Russian, Mademoiselle Petrovskaya. They said it was in connection with money transfers through Switzerland to America. We have dealt with this law firm in the past and they have done things for us."

"Money transfers?"

Haber raised his eyebrows and shook his head.

"We found her, this Petrovskaya, registered in a small hotel in the Old Town. You would not want to stay there."

"I'm at the Rosengarten."

"Good. Food, so-so."

Haber read from notes on his desk.

"The hotel is called the Monch. It's on Brunngasse. She is supposed to have been there for three days."

"And the name of the law firm?" asked Arthur.

"The law firm is called . . . I can't pronounce these names."
Haber gave the notes to Arthur. The firm was Jennings, Philpott &
Redfern, on Park Avenue, New York.

"So, someone from this firm called to ask about Tanya Petrovskaya, claiming that she was somehow involved in money laundering?" asked Arthur.

"Yes, that's what I'm telling you," said Haber.

"When did you let them know?"

"Let's see, it tells you exactly. Our response was at five thirty-five
p.m. yesterday; that's ten thirty-five a.m. New York time.

"And four thirty-five p.m. London time," said Arthur, thinking of
Sir Freddie and Richard Eikel huddled in the embassy corridor.

"Correct."

Arthur made a note of the law firm and the times of the calls.

"That's about all I know, my dear friend. Will you have time for
lunch or dinner? We could go back to the Odeon. You always loved
to dine where Lenin had coffee."

"That was a long time ago," said Arthur. "My tastes and politics
have matured—well, let's say seasoned—since then. How about the
Zunfthaus um Ruden?"

"A fine choice. You have grown up, finally."

Haber said he would love to lunch at the Zunfthaus, but right
now he had another appointment.

"Boring meeting about money transfers—real money transfers,
this time. To tell you the truth, I'm getting sick of these banks. They
are so big, so corrupt. Why can't we get back to chasing wine crooks?"

"Why not, indeed." Arthur sighed.

Haber's phone rang. He wrote notes of the caller's information on a piece of paper on his desk. *"Merci,* Charles."

"I had a man watch the Hotel Monch. A car, a brand-new dark blue Audi, an A6 Quattro, with a male driver has also been sitting outside the hotel."

"Russians?" asked Arthur, partly in jest.

"Non, non, non," said Haber. "Impossible. They don't drive Audis. They drive Fiats, maximum a thousand cc."

They both laughed.

"This car belongs to the new fleet of Audis owned by Panrustica, our latest global company to take up residence in Zurich. Perhaps you should go and take a look for yourself."

He rose awkwardly from his chair. "I'll come down with you. There's one more thing, talking of Panrustica."

When they reached the street, Haber suggested that they walk a little. They turned off the main road, down a side street, and Haber gave Arthur an Interpol ID card in Haber's name and a bunch of his own official Interpol visiting cards—in case Arthur found himself in a tight spot, a place he couldn't get into, or out of.

"You never know, my friend. You appear to be dealing with bandits."

"You're too generous," Arthur said.

"The last thing I have for you is quite distasteful, frankly," said Haber.

He told Arthur that the American law firm had confided in their Interpol contact that Panrustica's chairman, Sir Freddie, had a mistress.

"Name of Louise Beauchamp. She lives in Zurich, up on the hill. It seems they want to spread dirt around, for what purpose I really don't know," he said, throwing up his hands and giving Arthur a knowing smile.

"If they know, I thought you ought to know," he added.

And then they parted, Arthur promising to keep in touch.

★ ★ ★

Across a bridge over the Limmat River and through the Old Town
Arthur found the Hotel Monch. It was a three-story house turned
into a small hotel, badly in need of a facelift. Probably a few other
things besides. He was prepared to bet it was not in the guidebook.

He walked the length of Brunngasse, down one side and up the
other. On the corner of Neumarkt, a blue Audi, an A6 Quattro, was
parked, just as Haber had described. There was a driver inside but
sunvisors obscured his face. The driver would have a full view of the
entrance to the hotel, Arthur guessed. He resisted the temptation to
go and bang on the window. Instead he took the car's number and
walked into the hotel, his back to the Audi. There was no point in
advertising his arrival.

The lobby smelled of stale tobacco smoke and disinfectant
and Arthur could have written his name in the dust on the counter of the reception desk. He asked for Tanya Petrovskaya, but the
receptionist, an elderly, oversized woman who barely fit into the
space behind the counter, was on the phone speaking in French
about her dog's visit to the vet. After Arthur had coughed loudly
several times, she broke off to say that Mademoiselle Petrovskaya
had not spent a night in the hotel since she arrived two days ago,
adding, almost as an afterthought, that if she did not turn up tonight, the hotel was going to inform the police. Then she resumed
her conversation. Arthur picked up a copy of the *Zuricher Zeitung*
lying on the desk and walked out into the street, shielding his face
with the newspaper. Then he walked through the Old Town to his
hotel, the Rosengarten, on a quiet residential street, away from the
shops and close to the Kunsthaus, Zurich's best art museum. In his
room, he left the license number of the Audi on Haber's recording machine, in case it was a different car from the one Haber had
described.

He phoned Eva and left a message asking her to check out the New York law firm of Jennings, Philpott & Redfern and see if they had ever worked for Transgene, Panrustica, or anyone else interested in apomictic maize patents. Then he asked the operator for the number for a Louise Beauchamp. The number was unlisted.

Twenty-one

Matt Raskin lived in a dreary postwar block on Hirschengraben that reminded Arthur of Zurich's jarring mixture of architecture. Treasured medieval buildings along the banks of the Limmat, clean and comfortable cuckoo-clock chalets up on the hill, and in between were some of the most dismal, uninviting apartment buildings outside the old Soviet bloc.

Arthur was waiting in the lobby when the young American patent attorney arrived home from work, and he recognized Raskin easily from the *Chronicle*'s photo file. In the past five years, the young man had barely changed: curly, short brown hair, beard, and intense eyes peering through heavy-rimmed spectacles.

"Matt Raskin, sorry to bounce you," Arthur said in his best public school manner. "I'm Arthur Hemmings of Kew Gardens. You might know my name. It's about Professor Scott."

He was racing through his prepared spiel as Raskin eyed him with suspicion and perhaps a tinge of fear.

"I hate to be the bearer of bad news, but you may not have heard that Professor Scott has been found dead—drowned in the Thames."

Matt stared at him, his shoulders dropping slowly to a full slump.

"Sorry, I don't think I . . . would you say that again?"

"Professor Scott's body was found on Tuesday, drowned in the Thames near Lower Witton."

"Dead . . . drowned . . . no, I didn't know that." He spoke quietly with a slight British rhythm to his American accent.

"You are who?" he inquired, looking Arthur up and down.

Arthur took out his Kew ID.

"Arthur Hemmings of Kew? Yes, yes, I think I've heard of you. Maybe we've even met."

The young man was clearly off balance, not wanting to believe what he was hearing about his old professor.

"I know this is not the best moment, but I would like to have a chat about Scott's work. I'm supposed to be doing an evaluation—of the science."

"No, er, yes . . . of course," stammered Raskin. "Please come up. Sixth floor. Not the greatest place, I'm afraid, but I've been so busy. Never seem to have time to move, uh, to move house, even to think about moving."

The dimly lit elevator chugged down to get them, then lurched up to the sixth floor.

"You said drowned in the Thames?"

Arthur nodded. "Yes, his body was found at Queen's Lock. You must know it."

"I do, yes, of course. Just downriver from Lower Witton."

Raskin looked weak. He was pale and began taking deep breaths—puffing his cheeks and then blowing them out through pursed lips, fighting back tears, Arthur imagined.

The elevator stopped finally at the sixth floor.

★ ★ ★

Raskin's apartment barely had essentials—a living room and, Arthur presumed, one bedroom. The living area was uncomfortably furnished with cheap Swedish chairs and a futon. Several large unframed posters of art exhibitions were pinned to the walls, suggesting the occupant only planned a short stay.

Arthur apologized again for his intrusion, adding, as an excuse, a false excuse, that he had tried to phone Matt at his office.

"Yes, we have a problem," Raskin said as he pulled off his backpack and offered Arthur an uninviting chair. "They've gone crazy over security since hackers broke into the system."

"Hackers?" Arthur had not heard about this.

Raskin explained that as a patent attorney he had an office in the same building that housed the World Patent Organization, on Bahnhofstrasse. The WPO was a new, and somewhat controversial, organization run by the United Nations. There were still many quirks in the system, and a week ago the main computer had started erasing applications for biotech patents. Security had blamed outside hackers. There was a backup system, of course, but it had taken time to retrieve things that had been rubbed out, and they had lost data. Security at the WPO was tight as a result.

"Would you like a drink?" Matt asked Arthur, finally.

"A brandy would be great," said Arthur. "You look as though you could do with one yourself."

"Yeah, a brandy, maybe I'll have . . . in the kitchen. I'm sorry, I'm finding this all rather difficult." Matt let his backpack drop to the floor and slumped into a chair.

Arthur went into the kitchen, found an opened brandy bottle, and filled two glasses. Arthur then told Matt Raskin about the last forty-eight hours at Oxford, leaving out the mystery of Karen's poisoning, for the moment. Raskin was staring at the walls and taking gulps of his brandy. He didn't look like a drinker and Arthur worried that he might suddenly get sick or pass out.

Arthur explained that Kew was assessing how far Scott had progressed in the maize-*Tripsacum* chromosome ratios.

"Well, I didn't know about the most up-to-date results, of course," Raskin said.

Arthur took a sip of his drink. "I'll be frank, Mr. Raskin . . . , er . . . Matt, if I may. Our preliminary analysis at Kew suggests that Scott's research has blown the Americans out of the water on apomixis ratios—although so far we have been unable to confirm these tests with lab notebooks, or find the relevant DNA sequences. The British government would like to see the research patented in the name of Oxford University, naming its leading scientists and researchers, Professor Scott postmortem, of course.

"Big money is involved, as you will appreciate. Big egos—big scientific, business, and political egos. But I'm telling you things you already know."

Matt took a few more deep, uneven breaths. His eyes were darting around the room as he struggled to reply.

After a long pause, he said, "I must tell you that I find it very difficult to say anything about this right now, Mr. Hemmings, for many reasons. Could we talk about it tomorrow?"

Arthur was surprised. Raskin was shaken, but not shaken enough yet to do what Arthur wanted.

"Let me put it another way, more specifically this time," said Arthur. It was really too early to play his hunches, but time was limited.

"Tanya Petrovskaya—I think you know her—is in Zurich. She has brought research materials—presumably lab reports, seeds, greenhouse samples, and maybe even the key DNA sequences from Oxford—all someone might need to make an application for an apomixis patent to the WPO. You worked for Scott. Now you are a freelance patent attorney. You would be the perfect person to make the application. Perhaps Professor Scott has even asked you to do just that. There's one snag. Tanya Petrovskaya is being followed by agents who work for all those egos I was talking about. And they would like to sabotage Scott's project—in whatever way they can. They may even have access to some of the materials needed for the patent application, some of the seeds, for example, but not all of them. They will be trying to lay their hands on the rest of the material. Scott's death has changed things dramatically."

Arthur paused, searching for a good conclusion, one that would get this youth's attention. "These agents may already have been involved in criminal activity in the UK." He avoided the details.

"I'm not a cop," Arthur continued. "I'm here to try and ensure the best possible outcome for the British government, for whom I work as an employee of Kew Gardens and as a scientist. Frankly, I'm also here to find the best solution for science and humanity, although I don't expect you to believe that quite yet. In other words, if, by any chance, you are involved in making the application for Scott, I'm not your enemy."

Arthur disliked putting the situation so bluntly, at this awkward moment, to this intense young man. Several images of the next few days must have been coursing through Matt's head, none of them exactly inviting. The young attorney put his head in his hands for a long moment. Then he sat up, looked straight at Arthur, and offered his response—a calm, considered, legal response, despite his emotional state.

"I appreciate your frankness, Mr. Hemmings. But I also have my loyalties. I have given my word to a friend, my professor, who has suddenly died. That doesn't relieve me of my commitment to him, and in a way, it makes it more steadfast, more important that I should not fail him. Secondly, I am ethically unable to discuss the matter because the information you seek is restricted by attorney-client privilege, as you will appreciate. I hope you will not take this answer as anything against you personally. I do not want to be obstructive. I am as eager for the right outcome as you say you are, but I must repeat what I said before. I cannot talk about this now. I would be happy to meet with you tomorrow at . . . "

He hesitated. "I won't actually be in the office tomorrow. A late lunch, maybe, around one thirty. Shall we say the Limmat Bar?"

Arthur was impressed by the young man's recovery. He guessed, and it was only a guess, that Matt Raskin had not yet received the materials from Tanya. But he would receive them soon enough, probably within twenty-four hours. This was no time to pursue the conversation, but this was a time to lay out the risks.

"I admire your courage," Arthur said. "However, I must tell you that I believe you and Ms. Petrovskaya to be in some danger. I would like to fix a definite time to see you tomorrow. Can you tell where you will be before our lunch? Or give me a contact number? Here's my cell. Can you give me yours?"

Matt went to a desk and wrote down the number on the back of his business card.

"And now, Mr. Hemmings, I'd like to be alone, if you don't mind. I have many things to think about."

"Just one last thing, if I may," said Arthur as he rose to leave. "Nothing about science. A trivial question, possibly, but it's been bothering me. After Scott's disappearance, I went to his house to look through his papers. I came across two editions of *The Oxford Book of English Verse,* you know, the ones bound in red leather and printed on India paper."

"Yes, yes, I know the edition, of course. I remember Scott had one, possibly several."

"I was interested because I collect them, so I rather impudently inspected his copies," said Arthur. "One was signed to 'the Scholar' from 'the Gypsy' and dated Christmas last year. It was signed with the initials M. R. Those are your initials. That wouldn't be you, would it?"

"Um, umm," Matt hesitated. "I know Arnold's 'Scholar Gypsy'

well, of course. Who wouldn't, having been at Oxford, and especially working at the farm? That's where it was written, after all, or in a field nearby, so they say.

"It's true Scott's nickname was 'the Scholar.' He used to spend a lot of time walking in Whytham Wood—like the Scholar Gypsy of the poem. He and I used to read Arnold aloud together in his garden in the summer. He loved poetry. As to whether those are my initials. They are, of course, but I did not give the book to Scott."

Arthur felt he had gone far enough.

"Well, forgive me again; I've caused you enough grief. I'm staying at the Rosengarten near the Kunsthaus. You know it, of course?"

"Sure, of course."

"Until lunch, then . . . and be careful."

As Arthur walked out of the apartment building, he worried about leaving this vulnerable young man alone, but he had things to do. Matt's explanation about the security at the WPO had made him realize how sparse his knowledge really was about filing patents. An American friend, Tom Franklin from the University of Colorado days, who had become a patent expert, could help, he thought. Fortified by a bratwurst and sauerkraut from a stall in the Niederhofstrasse, he hurried past Tanya's hotel, once again on the way to his own. On the corner of Brunngasse, the blue Audi was still parked.

In his hotel room, Arthur punched in the number for Tom Franklin and waited. Franklin had been his closest friend in Boulder, where Arthur had done his masters in botany after leaving Oxford. Boulder was two years of intense fun interrupted, only periodically it had seemed at the time, by lab work and a Russian language course, which Tom had insisted they take together—to understand better both sides in the Cold War. Everyone agreed Tom was a genius, in and out of the lab. He played blues on an old steel-stringed guitar in local bars. Together they pursued Colorado's legions of coeds with variable success.

Tom had soared in the biotech realm. He became a professor of molecular biology at Boulder but quickly tired of the job and started his own institute in Seattle, working on biotech plants useful to developing countries. Tom was obsessed with the stifling effect of corporate patents—how big biotech companies had patented lab tools so that independent researchers, and especially developing countries, could never start their own biotech operations without paying heavy royalties. Tom was now inventing around those corporate patents, as he put it, placing his discoveries into a patent commons, like the open source software movement. He wanted biotech scientists to share the tools of innovation and had convinced an Internet millionaire to back a foundation—the Crucible Foundation—to oversee the ambitious project. Arthur approved of the idea, not only for agriculture but for medicines, but he was skeptical that it could work. He found Tom in his Seattle lab.

"What the hell are you doing in Zurich?" Tom asked.

"Too complicated to explain," said Arthur. "Just wanted to hear your voice and ask a couple questions."

"I know you're up to no good," he laughed. "What's the problem?"

Arthur explained about Scott and the rush to patent the apomixis work he had left behind.

"Trying to steal a march on Panrustica, are you? I don't blame you. If those bastards get an apomixis patent, it'll set back agriculture in the developing countries by at least a generation. Scott should have put his inventions into a protected commons."

"I think that was his idea," said Arthur. He asked Tom how long it would take to file such a patent—if you had the right lab materials and data.

A few days, Tom guessed, to mark up the application.

"Do you know Matt Raskin?"

"Very bright, just out of Harvard Law. One of the few recent graduates with a social conscience. I've never used him myself, but I know people who have. He's first-rate. He has been very interested in my Crucible Foundation for a protected commons for patents. Scott's work would be a perfect candidate for the Foundation, of course."

"I've just met him," said Arthur, relieved. "Had a favorable impression, but it's good to have your endorsement." He asked to be excused from small talk. There was a lot to catch up on, but it would have to wait, and he promised to call back.

"I know, queen and country first, right," he said, chuckling. "Good luck and keep your head down. Panrustica is not going to let this one go without a fight, and they fight dirty. Call me when it's over. It's time you came out here again—no excuses."

Arthur took a brandy out of the minibar and drank to his friend. It was too long since they had spent an evening on the town, and he was smiling at the thought as there was a knock at the door. It was the hotel porter with a fax from Eva—a company profile of Jennings, Philpott & Redfern. They had worked for Transgene regularly, enforcing patent rights. They were well-known corporate lawyers who had helped defend the tobacco and asbestos companies against class action suits. Eikel, Arthur knew, had worked with tobacco companies before joining Transgene, and that crowd had written the book on how to play low and mean in class action lawsuits.

Eikel. Richard Eikel. So, what else was up this polished southerner's elegant sleeve? He decided he would arrive at the Limmat Bar on the early side tomorrow, just in case.

Twenty-two

Matt *Raskin rested* on top of his bed that night, never really closing his eyes. Scott's death meant that the professor's plan to patent the apomixis research would take more than an ordinary investment of his time. It was no longer merely a botanist's protest, an expression of moral outrage from a distinguished Oxford professor who believed in the purity of science. He and Tanya were two youngsters without professional recognition and, perhaps now, without friends. Arthur had unnerved him with his uncanny guesswork about Scott's plan, if it was just guesswork. He had found Arthur to be sympathetic, an apparently caring scientist, but why should Matt trust him? Arthur had said that Tanya was already in Zurich and that she was being followed, but by whom? The suspect list included the CIA, MI5, the Russians, the Chinese, Panrustica, or any of the other agribusiness giants. They all had a stake in the outcome. Arthur Hemmings worked for the British government and it was an odd coincidence, to say the least, that he had arrived in Zurich on the eve of the handover of Scott's material. Matt had always understood that Scott's plan had its hazards, but hearing of the danger so clearly, so officially from Hemmings had rattled the young scientist. He also wondered how the vulnerable, exotic Tanya would react to the news of Scott's death. They had been very close—she and Scott. He even wondered about filing a patent for a dead man. He had seen posthumous patents before, although he had never completed one himself.

Once again he went over Scott's elaborate, far too elaborate plan for Tanya to hand over the apomixis file—which he hoped would include the seeds, lab notebooks, slides, and the DNA sequences. He took Scott's last letter out of his pocket, carefully unfolding the paper as though it were an antique vellum. He stared, once again, at the familiar writing in blue ink. It was a script that had long ago gone out of fashion with the retirement of older professors like Scott who would write their comments on student essays with a favorite fountain pen. Scott had sent the three-page letter Poste Restante, Zurich, the safest way, and Matt smiled at the paper in his hand, which now represented a personal, intimate farewell that would never be found on Scott's hard drive.

My dear Matt,

We have had some extraordinary good fortune in the laboratory. In our latest batch of maize, the chromosome ratios in the maturing plants have risen to 35:3. The F1 generation has proved to be vigorously apomictic. In addition, we have used SCAM to locate the apomictic genes on the relevant *Tripsacum* chromosome, using backcrossed chromosomes as indicators. We are, therefore, ready to apply for a patent which goes way beyond the American work.

I have been under intolerable pressure in recent days to sign an agreement for future research funds with Panrustica that would, in effect, give them an exclusive license on *anything* we produce, or patent, from now on.

I have no wish to be an impediment in the university's desperate search for funds. Believe me, I know how badly we need money. But I cannot, in all good conscience, do the vice-chancellor's bidding and sign away my rights—or the university's—to Panrustica, or any other multinational corporation, however "green" they are claiming to be. I therefore want to put our plan into action without delay. We have chosen next Friday at 11 a.m.

Tanya will come to Zurich with all the material, and I ask you to work with her in preparing the application. Your name must be included on the application. Your contribution while you were here remains invaluable. I am afraid that if we file the application from here, word will get out. Worse, there may well be some skullduggery. Apart from the vice-chancellor, I have had visits from Panrustica reps and, if you please, an oily diplomat from the U.S. embassy in London, who was accompanied by a man from the CIA whom I can only describe as a thug. They made the outrageous suggestion that I could be funded by the U.S. government—if I agree to certain conditions, of course. The vice-chancellor has said that if I do not sign the Panrustica contract, my funding (from the university through Ag & Fish) will end and I will have to give up my laboratory. As you know, I am already past official retirement age, so the financial consequences would not be heavy, but morally, I cannot support any deal. This invention must be available to all. I am worried that Tanya may have problems at the border, or customs, although the material she is carrying is not obtrusive. Once she is inside

Switzerland, I fear she may be followed. So be careful and don't rush to greet her. Maybe that's all my paranoia.

She will be at the Kunsthaus at 11 o'clock, as arranged. She has a foolproof plan which I have approved. Just follow her instructions. I can think of no better hands for our research to be in. Remember, there are people who do not want this to happen and they will resist it with every instrument in their considerable power. Once you have the papers ready, I will join you in Zurich.

> With my truest good wishes,
> Ever yours,
> A. S.

Matt knew that he had no option but to carry out the last wishes of the teacher he had so revered. Scott's voice of reason and morality followed his students for years after their graduation, always pushing them to use science for the betterment of humanity. He made them feel guilty for accepting any "preferment," as he always called it, money for a lecture to colleagues at a comfortable forum, which he considered an academic duty, and especially an honorarium from an institution or corporation.

As the clock on the Grossmunster struck eleven, Matt Raskin was sitting in the Café Munch across the road from the Kunsthaus. From his window seat he could see the entrance to the museum and the tram stop nearby. There were several people in the café, and he paid no attention to the man at the back, wearing a white cotton safari jacket, jeans, dark glasses, and a Panama hat.

Tanya was among the passengers from the next tram to arrive. He recognized her immediately. She was wearing the same blue denim jacket and tight black corduroys he remembered she had worn so often in Oxford. Her blond hair was tied in a short ponytail, and as always, she looked younger than her thirty years. She was beautiful, very beautiful.

She carried a small handbag, which was certainly not big enough to contain the papers and the materials from the lab, but that did not worry him. There was to be no exchange of the material in public. The plan was for her to leave instructions about where to find them. All Matt knew was that there would be two stops on this treasure hunt. The first was the Rodin in the Salle Moderne at the Kunsthaus. This was to establish they were both in Zurich. They were not to talk to each other. Tanya had suggested the Rodin at the museum as it was a favorite drop for Soviet spies during the Cold War. If either failed to turn up, they would repeat the procedure the next day. The second venue was James Joyce's grave in Zurich's cemetery on the hill above the city, where Tanya would leave a card in an envelope for Matt, marked "From the Scholar," in a bouquet of flowers. Inside would be instructions to retrieve the material. Timing was everything. Matt was supposed to arrive at the cemetery one hour exactly after the first sighting of Tanya at the Kunsthaus.

When this treasure hunt was over, Tanya was to disappear for a few days while he prepared a WPO application. She had said she would probably go to the mountains. If all went according to plan, she was supposed to make contact again on Monday. Scott had been going to join them later in the week.

Matt paid for his coffee, walked across the road to the museum, bought a ticket, and went directly to the Salle Moderne. Tanya was already standing in front of the Rodin in the middle of the room. Matt barely resisted the temptation to rush up to her. The uniformed guard, a woman, was watching from the other side of the room. Tanya went close to the statue, paused, then stepped back a couple of paces and moved slowly toward the exit, stopping briefly at the Munchs on her way out. Matt moved into the room toward the Rodin, where she could see him. When he looked up again,

Tanya was gone. He was supposed to wait five minutes, then catch a tram to the cemetery.

As the Grossmunster clock struck the half hour, Matt walked out of the Kunsthaus and along the Limmatquai. He did not notice the man in the Panama hat and sunglasses following a hundred yards behind him.

Twenty-three

Before boarding the tram to the cemetery, Matt bought a bunch of red tulips to put on Joyce's grave. It was Tanya's idea—he would look like just another admirer. The tram wound its way up the hill, past the university, making stops along the way. The passengers included a number of schoolchildren going to the zoo and old people returning home from a morning's shopping, or visiting the cemetery. Matt, trying to take his mind off the task at hand, started marveling at the Swiss pensioners, how fit they looked. The Swiss lived longer than any other nationality except for the Japanese, he had read somewhere. Maybe Calvinism prolonged life, or perhaps it was hiking in the mountains, or the alpine waters.

The tram reached the zoo terminus 6, opposite the cemetery, a minute before midday. On time, almost to the second. Everyone got out; the schoolchildren rushed to the zoo gates; the pensioners moved slowly into the cemetery, which was surprisingly crowded.

People were sitting on wooden benches, taking in the midday sun while they ate their lunch. Matt had been to Joyce's grave once before, and he remembered the bronze statue, small like Joyce had been in real life, with wire spectacles and a walking stick. Matt had been there in winter, and the statue had looked lonely and fragile in the snow. Now, in early summer, it was covered with gifts from admirers. Tanya was nowhere in sight, but he hoped she was watching him from a distance. Several people were in front of him, blocking his view. An old man in a tweed jacket put a daffodil in Joyce's lap. A tourist from Ireland, perhaps, on a pilgrimage. A woman in an overcoat stood in front of the grave, then did a little curtsy and moved on. The couple directly in front of Matt stood for a while and bowed their heads. Then it was his turn.

A sign in German, French, and English in the grass verge in front of the grave said Please Do Not Touch. But people had touched the statue, of course. The toes of Joyce's bronze shoes were polished to a handsome gleam from so many admiring fingers. Leaning against his shoes, among other bouquets, was a small bunch of alpine primroses, and inserted into the delicate green stems was a small white envelope, the size of a visiting card. In a black felt pen were written the words "From the Scholar."

Matt's hands were trembling as he bent down, placed his tulips beside the primroses with one hand, and picked up the envelope with his other hand, slipping it smoothly into his pocket. He turned to walk away, and the man behind him moved forward. It was the man in the Panama hat, still wearing his dark glasses. As the man approached the grave, Matt moved away, walked down the gravel path, and sat on a bench in between two pensioners.

He brought the small envelope out of his pocket and opened it. Inside was a ticket for luggage at the Bahnhof. He stared at the little brown ticket with its date stamp, three days ago. Tanya had done well. He put the ticket back in the envelope and slipped it into his pocket. He cast a quick glance around the cemetery, hoping to catch a glimpse of Tanya, but there was no sign of her. He did see the man in the Panama hat on a bench, directly opposite him. The man immediately looked in another direction. Matt noted the man's white cotton safari jacket and blue jeans. He was shortish, rather stocky. Just another admirer, Matt told himself, but he was feeling slightly uneasy. He checked his watch. It was 12:30. If he caught the next tram, he would be at the Limmat Bar in good time for his lunch with Arthur Hemmings.

Without looking at the man, he got up and walked back to the tram terminus. Two cars were waiting, and he boarded the first one, this one quickly filling up with schoolchildren carrying cardboard cutouts of animals in the zoo. There was no room to sit down. The man in the Panama hat got into the second car and found a seat, and then the tram took off. The children were shouting and giggling and bumping into Matt as he nervously glanced back at the man in the second car. He was looking out of the window, but Matt could see the reflection of his face in the glass and was convinced that the man was looking in his direction. A sudden panic gripped him. This man had been behind him in the line for the grave and must have seen him pick up the envelope. And now he was following him. Matt nudged the children aside and moved to the front of the first car, as far as possible from the man. The journey seemed to take forever, the tram stopping at each stop.

By the time they reached the Bahnhof Bridge terminus, Matt had decided that he would not go directly to the Limmat Bar, which was across the street. He had to know if the man was really following him. He would walk along the quai and buy another bunch of tulips at the flower stand to test his suspicions. As he was paying for the flowers, he glanced back and saw that the man had stopped a few yards away and was looking down at the river. Even as a newcomer to this subterfuge, Matt now knew he had a shadow, someone who didn't seem to care that he was noticeable, wearing a Panama hat. He moved swiftly from the flower stand, dodging traffic to cross the street, and as he looked behind, he saw the man turn and follow him. He sprinted the last few yards to the bar, crashing into a couple coming out. Inside, he spotted Arthur sitting at a table in the window and waved the bunch of tulips. Arthur rose from his seat as he saw the open look of terror on the young American's face.

"I'm being followed," Matt stammered. "A man in a Panama hat—he's been following me all the way from the cemetery. It's like you said it would be."

Arthur shook his head. Men in Panama hats? Cemeteries? A bunch of red tulips? Matt Raskin seemed to have lost it.

"Sit down, and calm down," he said, firmly. "And thanks for the flowers; I presume they're for me."

"This is no joke, Mr. Hemmings, look around the bar. A man in a Panama hat, dammit, and a white jacket, a safari jacket," Matt stammered as he sank into the easy chair.

"A safari jacket? Next you're going to tell me he has a shotgun," said Arthur, trying to make light of what, he knew, might easily be something more sinister.

"Yes, a safari jacket, a white safari jacket, and a Panama hat. Can you see him?"

Arthur remained standing and scanned the room. At the bar, with his back to Arthur, there was a man in a white jacket, apparently ordering a drink. And on the bar stool next to him was a Panama hat. He had a close-cropped head of blond hair. But Arthur told Matt he could see no such person and suggested that they both remain at the table, take it easy, and have a drink. He called over the waiter and ordered two schnapps, deliberately not giving the American any choice in the matter.

"Now, what have you been up to since I last saw you?" Arthur asked patronizingly, keeping one eye on the man at the bar. "By the way, last night I had a chat with a friend in the States, Tom Franklin, you might know of him. He runs a biotech institute outside Seattle and spoke very highly of you."

"Yes, I know of him, of course, he does excellent work," Matt replied, desperately wanting to tell his story about seeing Tanya, not listen to stories of Tom Franklin.

"But you have something to tell me, I can see," said Arthur. "I'm sorry, go ahead."

The waiter brought the schnapps and Matt took a large gulp, the glass shaking in his hand.

"I've seen Tanya. Well, only at a distance. It was part of Scott's plan, how to bring the material for the patent application to Zurich without anyone knowing—batty, yes, but it has worked, so far. I have a baggage ticket for the Bahnhof. I'm sure the material will be there. Tanya is very thorough. But I must tell you, Mr. Hemmings, that I'm through doing this alone. To hell with attorney-client privilege: my client is dead. I need your help."

"You have it," said Arthur, still watching the man at the bar. "Now, if you don't mind, I have a plan of my own. In case you were actually followed, just in case, this is what we should do. We will now leave the bar together. At the door onto the street, you will leave as quickly as you can without seeming to be in a hurry. Once outside, go to the Niederhofstrasse and get lost with the tourists. I'll be right behind you and meet you back at the Rosengarten."

Arthur saw the blood drain from Matt's face as he grabbed Matt's arm and lifted him out of his chair.

"Let's go," he ordered, pushing Matt toward the door. The man at the bar was watching them and easing himself off his bar stool. As Arthur and Matt drew level with the bar, Arthur pushed Matt toward the exit.

Without a moment's hesitation Arthur turned toward the blond man, put his left foot firmly on the ground, and swung his right leg up into the man's crotch. Arthur knew he had scored a direct hit when he felt the tip of his loafer sink into the soft part and the man shrieked in pain and sunk to the floor. Arthur picked up two glasses of red wine off the bar and threw them at the man, staining his jacket a deep purple. As the man struggled to get up, Arthur kicked him again.

The astonished barman leaped onto the bar and lunged at Arthur. Arthur shouted "Police," flashed Marc Haber's Interpol card, put 200 francs wrapped around one of Haber's business cards on the counter, and yelled to the barman to call the number on the card. Then he ran out into the street.

Arthur sprinted into the Niederhofstrasse hoping to find Matt, but there was no sign of him. He was looking back as he ran, but there was no sign of the man. A few quick turns into alleys and he was in the Rindermarkt, then the Neumarkt. Tourists were cursing him as he bumped into them. When he finally came out onto the Seilergraben, a broad main street, he skipped across the road to a waiting tram, catching it as it took off, his arm stuck briefly in the closing door. An elderly man looked at him disapprovingly and Arthur smiled back at him. The next stop was the Kunsthaus, a hundred yards from the Rosengarten. He had to admit he had enjoyed himself. He was looking forward to telling Haber about the bar brawl and making some real trouble for this blond-haired thug.

He arrived at the hotel just as Matt was walking into the lobby.

"You just cost me a sore foot and two hundred francs for the barman," said Arthur, smiling. "But I'm very glad to see you. Are you all right?"

"No," said Matt, his whole body trembling now.

"Come up to my room. I've got to change, and we haven't long. I ordered a car for six o'clock."

"A car?"

"Yes, we're going to Bern—after we've been to the Bahnhof, of course. Have another drink."

Arthur thrust a miniature bottle of brandy into Matt's hand and changed into his spare green shirt and the light sweater Eva had advised. Arthur wondered how this guileless youth could survive the next challenge, filing the patent. He grabbed Matt by the arm and led him to the elevator and down into the lobby. The Fiat rental, a compact 1,000 cc model, was waiting for them outside the hotel entrance. Arthur took the back route to the Bahnhof, via the Seilergraben, to avoid the traffic. He parked outside the station and looked at Matt's damp and pale face.

"Feeling all right?"

"I'm about to throw up."

"Shouldn't have drunk all that brandy."

"It's not the brandy. I'm just not used to this kind of subterfuge. I'm a patent attorney, not fucking James Bond."

"Let's go and get the stuff," Arthur said, patting the young man on the shoulder. He would have to remember that Matt was not his partner, someone schooled in the cagey arts. He was an innocent, caught in a nasty little war.

The luggage office was in the basement of the station and there were two people in front of them in the line, a student claiming a rucksack and a man retrieving golf clubs.

Funny, thought Arthur, I always believed a redeeming feature about the Swiss was that they don't play golf, not enough flat surfaces. Arthur was watching the golfer and eyeing Matt, who looked increasingly faint.

"Cheer up, young man," he whispered in Matt's ear. "The worst is over. Take a look around and see if you can see anyone in a Panama hat."

"Please, Mr. Hemmings, I feel sick."

It was their turn for the luggage: the golfer, apparently, was just a golfer. Arthur handed over the ticket plus five francs. The man returned with a battered aluminum case, the kind photographers use to carry cameras. Arthur grabbed the case and they headed back to the car.

"That's Scott's case. I recognize it. He used to keep his lecture slides in it," Matt said as they pulled out of the station.

"Good, then we have the treasure. Tell me about it on the way to Bern."

The traffic was flowing smoothly now. By late Friday afternoon most Zurichers were well on their way to the mountains for the weekend. Arthur and Matt would be in Bern for dinner.

On the way, Arthur had planned to question Matt about his relationship with Scott, what he knew about Tanya's past, what he knew about the DNA sequences. Sooner or later, Arthur had to tell him about Karen Lichfield, but Matt had already put the passenger seat back and had closed his eyes. He would sleep until they had reached the outskirts of Bern.

Twenty-four

As he drove beside the River Aare into the Swiss capital, Arthur remembered the city from a visit several years earlier. If it weren't for the hulking Bundeshaus, the nation's oversized parliament buildings, and the trams, Bern could be an alpine market town. At its center, the medieval clock tower rose above cobbled streets and presented its musical puppet show to admiring Bernese every hour on the hour. From the hillside on a clear day, you could see the peaks of the Jungfrau, Eiger, and Monch. Bern was scrubbed clean, inside and out, and at this time of year, it was festooned with scarlet geraniums, the city's official flower. It was a place for ordered, scientific people, like Einstein, who, as clerk at the national patent office, had developed his theory of relativity. Now the city boasted its attachment to science of all varieties, a perfect choice for what Arthur had planned.

A hundred yards from Einstein's old patent office, tucked away between the half-timbered houses, was Arthur's destination, a garden and a small greenhouse, surrounded by a brick wall. The Bern Physic Gardens had been breeding rare herbs since the 1800s and, for the last two decades, a Bern University botany professor, Alfred Geiger, had been in charge. He was Switzerland's leading specialist in maize, a crop hardly grown in the mountainous nation, but one that the government's botanists knew well because of Switzerland's agricultural work in developing countries, especially in Africa. As head of the Physic Gardens, Geiger had been a regular visitor to Kew, and on several occasions, he had been Arthur's dining companion.

A few years ago, during Arthur's extravagant phase of putting truffles in his soups, the professor, who had a license to hunt truffles in the Perigord, supplied the costly ingredient either by mail or sometimes, more pleasantly, in person. Arthur and the professor had become good friends, and even after Arthur's enthusiasm for these exotic dishes waned, their friendship had continued. Arthur and Geiger saw eye to eye on many things, especially the potential harm to pure science by the corporate takeover of university laboratories. In Arthur's small circle of friends, Professor Geiger was affectionately known as "Herr Truffle."

Before the drama in Zurich, Arthur had anticipated Matt's need for seclusion and perhaps a small laboratory and even, eventually, a greenhouse, to help shepherd Scott's application through the World Patent Organization. Geiger's Physic Gardens offered such a haven. Few people knew of the rare herbs growing behind the walls, and there were even fewer visitors. For most people interested in the plant world, Bern's Botanical Gardens, on the other side of the city, were a much greater attraction. As luck would have it, Professor Geiger was at home when Arthur had called and instantly warmed to the idea of being part of the apomixis patent. When Arthur explained the Geiger connection to Matt as they arrived in Bern, Matt smiled for the first time since Arthur had met him. He was happy, even eager, to disappear for a couple of days.

★　★　★

Shortly before six o'clock, the little Fiat with its priceless cargo pulled up outside the professor's house in Gellerstrasse, next door to the Physic Gardens. Geiger answered the doorbell immediately, his short, wiry frame topped with a full head of white hair so long it merged with his beard. The effect was a fluffy halo around his already round face. He peered at Arthur and Matt over his wire reading glasses with a look of paternal concern.

"I was beginning to get worried," he said as he hugged them in obvious relief.

Arthur introduced Matt as Geiger ushered them inside. He lived alone and the front room was overcrowded, to put it kindly, with family relics. A high-backed chair near the fireplace, Geiger's chair, was surrounded by piles of books on top of which sat a coffee mug, with the dried-out remains of the morning's brew. The sofa was covered in newspapers and scientific journals. As Geiger darted about the room, clearing places for his visitors to sit, he invited Arthur and Matt to take a quick tour of the gardens.

"You must see my teff specimens," he called after them as they went out the back door, past the garage where, Arthur remembered, Geiger kept his old Fiat, a tiny 600 cc model known in the sixties as the *topolino*—a "mousecar." When Arthur first met Geiger, the car was, even then, a relic, a faded red machine that looked as though it might not make it up the hill. Arthur patted the car affectionately and then took Matt, still clutching his suitcase, to the greenhouse and showed him several magnificent teff plants with their tiny dark brown seeds.

"The pride of Ethiopia," Arthur announced to the puzzled young American. Ethiopians, he explained, use teff to make *injera,* the spongy white bread with the consistency of a towel that is Ethiopia's national staple. "Now it's even grown in America, in Idaho, I think," Arthur announced, proud of being able to supply the latest

information on this arcane crop, but Matt's expression was blank.
He had other things on his mind.

Back in the house, Geiger brought chairs around the coffee
table, where Matt placed the aluminum suitcase. Arthur asked Geiger if he could draw the curtains. Then the three men sat down
and stared at the battered case, like sailors about to open an old sea
chest.

"Well, let's get on with it," Arthur urged. Matt, who had been looking at the case in a trance, rolled the numbers on the combination lock.

"How do you know the number?" Arthur asked.

"Easy," said Matt. "Scott thought it would be simpler if all his
slide cases had locks with the same number. He chose 1860, the year
the Oxford museum was completed."

"Of course," said Arthur, as the lid of the case sprung open.

He and the professor joined in a round of applause. Matt was
taking his time, annoyingly. He raised the lid slowly to reveal several
little white cotton seed bags, which Arthur noted, with satisfaction,
were labeled with codes beginning with NS and LG, no SP. A separate box contained a number of glass slides. There were seedlings
in special plastic tubes, clouded with condensation from the moist
soil, a collection of papers, and two CDs in plastic containers.

Matt reached first for the papers, leafed through them, and
smiled.

"We have the lab reports," he announced. "They are copies, but
they'll do, for now. And yes, the CDs must be the DNA sequences."

Arthur led another round of applause, and this time Matt joined
in. Geiger went to the kitchen and came back with an opened bottle
of schnapps and three thimble glasses. They toasted Scott and Tanya
Petrovskaya.

Matt took a closer look at the copies of the lab reports.

"I assume Tanya left the originals with the lawyer in London.
That was the plan—in case she got intercepted, or whatever."

"Do we know the name of the lawyer?" asked Arthur.

"I do," said Matt. "But that's privileged information for now."

Well, well, Arthur said to himself. This young man was rising to the occasion, at last accepting his responsibility in this high-stakes adventure. At least, that was what he hoped was happening.

Arthur was about to settle down with the bottle of schnapps and tell Geiger the story behind the aluminum case when the doorbell rang.

"Are you expecting anyone?" Arthur asked the professor.

"No one," he answered.

There was no easy way of finding out who was at the door without the person outside seeing him through the window. Arthur told Matt to close the case and take it, and himself, upstairs.

The bell rang again, a longer ring this time.

"I can handle this," said Geiger, moving toward the door.

Arthur was not so confident, but he had no better idea.

There was a small hallway just inside the door, enough room for Arthur to place himself so that he would be behind the door when the professor opened it.

As the bell rang for the third time, there was a sharp rap on the door knocker. Geiger coolly opened the door.

"Good evening, Herr Professor," said a man's voice. "I am Inspector Gallen of Interpol. I'm sorry to disturb you this late at night, but I have orders from our Zurich office to check on you. They had information that you might be in need of assistance—that you had an intruder at the Physic Gardens. There is a gang at work stealing exotic plants, as I'm sure you know."

"But that was weeks ago," said the professor calmly. "I reported the incident, a man broke into the gardens, but there has been no trouble since. I'm familiar with the reports of the gang, of course, but nothing was missing. I concluded that the intruder was probably a vagrant seeking shelter. We had one like that years ago."

From behind the door Arthur was willing the professor to ask for the inspector's ID, but he did not.

"To complete my report I would need to inspect your gardens," the man continued. "Would now be convenient?"

Arthur held his breath, waiting for the professor's reply.

"Tomorrow morning would be better," Geiger said firmly.

"Thank you, Herr professor. Tomorrow morning then," the man said. "Let's say nine o'clock. Good night."

"Thank you, Inspector," Geiger replied, still calm, and closed the door.

Arthur breathed normally again.

"You did marvelously," he said, giving the professor a hug, but the old man looked shaken. Matt came down from upstairs still clutching the suitcase.

"It's so strange," Geiger said. "I did make a report, but it was three weeks ago and no one ever came to see me at the time."

"It may not be so strange," said Arthur. "I'll tell you why in a minute. Just now I need to make a call." He was thinking of Marc Haber's story of the New York law firm that had made contact with Interpol; perhaps there was a connection.

He took out his cell phone and dialed Marc Haber, at home.

"You seem to be having fun," Haber said, chuckling. "I had a call from a barman at the Limmat who accused me of assaulting one of his customers and throwing red wine all over the bar."

"Oh, yes," said Arthur. "Sorry about that."

"Never mind, it's all sorted out. That's why I gave you the cards. Do you have news of your Russian?"

"It's not about the Russian. I'm in Bern."

"Good, nice place. Show your Russian the bears."

"I'm actually with a mutual friend of ours, Professor Geiger. You remember him from the wine days?"

"Of course, a wonderful man and a real patriot."

"We just had a visit from an Inspector Gallen of Interpol."

"You had what?"

"A visit from a man who said he was Inspector Gallen from Interpol. He claimed to be following up a report about an intruder who had broken into Geiger's Physic Gardens—three weeks ago."

"Three weeks ago—and he's calling on Geiger at dinnertime?"

"You have it exactly, Marc. He said he wants to come back in the morning, at nine o'clock."

"Leave this with me. I'll call you back. And in the meantime, don't answer the door."

Geiger turned to Arthur. "So, you think he was not from Interpol?" he asked, smiling.

"Well, what did you think, Herr Truffle?"

"Of course, I knew he wasn't a regular inspector, but I learned a long time ago, during the war, not to confront impostors. It's better to buy time and think of a way out. We have until tomorrow morning, supposedly."

Arthur truly admired Geiger. Britons of Arthur's age despised the Swiss for their wartime neutrality, but he knew Geiger's story was very different. In prewar Switzerland, government policy was to refuse entry to Jewish refugees from Germany. The Geigers had helped refugees enter the country, smuggling them over the border, taking them into their homes, hiding them even from their neighbors. Now here was the professor giving Matt shelter from people who would harm him, harm them all, perhaps.

Marc Haber called back. There was no Inspector Gallen in the Bern Interpol office. There had been no follow-up of Professor Geiger's report of an intruder. The exotic plant gang had not been heard of for months.

"You need a real policeman to look after you," said Haber. "I don't know exactly what you're doing with Geiger, but I can guess it's about the patent. I'm sending someone who can watch the house until you're finished—at my expense. You are my guest."

Arthur was overwhelmed by his friend's generosity. The guard would be one of Haber's retired colleagues, moonlighting, no doubt.

He told Haber that he had to leave that night to fly to London to attend Scott's funeral and wouldn't be back until Monday. "I'm worried about leaving Geiger on his own, even for an hour, with people like Gallen around."

"You won't have to: my man will stay in the house. His name is Peress. François Peress. French, but efficient."

Arthur gave him Geiger's address and hung up.

A few minutes later, Arthur's phone buzzed again. François Peress was outside in his car. Arthur went out to meet him. He looked a decent sort, about sixty, well built, radiating security. Arthur brought him inside.

"There are people out there who are up to no good," Peress said, as he shook Geiger's hand. "You will be safe with me."

"Don't worry," said Geiger. "I'm not as defenseless as I look." Arthur imagined an old blunderbuss somewhere in the attic. He hoped it would not come to that.

As Arthur set out for Zurich, Eva called to say Harry Torrens could find no trichothecenes in Karen Lichfield's samples, either the blood or the Band-Aid.

"That's very odd," said Arthur. "The symptoms as reported matched perfectly. And there's no doubt she was working on them. Ask Harry to test for *Abrus* and aconite. It's a long shot, but time is on our side, just."

About halfway to Zurich, Matt rang.

"Tanya called from a pay phone, as planned. I told her I had received the suitcase and everything was in order. I said I would have the application ready by Monday. I didn't tell her where I was. I didn't give her a chance to ask about Scott. She said she was going to the mountains for the weekend and would be back in Zurich on Monday afternoon."

"Fine," said Arthur. "But you shouldn't talk anymore on the cell phone."

Actually, he thought, it was not fine. Not fine at all. He was uneasy that they were communicating, and he remembered the blue Audi at the corner of Brunngasse with its view of the Hotel Monch. They could follow Tanya into the mountains. And then what?

Twenty-five

Oxford University looks after its dead, and on Saturday morning a lavish half-page obituary of Professor Alastair Athelston Scott appeared in *The Times,* with a picture taken during easier days.

Arthur picked up the paper from the doormat, opened the French doors onto the patio, letting in the morning sun, and settled down to read the digest of this man's already shortened life. Scott was one of the last purists, the paper said, a scientist who believed in science for the public good, a member of a breed about to be as extinct as some of the specimens in the University Museum, where the professor had worked since 1958. It mentioned his invention of the SCAM process, as well as something Arthur didn't know—that he was the grandson (on his mother's side) of a nineteenth-century botanist and explorer who had contributed many rare species to Kew Gardens, one Archibald Urqhart of Glasgow.

The obit confirmed that he was survived by a sister, Emily Mitchell, of Sydney, Australia. The rather large picture of the professor was from a walking tour, somewhere in the highlands, the bleak moorland with its secretive creatures lost in a gentle blur. Arthur imagined every dedicated rambler sighing over that photo. The professor was wearing the uniform for the moor's human intruders: plus fours, a tweed jacket, and a tam-o'-shanter. He was even leaning on a shepherd's crook. Arthur grimaced at the caption, "Gentle genetics genius loved nature." No poets at Rupert Murdoch's flagship newspaper, he thought, and then began surveying the day ahead.

To take full advantage of the outing to Oxford for Scott's funeral, he had asked Sydney if she wanted to go along. She had accepted the invitation eagerly, giving him a moment of male pride until she explained that she had never been to Oxford.

In his bedroom cupboard, he rummaged for something dark enough to wear. He had not bought a suit since a student friend was married, some twenty years ago, and he was not yet of the age to acquire a special outfit for funerals. His black linen jacket, a black turtleneck, and a pair of gray pants would have to do. Not proper enough, he realized, but it was the best of the options scattered across his untidy bedroom.

For the outing, Sydney would be favored with a ride in his '62 Morgan Plus Four two-seater. It was the car's first appearance since the previous summer, and its dusty black body could have done with a wash, but Sydney's face lit up when the elegant old racer, top down, drew up outside her cottage.

It was a little treat, a homage, she knew, but she too had brought her own surprises for the day, since Arthur was accustomed to seeing her dressed for lab work or gardening. Today's simple, sleeveless linen dress was black for the funeral but also short enough and cut low enough to remind Arthur of earthly pleasures that still needed to be sampled. For the service, she carried a black straw hat, and it was her only decoration. She wore no jewelry, and no distractions were required in her case. Pleased she had come, he finally found the courage to tell her that she looked "very pretty." She laughed, signaling she knew the compliment had been difficult for one with his background, and she thanked him, a slight blush on her neck betraying her own pleasure.

The ride gave Arthur a chance to show off the Morgan, and Sydney let out a little giggle each time he pushed the car a little faster around a bend in the road. He was quickly discovering that Sydney was a far cry from the skinny mannequins he sometimes courted, fewer and fewer these days, or the typical lab researcher with whom conversations ran dry usually before the second course had arrived. Sydney had catholic interests and was persistently curious, asking surprising questions, even about aging sports cars.

When Arthur proudly told her the Morgan had won many cups at Silverstone races and could go from 0 to 62 mph in 7.5 seconds with a top speed of 120 mph, she immediately challenged him to prove it. He stopped the car in a side road, brought it back onto the main road and zipped it up to 62 with Sydney looking at her watch.

"Eight seconds," she giggled. "Not bad for an oldie."

As they continued to Oxford, Arthur called Merrill to report in. For once, Merrill sounded as if roused from sleep; he groused that it was Saturday—early Saturday, he noted, with some irritation. Arthur resisted a comment at his friend's expense.

"Where are you?" Merrill growled.

"We'll be in Oxford shortly," Arthur replied.

"We?"

"Yes, myself and my Morgan, that's we in my book," said Arthur, with a wink to his motoring companion. "Call you later."

This was not the time for another of Merrill's snide remarks about his budding relationship with Sydney. Arthur hung up before his friend could wake up enough to cause trouble.

Twenty-six

*A*s they entered *Oxford,* Arthur offered Sydney a quick tour.

"It's why I came, Doctor," she replied. "One of the whys, I should say."

Arthur had performed this routine before, for other women he tried not to think about now, and knew he was good at it. He could edit the history of Oxford's landmarks into a few lines, depending on the route. Today it began at Worcester College, where Thomas De Quincey, author of *Confessions of an English Opium-Eater,* had been a student in the 1800s. There was the Ashmolean museum, originally endowed with biological rarities collected by the John Tradescants, the seventeenth-century royal gardeners. And here—he pointed to the seventy-foot-high stone cross with three clerical figures—was the Martyrs' Memorial, where bishops had been burned at the stake.

"What for?" asked Sydney.

"Heresy, of course." Arthur could not remember what heresy and hoped she would not ask.

Then there was Balliol College, whose fabled Benjamin Jowett is supposed to have said, "I am master of this College. What I don't know isn't knowledge." The current vice-chancellor was a Balliol man, he added with a quick raise of the eyebrow at Sydney.

And finally, here was Magdalen—the college of Oscar Wilde, Alastair Scott, and also of a lesser-known botanist from the Royal Botanic Gardens at Kew, Dr. Arthur Hemmings.

"Then you knew Alastair Scott?"

"Thank you, Sydney, but not exactly. He was seventy-five."

"Sorry," she said, suppressing a healthy laugh.

About two hundred people came to the eleven o'clock service, more than Scott would have drawn had he died in his sleep, Arthur guessed. The professor had become a recluse in recent years, but now reporters and TV crews hung about inside and outside the chapel, a full house.

Arthur and Sydney slipped into a pew at the back with a couple of minutes to spare, and Arthur checked the order of service. It was simple and short, mercifully. The boys' choir would do most of the singing and there were to be two speakers, the vice-chancellor and a man named Edward Dalton, whom Arthur ascertained from the usher was a college friend of Scott's from their student days at Magdalen. Mr. Dalton lived in Tunbridge Wells.

The service opened with the procession of a dozen dons, headed by the vice-chancellor, shuffling down the aisle in their academic finery, black gowns flowing with silk hoods of red and white. At the coffin, they split with surprising precision into two lines, six on either side. They turned, faced their departed colleague, and bowed.

"Meiosis," Arthur whispered in Sydney's ear. "The perfect but un-

explained natural division of long colored threads of organic material in the nucleus of the cell—*Shorter Oxford Dictionary.*"

"Shush, behave," Sydney admonished him. But there was a light smile on her face. The man next to him cleared his throat, disapprovingly.

The dons took their seats in the front pews, and the chapel grew quiet as the vice-chancellor strode to the pulpit. Arthur had no idea what to expect. His eulogy began with Scott's contributions to British science, to the academic institution of Oxford, and to his students, who loved him.

Nothing new there. He might as well have read out the *Times* obituary, Arthur noted. But then Professor Goodhart cleared his throat, an apparent warning of more important thoughts to come. He chided Scott for being out of touch with modern times, a gentle scolding that quickly turned into an outright challenge to the deceased now lying defenseless a few feet away. As if he were speaking to trusted allies, not to this group of mourners, Goodhart bemoaned the "well-meaning people" taking pure science too far, and warned that university life could not, and would not, stand still. Like all living organisms, Goodhart intoned, it must evolve. The academic community could no longer labor in that great, shining, ivory tower it had once inhabited. The mourners began to shift in their pews and glance at each other in discomfort. This was a speech for another time, but Goodhart seemed caught in his own rhetoric. It was as if he could not help himself, and Arthur spotted the journalists taking notes with maniacal glee.

"We must be prepared to accept new relationships with government and business, especially with the new life science companies," he lectured the stunned congregation. "We must be a fully integrated part of the global community."

Arthur thought about Matt, even Tanya, and found his anger mounting. Goodhart's parting words were unforgivable, in Arthur's view. "Even as we bury our dear colleague, we must embrace the fu-

ture. Oxford botany will again be the best in the world." Implying
that, under Scott, it had not been.

Arthur looked up at the chapel's vaulted ceiling and let out a
long, very deliberate, and very loud sigh. This time, the man next to
him did not protest. Sydney was silent and, Arthur noticed, uncom-
monly still.

Edward Dalton now walked to the pulpit. From his attire, he
could have been a banker or a lawyer, perhaps both. He wore a perfectly fitted pinstripe suit—from Savile Row, no doubt—and a shirt
of striped pastels. The maroon silk tie matched a silk handkerchief
folded like origami into his top pocket. To complete the picture,
Dalton had a bright pink face and smoothed silver hair that curled
slightly at the back. In his working life, Arthur imagined, he had
probably spent as much time at the club bar as he had at the office.
His somewhat unsteady gait, the way he pulled himself up, suggested
that he might even have taken a small detour to the club that very
morning.

It quickly became apparent, however, that whatever his profession, Mr. Dalton was no ordinary stuffed shirt. He had no intention
of delivering a solemn eulogy about his lost friend. Quite the opposite. The mourners quickly warmed to amusing stories of Scott's
undergraduate days—punting parties on the river, climbing into
college after curfew, regular fare but a welcome relief from the vice-
chancellor. But he was not really reminiscing, the audience would
soon realize, so much as softening them up for his response to the
vice-chancellor's vicious attack.

Allegations that Alastair Scott, by some error of his own judgment or, worse, through negligence, had been disloyal to the university were false, "a calumny, a monstrous slur on the character of
a dear, departed friend," Dalton fairly shouted into the chancery.

"My friend, Alastair Scott, died in a courageous attempt to resist
the rising tide of outside interference with scholarship. His lead-

ership will be missed in the university, in the world, and even by those who besmirch his reputation."

The silence that met his conclusion was broken only by Dalton's noisy footsteps on the stone-flagged floor of the chapel as he walked back to his seat. The chaplain quickly rose to his feet and announced the last hymn, "Jerusalem." Arthur thought he detected a slight tremble in the chaplain's delivery, echoed by the unsteady quavers in many of the voices now around him.

Following the commendation, the academic procession filed out, led again by the vice-chancellor, his face now stony, his eyes fixed straight ahead. Outside the chapel, Dr. Goodhart deliberately avoided Edward Dalton, who was being mobbed by reporters and television crews, and kept going.

"No, I did not plan to say what I said and certainly not in the way I said it," Dalton was telling a bouquet of microphones. "But I felt the vice-chancellor's unforgivable address needed a reply. I have nothing more to add."

Arthur managed to slip his official Kew visiting card into Dalton's hand and received an acknowledgment, a nod sufficiently positive, he judged, to think that Dalton might soon give him a call.

Inspector Davenport was there, in his uniform. Arthur drew him away from the reporters.

"Our initial analysis suggests that it was not trichothecene poisoning," Arthur said of Karen's samples. "I'll keep you informed, of course. Any news about Scott's autopsy?"

"They have found traces of a barbiturate in Scott's blood, and the time of death, they think, was Saturday. It'll be a few days yet. We're dragging the river. Nothing so far."

"I'm a little curious," Arthur said. "Miss Richards didn't come to the funeral. You'd have thought a good friend and neighbor would have wanted to be here."

"She's in Lyme Regis with her sister, as you probably know," said the inspector. "We've seen her, and she said she knows nothing. Keep in touch."

The inspector was ushered away by his aide as Fred Barton spotted Arthur.

"Hello there, Dr. Hemmings. Pretty hot stuff for a funeral, wasn't it. Can we have a word?"

"Not now, Barton. Call me later," said Arthur, giving Fred a wink and leading Sydney into the quad and away from the crowd. He wanted to hear Fred's news, but now was not the time, for all sorts of reasons.

As they walked toward the Cherwell, Sydney broke the silence.

"Whoa. You Brits certainly know how to do a funeral," she declared. "Nothing missing there. Pomp. Circumstance. Slam the home team. Bite the hand that feeds you. What happened to England's green and pleasant land?"

"Pretty impressive, wasn't it?" agreed Arthur, as they moved beside the riverbank on Addison's Walk. "I'm sure the professor would not have had quite the same send-off at, say, Harvard or Yale. But British academics, and apparently also friends of academics, are really upset about this corporate invasion stuff. They feel threatened and for good reason."

"So do you think Scott was murdered?"

"I don't know, but there are some desperate players in this game. And I'm beginning to believe some of them are, in fact, evil," Arthur said, although he had no intention of letting Sydney know about his trip to Zurich.

"Evil?" asked Sydney. "What exactly do you mean? Is Panrustica evil? The greens would say it is."

"That's the age-old debate, isn't it," said Arthur. "Should we, like Saint Augustine, believe in original sin, or like Rousseau, believe humans are basically nice but open to corruption, or like Freud, believe heinous acts result from unresolved conflicts of the human psyche. I believe that Panrustica, like any large corporation, is not an inherently evil institution, but it has immoral, unscrupulous agents, who will not shun evil acts to achieve their ends. They are, if you like, of the school of whatever is not nailed down is mine and whatever I can pry loose is not nailed down. If people get in the way of such a philosophy, they will come to harm, sooner or later."

"Anyone of that school in mind?"

"Yes, but you haven't met him and I hope you never will."

"Good to know it's a he."

Sydney put her arm through his, the way she had done that evening at Kew, and rested her head lightly against his shoulder. She was not inviting a response, not forcing the pace. Rather, it seemed to him, she was being tender, trying to understand the tragic circumstances of Scott's death, and the possible dangers to Arthur, if the professor had indeed been murdered for his seeds.

Whatever its source, her mood suited Arthur's need. He wanted to forget about Scott and Tanya and apomixis and the whole damn patent race—if only for one glorious afternoon.

As if she had been reading his mind, Sydney suddenly said, "Arthur, I was thinking as we were driving down here. I have been out with you several times, I have worked with you in the lab, I know your reputation as a first-class botanist, but"—she paused—"I feel I don't really know who you are."

"An enigma, Sydney. I was born an enigma."

"Well, I've got to start somewhere, so do you mind if I ask you a delicate question?"

"Of course not," he answered.

"On the way down in the Morgan—which I just loved, by the way—and also in the chapel, I had the opportunity to study your profile . . ."

Arthur slowed their progress along the riverbank, lowered his head, and looked down at her quizzically, hoping that she was merely mocking him. She was smiling up at him, a smile of deliciously faked innocence.

"Yes . . . and?" he said, readily and enthusiastically playing her game.

"If I may say so, you enjoy a nice profile and an especially fine nose."

"Well, thank you, Sydney. I may say you are not the first to have remarked upon my nose."

"May I ask," she continued, "is that from your mother's or your father's side?"

"A good question," he said, resisting a smile, "the kind of penetrating inquiry one might expect from a geneticist. As a matter of fact, this nose comes from both parents. The beginning of my nose comes from my mother, who had a solid English/Irish nose, large but straight. The second part, farthest from my face, the tip, you might say, comes from my father's mother's ancestors, who were Huguenots. Their noses turned downwards at the tip, like mine. It has been said that the trait of turning down at the tip was selected out and became dominant in France before the Huguenots came to England in the mid-eighteenth century."

Sydney was beginning to giggle, a soft giggle that invited him to continue.

"A turned-down nose," continued Arthur, "had a better opportunity to extract the full aroma from the wineglass than, say, an upturned nose, which was entirely inappropriate for such a task. The Huguenots, as I am sure you remember from your history lessons, made the finest wine tasters, better by far than their Catholic brothers and sisters. I inherited the Huguenot variant—without the fine sense of smell, unfortunately. That is not to say I cannot smell; I can, but not as well as my French ancestors. Even so, I am proud of my nose—and my ancestors, for that matter."

Sydney's giggle turned into a full-blown laugh, and she could no longer rest her head against Arthur's shoulder.

"Can't you cancel that dinner tonight?" he asked her, moving his hand around her shoulders and giving them a long firm squeeze that had the effect of bringing her face close to his.

"If only," she sighed. "Dinner with my aging parents is a command performance. Sorry, I see them so rarely these days."

Her remark brought Arthur's fantasy to an abrupt end. He was suddenly reminded of his own parents. They had been killed in a car accident ten years ago on the outskirts of Oxford, one of those freak motorway accidents that happen when everyone is going too fast. One car had touched another, swerved into a different lane, and within seconds a dozen cars had piled up. Arthur's parents perished in the middle of the pile. Unlike many of his peers, Arthur had grown closer to his parents since leaving Oxford, and for several years after their deaths, he could only relieve his frequent bouts of melancholy by visiting the village where they had lived and by taking long walks in the Oxfordshire fields.

Now even the family home was off-limits. Neither he nor his younger sister, Madeleine, had wanted to live in the place. Madeleine had become a professor of geology at Keele and wanted to sell the house, but Arthur thought he might move back there, one day, if he could find the right mate. So they rented it to a family from London, and he had honored a promise to himself, and certainly to renters as well, that he would not hang around like an old ghost.

Arthur was wondering whether this was the time to introduce his family's tragedy when his cell phone made the decision for him. "I thought I'd switched that damn thing off," he muttered, crabbily.

It was Fred Barton, one call Arthur had to admit he actually wanted. Arthur suggested a pint at the Badger in half an hour, which was about as long as it would take to get there, and Barton agreed.

They went back to the Morgan, which was covered in parking tickets. Arthur peeled them off the windshield and stuffed them into a nearby trash bin, nodding reassuringly to Sydney, who was looking worried, and they headed out for Lower Witton.

"The tour continues, my dear Sydney."

She looked hesitant.

"Don't worry, we'll get you back to London in time for dinner."

"Arthur," she said, frowning, "I think I'd better take the train."

He took a deep breath and nodded. "I hate to say it, but you're right." He saw images of Fred Barton at the Badger. That alone could suck time out of the rest of the afternoon. And then there was the Morgan, on its first outing after the winter, an old thoroughbred whose reliability was not to be taken for granted.

The London train was already in the station. As Sydney was about to get out of the car, she grabbed Arthur's head firmly in her hands and gave him a soft kiss on the lips.

"Thank you. I loved it. Every minute of it." Then she was gone.

In the rush she had left her scarf on the seat, and he picked it up, folded it neatly, and put it in the glove compartment. Pity she's an American, he thought, as he turned the Morgan into the Botley Road and headed for his rendezvous. But why should that always be a pity? he asked himself. It was time to get over the sour memories of his disastrous marriage thirty years ago.

Twenty-seven

T he Badger was filling up with the Saturday evening crowd as Arthur pulled the Morgan into the parking
lot at the back. He spotted Barton's green TR, recently
waxed, by the look of it. He had not mentioned to Fred about his
own passion for old sports cars: it would be a pleasant surprise for the
amiable reporter. Before he went inside, he called Eva Szilard. Eva
had her answering machine on. Probably at the theater, he thought.
She often went on Saturdays, to the matinees—and then had a few
glasses of wine to top it off.

"Eva, two things please. Could you find a Miss Ida Richards in
Lyme Regis? I don't know another initial, sorry, but there can't be
many Idas. I'd like to see her tomorrow morning, first thing. Number two." Eva's beeper ended his message and Arthur snorted at the
dead line, then called again.

"Number two, there's a banker type by the name of Edward
Dalton, lives in Tunbridge Wells. He spoke today at Scott's funeral

and I would like to see him tomorrow, late afternoon. I gave him my card. It's a bit of a stretch, Lyme Regis in the morning and then back to Tunbridge Wells, but it could be done. Thanks."

Arthur felt better after the call. Miss Richards had been on his mind, a missing face in a puzzle that still had more than a few missing pieces.

Fred was inside the pub talking to barman Bill.

"Evening, Doctor. Some funeral, eh? I've given the vice-chancellor a prominent position in my story. What an asshole. Honestly. Talk about a broomstick up his bum."

"My thoughts precisely, Barton." Arthur moved in beside the *Chronicle*'s man and raised his voice above the din. "So what's been going on in picturesque Lower Witton?"

"Nothing going on here, Doctor. Only murders or suicides, or whatever, of university professors and poisoning of young researchers, surprise visits by doctors from Kew Gardens, out-of-season, er, fishermen, and scientific miracle plants. Nothing at all, really."

Arthur suggested they go outside. He wasn't drinking.

They went out into the garden, but it was also crowded with the evening's celebrants, so they moved into the parking lot.

"Come on your bike?" asked Fred, chuckling.

"Yes, it's over here," said Arthur, moving to his Morgan.

"You're a sly one. This is yours? It's a cracker. What year?"

"Sixty-two."

"Excellent year." Burton laughed. "For Bordeaux too."

"I've not much time," said Arthur, shutting down the banter that they both could have enjoyed all evening. "I'm really sorry about Karen. Hear anything?"

"Nobody knows. The vice-chancellor is in control of information, and that means zero. I did hear that Davenport is in the shit with Goodhart for allowing samples of Karen's blood out of the hospital. You wouldn't know anything about that, would you, Doctor?"

"Nothing," said Arthur, looking Fred right in the eye.

"I thought not. I also heard the autopsy on Scott is about to be released. Apparently it says they found a significant quantity of a sleeping pill in the professor's blood, no identification of the drug yet. Also, the time of death is put on Saturday afternoon, before the break-in."

"Thanks, that's useful," said Arthur, not wanting to deprive Fred of his scoop. "We can trade. I have a scoop for you. But you have to come with me to Zurich on Monday."

"Zurich? You must be joking. Gnomes? Calvinists? Small bankers who ruined my parents' life speculating on our great British pound sterling? No way."

"Fred, trust me, this could be the high point of your career."

"Or bust it."

"That's possible too."

"So, what are you? My guardian angel? And what am I? Your Boswell?"

Arthur was certainly not asking Fred along for company, although he liked him. The truth was that he thought Fred might be useful. A few controlled leaks might help the case along, and Arthur was willing to take a gamble with this local reporter.

"Do you have something better to do on Monday?"

"Not offhand," Barton answered.

"So, come to Zurich."

"And what, may I ask, will I do when I get there?"

"You will solve the mystery of the Scott case for your readers—well, part of it. But you will have to buy your own ticket. Bring a credit card. Meet me at Heathrow, terminal one, on Monday morning at eight o'clock at the SWISS check-in desk for Zurich.

"And if you breathe a word to anyone about this, the deal's off. I will deny everything," Arthur said as he climbed into the Morgan and drove off, leaving Fred with a glass in his hand and a look of deep satisfaction spreading over his soft face.

On his way back to London, Arthur called Eva. She had been at the theater, as he had suspected. A Royal Shakespeare Company production of *Midsummer Night's Dream,* not as good as its billing, she had concluded. And she had come home to see Arthur on TV, a crowd shot during the coverage of the funeral.

"You do get around," she said, approvingly.

"Thank you, Eva. Any luck with my next victims?"

"Edward Dalton wants to see you. In fact, he seemed very keen. As though he had been waiting for the call. Who is he?"

"A banker, or a lawyer, or both," said Arthur. "All I know is that he lives in Tunbridge Wells. What about Miss Richards?"

"Yes, she will be waiting for you after breakfast. You'll be able to get to Lyme on the first train out of Waterloo. I've left you details on the kitchen table. By the way, I thought you'd like to know her full name is Ida Molly Richards, and everybody calls her Molly. She worked as a librarian at the Chelsea Physic Gardens in the sixties. She's an old lefty, like Scott. Traveled to the Soviet Union several times in the sixties and seventies, on friendship tours, according to my usual sources. Might be something there. I never liked the name Ida, did you?"

He thanked her and hung up. Indeed there might be something interesting. Molly Richards. M. R.

Twenty-eight

When Arthur arrived home, the place seemed to be covered in messages from the women in his life. Lucky man, he thought, as he opened an envelope that had been on the doormat. Inside was a postcard of the Empire State Building. He smiled. No mystery there. "Thanks for Oxford. Good luck tomorrow, wherever you're going. Sydney." This young American woman was scoring a lot of points on a willing target.

Inside, on the kitchen table, was a note from Eva, including Miss Richards's address in Lyme Regis. The 6:08 a.m. express from Waterloo to Axminster would get him to Lyme by about 8:30. Midsixties all weekend. A nice place for breakfast—the best in season was the grill room at the Mariner's Hotel.

Dalton would see him on Sunday evening for tea or cocktails, whichever he preferred. She had included his address in Tunbridge Wells. The trains also left from Waterloo and took about forty minutes.

Arthur thought for a moment about Eva and Sydney—two very different people he sometimes wished he could meld into one. Then he picked up his phone, which was blinking urgently. Eight messages, *eight,* from Merrill. He called him at home, hoping Merrill would be out and he could leave a message, but Merrill answered on the first ring.

"You're in triple trouble, boyo. First of all, Williams is, I would say, slightly put out that you were not in St. Petersburg. Secondly, Sir Freddie somehow knows you have been in Switzerland and he has complained to Williams that you know where Ms. Petrovskaya is and you are not cooperating. And third, Williams thinks you've been stirring it with the local press in Oxford. Have you?"

"Innocent, totally innocent," Arthur offered, wondering how Sir Freddie had learned of his whereabouts.

"Since you've been snooping around the back streets of Zurich, tell me what you know about Ms. Petrovskaya."

"She's there, but I never met her."

"So, when are you going to meet her? You've got to keep me in the loop, Arthur. I'm the closest thing you've got to protection around here."

"Maybe I'll never meet her. Merrill, I've had a long day."

"Oh, yeah, one more thing, about your day. I saw you on TV in Oxford with guess who? Ms. Rodgers. Very nice-looking in her funeral outfit. Sure, you've had a long day.

"And this Edward Dalton. Who is he? He looked drunk to me. I saw him on the evening news outside the chapel. He looked pissed. Was he pissed?"

"Drunk with revenge, maybe," replied Arthur calmly. "The vice-chancellor is a foolish man, Merrill. You know that. His rant about Scott was uncalled-for. Dalton defended his dead friend. That's what happened."

"But who the hell is Dalton?"

"You mean you don't know? I thought the ministry organized the whole thing, one of your PR stunts. Scott came off badly. Isn't that what you people are looking for?"

"Arthur, we had nothing to do with it. Nothing."

"Then where did Dalton come from?"

"I don't know, but I have my suspicions. Bloody disaster, it's a bloody disaster. Number Ten's gone bananas because they hoped the funeral would put an end to the Scott story."

"So, who's under suspicion here, my dear Merrill? Besides me, of course."

Merrill said the secret service could have put Dalton up to giving a speech. The ministry had been waging a running battle with old MI5 members over university ties with industry, he said. They had taken the side of the professors like Scott, mainly because of old "associations." It went back a bit, to the Cold War, even World War Two.

Merrill pitched his theory in characteristically sparse language. In the good old days, Oxbridge profs helped the spooks out with their dirty tricks. The professors loved the work: it got their blood up. And the spies loved the access to all that brainpower. But times had changed. The secrets used to be military secrets. Now they were industrial secrets. No more trips to Oxford. Now professors were bought by industry—for large sums. No more dining at high table for Her Majesty's lowly agents. The service had to deal with the companies, people like Richard Eikel. It was more complicated, in many ways distasteful. When the company had roots in America, the Brits were often cut out completely. In short, the older members would have liked to go back to the way things were.

"I suspect Dalton is one of theirs," said Merrill. "They're always doing shit like that, clever, clever stuff but, frankly, unhelpful."

"So, while we wait thirty years for this file to be declassified, our dear Minister Williams of Ag & Fish wants to blame me for all this?"

"Don't take it personally, Arthur. Aneurin Williams is a politician. He's got to explain this fucking mess. Number Ten is not going to believe any inside stories about MI5. It's politics. Williams is paranoid Britain is going to lose this patent, on his watch."

"It's a big pile of *merde*, Merrill; that's what it is and you know it," said Arthur. "There are no heroes in this story and the villains have so far eluded us."

Arthur hung up with Merrill bleating "Call me" as his plaintive goodbye. Arthur took the dirty clothes out of his duffel bag, stuffed them into the laundry basket, and checked the closet. There were still a few more green shirts and a pair of khaki pants. Enough. He called a cab for 5 a.m.

Twenty-nine

The 6:08 a.m. from Waterloo to Axminster left on time, almost to the second by Arthur's self-consciously overcalibrated watch. He had bought a first-class ticket—he had earned it, he told himself—and put the seat back as far as it would go. There were only two other people in his carriage, a flaxen-haired youth of college age and a middle-aged woman, rather plain, reading the *Observer*. She didn't look up as he sat down in the middle of the car, between his two traveling companions. Before the train left the station, he had dozed off. At Salisbury, he opened his eyes just enough to see the cathedral spire silhouetted against a brightening sky, then drifted back to sleep until the train pulled into Axminster. The woman from his carriage was in the taxi queue behind him, three or four people down the line. Several taxis were waiting, and he took the first in line. It dropped him at the Mariner's Hotel a little before 8:30 a.m., as Eva had planned. A perfectly executed excursion was indeed a rare and pleasant thing, he reminded himself, after the hurried, improvised travel of the last few days.

He ordered a full-court English breakfast with fried eggs, bacon, agonizingly good pork sausages, baked beans, toast, thick-cut Seville orange marmalade, and several cups of Earl Grey. After so much Swiss ham and cheese and little, silver packets of La Vache Qui Rit, this was a meal that could only bring a successful day, or so he hoped. Arthur raised his teacup in a silent toast to Eva, who had made the trip possible.

Looking out of the hotel window, for a moment he longed to be one of the tourists ambling through this once-quiet Dorset seaside town. He stared down toward the Cobb, the landmark crescent of seawall first raised in Tudor times, an artificial barrier that had turned this fishing village into an important harbor, trading center, and smuggler's haven.

The Hemmings family, his parents and his younger sister, Madeleine, had spent several summer holidays at Lyme with Uncle Phil, his mother's brother, who had lived there until it became too crowded for him. The children had hunted for fossils along the shore of Charmouth Bay, tiny, coiled ammonites encrusted with iron pyrites—pure gold, they pretended. And they had dug out cone-shaped, jet black belemnites, which, in their make-believe stories, became fossil dinosaur teeth. For Madeleine, these discoveries ignited a passion for paleontology, a life's calling born on those wonderful holidays. The adults had happily bowled on the green by the pebble beach while Arthur and his sister bit into peppermint chocolate ices and chased each other along the Cobb. They threw a sixpence in the model red, white, and blue lifeboat for good luck and because they so admired the boatmen in their yellow oilskins, braving storms to save lives. If he had time, and the model boat was still there, Arthur promised himself, he would make a contribution later. With things going as they were, it couldn't hurt.

★ ★ ★

Shortly after nine o'clock he walked up the hill, along Ship Street, and past the cottage with its thatched roof shaped like an umbrella. Small children and their mothers were walking down the hill, armed with buckets and spades and large, colored plastic balls, to play on the beach. The summer holidays began early in Lyme Regis.

It took him only a few minutes to reach Miss Richards's house in Buddle Lane. Built into the hillside, like so many houses in Lyme, this one had false timbers in the style of the turn of the century. In the small front garden the roses were in bloom, the borders bursting with herbs, hyssop, savory, and thyme. Branches of a golden genista trailed over the front door. A gardener clearly lived here, Arthur thought, taking a deep breath, trying to identify the medley of scents, as he pressed the bell. The top half of the door was decorated glass, Victorian-style, and he could see the tiny outline of Miss Richards coming toward him. She must have been waiting.

As the door opened, he quickly gave his name and place of business, Kew Gardens, and put out his hand in greeting.

"Oh yes, Mr. Hemmings," she said knowingly, her head tipped ever so slightly to one side. She took his hand, a firm grip, a lot firmer than he had expected from this frail-looking woman.

"Your colleague, Eva I think her name was, said you might call if there were any loose ends," Miss Richards said, well in control.

Loose ends, Arthur thought with a smile. Eva had a way of putting people at their ease, even vulnerable old ladies. This one was in her late sixties, he guessed, and perhaps not vulnerable at all. Britain was full of elderly women like Miss Richards who, in reality, were anything but grandmotherly.

"Well, I'm sorry to be so early, and I don't want to disturb you if this is not a good moment," said Arthur as he moved into her entrance hall, "but I do have a couple of things I'd like to ask, if you don't mind."

"Not at all," said Miss Richards. "Have you had breakfast?"

"Yes, thank you." He was on his best behavior and she was the kind of woman who would notice.

"Good, so have I. Then may I suggest we go for a walk; it's such a nice day and my sister is not up yet. I'd rather not disturb her. She had a bad night."

"I'm sorry."

"No, it's not terrible, just, uh, respiratory problems. She suffers so much from the pollen at this time of year. Would you wait while I get my coat?"

Miss Richards disappeared down the hall, without inviting Arthur inside. He noted that she kept her small frame perfectly straight and walked rapidly for her age. *In command* was a phrase that seemed to fit, at least of herself and her modest surroundings.

The door was only half open, but Arthur could see down the hall and into the back room. The furniture appeared to be mostly old, with Oriental rugs and chintz-covered chairs, and on the walls were seascapes in ornamental gilt frames. There was a musty smell, a sourness that came from too many sealed windows and not enough recent dry cleaning. This was a house for the elderly, and Arthur felt enclosed, as if he needed to whisper and breathe lightly.

Not wishing to be caught snooping, he took several steps backward and into the front garden, again appreciating the fragrances. He was sniffing the roses when Miss Richards reemerged wearing a light blue cotton raincoat and a matching sou'wester, which made her look even smaller. He guessed that she was barely five feet tall, and on her small feet she wore a pair of brand-new navy blue and white tennis shoes, the kind they wore on the bowling green.

"Lovely roses," said Arthur, as they walked through to the gate. "Are they from around here?"

"How astute of you to ask that question, but then you are from

Kew." She smiled. "Yes, they come from the manor house at Cranborne, which is a few miles away, as you know. John Tradescant the Elder was gardener there, and he put in so many wonderful varieties. We were very lucky to get one or two. They are not hybrids, you know. I won't have anything to do with hybrids." She made them sound tawdry, like fake jewels.

"At Kew we have many Tradescant varieties, both Younger and Elder," said Arthur, in an effort to match his energetic companion. But Miss Richards was determined to keep the upper hand.

"Yes, I know, I've been to Kew many times. But some of the best Tradescant roses, that I've seen anyway, are at Cranborne," she insisted, her triumphant tone leaving Arthur willing to concede the first round.

As they walked down the hill toward the Cobb, Miss Richards did not stop talking. It was as though she had a script, a well-rehearsed text. She stifled Arthur's planned interrogation by preempting his questions.

"You will want to ask me how long I had known the professor," she said. Arthur nodded and resigned himself to listening, carefully.

They had met at the museum, before Alastair and his wife came to live in Squitchey Lane, she recounted. It was the summer of 1962 and Miss Richards was working in London, at the time—as librarian at the Chelsea Physic Gardens, she added, with obvious satisfaction in her own botanical achievement. Every day she traveled up to London; every evening she returned to Squitchey Lane, to the house her parents had bought for her and her sister just after the war. She was an avid gardener even then and went to all the botany lectures at the Oxford museum. She still remembered the first time she had heard Alastair Scott. He had given a talk about plant breeding.

"I was fascinated. Of course, I didn't understand the science fully. And when Alastair and his wife, Jane, moved in next door, I was thrilled to have such a marvelous person nearby, but I couldn't show it because that might have got the relationship with Jane off on the wrong foot."

Arthur took her to mean that she did not want Jane Scott to realize that she was interested in Jane's husband, which she clearly was, even at that early stage.

Jane was a "decent sort," Miss Richards explained, a lecturer in English at Somerville, a bluestocking. "Alastair and Jane would sit in the garden and read poetry aloud to each other. I could hear them, over the hedge. They were very attached, and in their spare time, they went rambling, hiking all over the wildest patches of England. But Jane was never much of a gardener, not like Alastair. She liked to admire, not to dig, and toward the end she watched the seasons from her chair, then her bed. He built the garden around her. He was desperately upset when she died two years ago, poor Alastair."

She took a moment to catch her breath and stared out beyond the Cobb to the open sea, and then she started up again.

"It was at this time that my sister, Ethel, moved down to Lyme for the sea air. I should have come down here to be with her then, but I like a busier life than she does. I became very friendly with Alastair," she said as her face softened. "We kept each other company." Arthur was wondering what sort of company, when she provided her own answer.

"You will want to know whether we became lovers. We did not," she said emphatically. "It would not have been appropriate. I found him very attractive, of course. And so did his female students. They simpered and maundered at his lectures. But he was so wrapped up in his work that I suspect he didn't notice."

She paused, to catch her breath again, not to allow Arthur a question.

"The Russian girl, the one who has disappeared. There is a story there."

Arthur did not respond. He did not want to stop the flow.

"Alastair Scott, as a young man, had fallen in love with Tanya Petrovskaya's mother," Miss Richards explained quietly. He had told her the story only last year, after several drinks.

"It was in the sixties—before Tanya was born. Like many British scientists of his generation, he was fascinated by Soviet science in post-Stalinist Russia—especially how they were going to catch up after the Lysenko affair. He had been an active member of the British Soviet Society, and although most of them were Party members, Alastair was not. They organized cheap trips to Russia, and he went a couple of times to Moscow and St. Petersburg, nothing out of the ordinary, as I said, for British academics at that time. Tanya's mother was a translator for Intourist, the Soviet travel agency. The way Alastair described her, she was a very beautiful woman, tall, slim with fair hair and high, Slavic cheekbones, much like Tanya.

"The affair was one of those long-distance romances, you know, I'm sure, Mr. Hemmings." She eyed him for signs of recognition, and he smiled and raised his eyebrows to signal he knew about such things quite well, certainly better than she did.

"These affairs are intense, for a short while—especially when conducted across an inhuman barrier like the Iron Curtain. Alastair wanted to leave Jane and bring Tanya's mother to England. He even started the paperwork with the embassy without telling Jane anything. But the Soviet bureaucracy killed the romance. He never heard anything from the embassy. And gradually the affair tapered off.

"Is that the first time you've heard that story, Mr. Hemmings?" Arthur nodded.

"Yes," she said slowly and deliberately. "I'm probably the only one who knows." She seemed to take pride in her own private knowledge of Scott's personal life.

By now, they were close to the Cobb. The tide was out and Arthur caught a strong smell of drying seaweed, the smell of those family holidays. He spotted the little model lifeboat, still fixed to the wall where it had always been. He put a pound coin in the slot and then suggested they sit on the seawall. He didn't want Miss Richards to get tired, but he also wanted to indulge in his own nostalgic moment.

"I'm not tired, if that's what you think," she said, sharply. "I come down here every day. Let's walk to the end of the Cobb, and then we can sit down when we get back."

Thirty

Miss Richards finally agreed to rest on a wooden bench overlooking the Cobb. *Perch* would be a better word. She sat a little to the side, to emphasize that the stop was only temporary.

A few weeks ago Alastair had knocked on Miss Richards's door, she said, as she resumed her story. It was late and she could smell alcohol on his breath. He wasn't drunk; he was never drunk. He was terribly depressed. He could be very glum, she explained, especially after Jane died, and he asked if he could come in and chat. She had offered tea, but he asked for Scotch.

"The pressure from the vice-chancellor to sign up with the multinationals had been intensifying, he said. But it was worse than that. An official from the American embassy came to see him offering big research grants from Washington, that sort of thing. The Panrustica company had begun to threaten him. One of their executives told him that if he didn't agree to the contract, they would destroy his reputation. He didn't know what they were talking about, but he had no doubt they were serious and that they knew how to hurt him, how to undermine a fine reputation that had taken decades to build. He assumed they were referring to his trips to the Soviet Union during the Cold War, perhaps even to his affair with Tanya's mother."

She paused.

"The worst torture is always when you don't know, isn't it, Mr. Hemmings?"

A week later Scott came to see her again. He had been called to London—ostensibly for a regular budget meeting with Ag & Fish—but when he arrived at the ministry, he was told by the security guard to go to a different building nearby. In a small room that was bare except for a table and two chairs there was a man, rather short and in his forties, Alastair guessed, a man whom he had never met. The man introduced himself as Mr. Simpson, from MI5.

Arthur wondered about Miss Richards's apparently capacious memory—and how much of this story might be imagined.

As if reading his thoughts, she said, "I remember the man's name was definitely Simpson because of Simpson's in the Strand. Without any preamble, Mr. Simpson accused Alastair of taking money from the Russians all those years ago."

"From the Russians?" asked Arthur, incredulously. "When?"

"In the sixties," she continued. "Alastair was completely taken aback. He couldn't believe what was happening to him. Mr. Simpson said MI5 had been told by a reliable source that during the nineteen sixties, when Alastair had his first contacts with the Soviet scientists over apomixis, he had received several payments from Soviet agents. The money had been given in exchange for information about his own laboratory work, Mr. Simpson said. MI5 wanted Alastair to answer several questions about the alleged payments. Mr. Simpson gave actual dates on which he was supposed to have received the money. The total was something like fifty thousand pounds, which was a lot of money in those days. Alastair was furious. The allegations were lies, all lies, he repeated to this hard little man.

"But Mr. Simpson insisted that the source of the allegations could not be ignored and the inquiry had to go ahead. It would take several months, he said, and Alastair would not be allowed to leave the country during that period. He was also forbidden to publish any of his apomixis results, or any other scientific data, until the inquiry was complete.

"Forbidden to publish?" Arthur interrupted.

"Yes."

"I've never heard of such a thing."

"Neither had Alastair. He asked what on earth his current research had to do with accusations forty years ago, and Mr. Simpson replied that because part of Alastair's salary was paid by state funds—as in all universities—Alastair was being treated as a government employee. He had to follow the rules for civil service employees under investigation.

"Alastair didn't sleep for days, worrying about the charges but especially wondering who had made up these lies about him, and for what purpose. The meeting with Mr. Simpson was about a week before his death."

Miss Richards stood up.

"Mr. Hemmings, do you mind if we walk a little? I feel in need of some movement, otherwise I will get stiff. We could take the cliff path; there's a beautiful view of Golden Cap, although of course at this time of day, with the sun coming from behind the cliff, the view is not at its best."

She got up, and Arthur walked beside her, moving briskly to keep up. They were soon walking freely along the cliff path with a pleasant light breeze coming off the sea. Without prompting, she continued her story.

On the day before he died, Alastair told her that he had received a call from Mr. Simpson. The internal inquiry had determined that

Alastair must face a tribunal and answer questions that had not been resolved. He would be called to appear within the next two weeks.

She paused again.

"When he came and told me this, he was in a terrible state. I had never seen him like that. He was shaking, his hands were shaking. I did not smell drink on his breath. I made him some hot cocoa and gave him two sleeping tablets that I use myself. It is a prescription medicine, quite mild. I have the bottle if you want to see them. He took two pills and lay down on the sofa. I covered him with a blanket and he went to sleep immediately. I went to bed. At dawn, I got up to make a cup of tea, but he was still asleep. I was a little worried, but he was breathing normally. He was in good physical condition, you know, for his age, just exhausted. So many nights without sleep.

"In the morning, he seemed much better. He suggested that we should go for a walk along the river. He wanted us to ride bicycles. I have a bicycle but I have not used it in years. I persuaded him that we should go in my car, in my old Mini."

"This was the Saturday morning before the break-in at the museum?" asked Arthur.

"Yes. Exactly."

Miss Richards said they drove out to Lower Witton, parked the car at the university farm, took a rug and a flask of coffee, and walked to the river.

"We found a secluded spot, spread out the rug, and talked about the inquiry. Arthur drank a little coffee."

She paused, as if recalling the setting.

"He was so down in the dumps," she said, "totally despondent, angry. He could not believe what was happening to him. He said he had thought of holding a public meeting at the museum to tell the world, as he put it, about the false accusations, but he couldn't summon the energy.

"In any case, he felt it might have made matters worse. He was sure that he would be cleared by the inquiry and then no one would ever know about the charges. Mr. Simpson had promised him that was how it worked. If he made a to-do about it, there would always be some people who would believe that he had taken the money. He was totally stuck, really."

She paused. Arthur was about to begin his questioning when she suggested that they sit.

"I am getting a little tired," she admitted.

They sat on a wooden bench and she took off her coat, shook it slightly, and then placed it over her lap. Looking straight ahead, out to sea, Miss Richards presented a striking profile. The gray hair was combed back and done in a bun with old-fashioned pins, Arthur noticed, since one had worked its way out and stood perched at one side, ready to fall. As he studied her prominent nose and strong chin, she reached up and pushed the pin back into place. She must have been attractive at one time, and he wondered if there had been men to take advantage of the fact. Then she interrupted his silent assessment.

"Mr. Hemmings, I . . . I do not know you, but you seem to be a decent man. You are here in some official capacity, the exact nature of which I do not know either, and I don't really want to know. But you are not a policeman, I can see that. You are a botanist from Kew, but we are not discussing botany, are we?"

Arthur understood she didn't want an answer. He shook his head gently.

"We are discussing the life of a brilliant man who met a tragic end. I assume that you will have to make an official report of some kind about our meeting. Why don't we walk home now; I'll make a cup of tea and tell you the rest of the story."

Arthur agreed. During the short walk back to Buddle Lane, Miss Richards fell silent. Arthur made small talk about his family holidays in Lyme, about collecting fossils at Charmouth and walking on Golden Cap; he did not want to upset Miss Richards before she had finished her tale.

★ ★ ★

Back at her house, she showed him into the front living room, where net curtains filtered the late afternoon sun, leaving the room closed and gloomy. Arthur looked around the room. It was filled with family heirlooms, each of which seemed to have occupied its appointed space for many years.

The centerpiece, a cupboard with a curved glass front, housed an assortment of flowered bowls and a collection of painted egg cups. Next to it stood an open bookcase with clothbound volumes with faded spines. There were two armchairs, with white lace antimacassars facing the fireplace. A gas fire had been fitted into the grate, the only concession to modernity. There was no television, not even a radio. If those amenities existed, they were somewhere else, wherever Miss Richards and her sister really lived in this house. The room into which he had been invited was small and stifling and made Arthur feel large and clumsy. He cringed at the sight on the mantelpiece of several china figurines, including Mr. Pickwick and a pint-sized Toby jug of Winston Churchill. On the wall was a fading watercolor of the Cobb. It was the typical home of a British middle-class pensioner.

"Do sit down, Mr. Hemmings. I'll make a pot of tea," she said and disappeared.

The chair facing the window clearly belonged to Miss Richards. On a table beside the chair were gardening books and a pair of knitting needles punched into a ball of pale blue wool. Arthur sat down in the other chair.

He heard a woman's voice calling faintly from the next room.

"Molly, Molly? Where are you?"

"Coming, dear," replied Miss Richards from the kitchen.

Arthur could hear only muffled voices in the other room for a few minutes until Miss Richards returned with the tea tray and an assortment of chocolate biscuits and sponge cake.

"Was that your sister?" Arthur asked. "Is she feeling better?"

"Much better, thank you," said Miss Richards. "The pollen count is down. Poor dear, she does suffer so."

Must be more than pollen, Arthur thought, as Miss Richards poured the tea into dainty bone china cups and offered Arthur a slice of sponge cake. She settled into her chair and took a deep breath.

"What actually happened on that terrible Saturday afternoon is this," she began. "We were sitting on the rug on the riverbank. There were bulrushes and long grass. It was so perfectly peaceful. I could take you there. I was fully stretched out on the blanket, feeling helpless because Alastair was inconsolable. We had talked about everything, gone over what could be done so many times, and never reached any solution. I had done my best to revive his spirits, but I had failed. I knew I had failed. Our conversation had come to a close. We had been sitting in silence for some moments when Alastair got up. He said he was going to stretch his legs and when he came back, we would go and have lunch at the pub.

"I knew then that he was not going to stretch his legs. But I knew there was nothing I could do about it, and maybe nothing I should do about it. This sounds awfully weak and cowardly, but I was in a kind of trance.

"I knew that as he walked off down the riverbank, that was the last I would see of him. I did not try to stop him. I started to sob, for myself as much as for him. I was just staring into the river. And then I heard a splash, a barely audible splash, not much more than a moorhen startled from its nest." She paused and kept her eyes down.

"You see, the river was almost in flood, there had been so much rain. He couldn't swim, you know. I didn't move. I didn't cry out. I just sobbed, uncontrollably for I don't know how long. And then I got up and I walked the other way, back to my car."

Arthur was looking at her, straight in the eye, staring hard. She wanted him to believe that Professor Scott had committed suicide, a hundred yards or so away from where she was lying on the bank, and knowing that he couldn't swim, she had not tried to save him. He was about to tell her that he found her story incredible when she spoke again, in a voice now weak and barely audible.

"I was as powerless to save him as he was himself. There are some forces that you simply cannot defend yourself against, aren't there, Mr. Hemmings?"

She was staring out the window into the front garden. No tears, no emotion. This tough, resolute woman had devised her own way of coping with Scott's death. She had practiced, over and over, telling a story she hoped would be accepted—whatever part she had really played.

"Now, Mr. Hemmings," she insisted, turning to face him. "You have several questions, don't you? I can see. You would like to ask me about the milkbottles, I daresay."

Arthur was taken aback. He had a question about the milk bottles, of course, but how could she have guessed?

Miss Richards said she knew that she had made a mistake as soon as she told the police about the milk bottles on Scott's doorstep. Alastair, of course, had not had milk delivered since his wife had died, she said.

"The problem was, I was getting anxious about the whole thing. As I told you, Alastair drowned himself on Saturday afternoon. After the break-in was discovered, the police came round on Monday. They didn't seem too concerned at that stage. They thought he had gone on one of his hikes. But I panicked. I said he had definitely gone away and I blurted out the story of the milk bottles. Very silly of me."

"Quite understandable in the circumstances," Arthur said. It was time to stop being so accommodating to this cunning old woman and her little lies and maybe, also, a few big lies.

"What do you mean, 'quite understandable,' Mr. Hemmings?" she said, keeping her head down.

"Well, Miss Richards," he began. Arthur did not want to accuse this woman, only to press her to go beyond her rehearsed script. "I believe there may be other things you haven't told me, perhaps more important things."

"Do you really?" She smiled. "Yes, I must try and put that right. I don't want to be unhelpful."

"Did you and Professor Scott ever discuss his committing suicide, and did these discussions ever reach the stage where you agreed to help him commit suicide?"

Her gray eyes were staring at him, but they revealed nothing. She held her hands in her lap, a woman trained to look poised in the face of any unpleasantness.

"What a preposterous suggestion. I was trying to keep him alive, trying to prevent him from giving in to those bullies who were intent on destroying him. I see now that I should never have told you these things, these private things. You have no right to be asking such questions."

Realizing that he was probably close to being thrown out of her house, Arthur interrupted.

"About the *Oxford Book of English Verse*. The one you wrote in, and signed your initials M. R. Those are your initials, Miss Richards, aren't they?"

"My goodness, what a sleuth you are, Mr. Hemmings. Yes, they are my initials, indeed. I gave the book to Alastair at Christmas. And to Alastair I was Molly, of course, as I am to all my friends."

"So," said Arthur, "in the poem the scholar is lured away from university life to live with the Gypsies. You wrote in the book, 'Together we will end the knocking on Preferment's door.'"

He stopped for a moment and let the silence gather around them. Then he spoke, in a whisper as if the conversation were now confidential, just between the two of them.

"I must ask you again, Miss Richards. Had you agreed to help Alastair commit suicide?"

She jerked her head away from him and looked toward the window.

Arthur sat frozen, waiting for a response, but she seemed ready to outwait him.

"Miss Richards, did you have a pact with Professor Scott to assist in his suicide?" Arthur asked, no longer in a whisper. "The autopsy has revealed the presence of a sleeping pill in his blood. Did the coffee you gave him from the flask contain your sleeping tablets, a dose that would have sent the professor into a deep sleep?"

She was silent and still, looking out of the window.

"Did you then push or roll him off the rug into the river? As you mentioned, the river was high; it would not have required much effort, and a man's body rolling into the swollen river hardly makes a sound."

Miss Richards remained silent for what seemed like a long time but was only a minute, Arthur guessed, maybe two.

Then she took a deep breath and shook herself slightly before raising herself out of her chair and addressing him directly.

"You must excuse me, Mr. Hemmings, I think I hear my sister."

Arthur heard nothing; no one was calling.

She left the room and came back almost immediately.

"And now, Mr. Hemmings, I'm sorry, but I really must ask you to leave," she said. "My sister needs my attention. Please do call again if you have any more questions. I would only ask one thing. Whatever you write in your report, please be respectful of Alastair. He was a very brilliant and a very dear man, and he was in great pain just before he died."

Arthur promised to respect Scott's memory, but he imagined the police and the media would not be so tender. He walked out of the room, opened the front door, and let himself out, and as he walked down the path, he heard Miss Richards close the door softly behind him.

At the Mariner's Hotel, Arthur ordered a cab to Axminster, reluctantly abandoning his hope of a nostalgic walk around Lyme on his own. In the taxi, he made a note to call Eva. There was one part of Miss Richards's story that could be checked out. If she had driven to the river with Scott in her Mini and parked at the farm, her arrival would have been recorded on Mr. Hendon's videotape.

As he boarded the train, he cast a quick glance down the platform. At the barrier, he saw the same woman who had been in his car on the outward journey.

Well, well, he thought, if this woman is following me, I must be doing something right. Quite suddenly, he felt a lot better about his inquiry. He dozed most of the way to London. There was no sign of the woman when he reached Waterloo station for his connection to Tunbridge Wells. Maybe she had completed her assignment. Maybe her appearance had been a coincidence.

Thirty-one

The last time Arthur visited Tunbridge Wells, it was the year of Sputnik, 1957. That autumn, the Soviet Union launched the earth's first orbiting spacecraft, shattering the myth of Soviet scientific backwardness. Arthur was only five years old at the time, and the memory of Sputnik flashing its triumphal message across the night sky was one of his earliest.

In this garden suburb where Tories go to die, as the saying goes, the master of the house where Arthur was staying with his parents would yell, "*Svoloch*" in Russian—street slang which his father much later told him meant "fucking trash"—each time Sputnik came into view. The story had been told and retold in the Hemmings household as he was growing up so that, young as he was at the time, it had become a durable memory. Quite why his father spent time with this man Arthur was never sure, except that his father was a physicist who worked on space matters. Later, when telling his "Where were you when Sputnik was launched?" story, Arthur would recall the incident. It was with this memory in mind that he arrived at Tunbridge Wells station and took a taxi to the Dalton residence. He had really no idea what to expect from this next encounter, except that Dalton presumably had welcomed another chance to defend his dead friend. Maybe Merrill was right about the rivalry between the young and old factions of the services. It made sense. And maybe Dalton was the messenger for the veterans.

The Daltons lived in the same neighborhood he remembered, if only vaguely, from the Sputnik visit: mock Tudor houses, lead-latticed windows, gravel driveways, and perfectly tended gardens. Arthur was surprised to find the dapper Edward Dalton of Scott's funeral dressed in jeans and a blue short-sleeved shirt and mowing his lawn with an antique manual machine.

"Arthur, great to see you again, it's been a long time," Dalton greeted him like a close friend. "Have a good trip?"

Arthur was taken aback, since he had only given the man his card at Scott's funeral. Perhaps that was how the people of Tunbridge Wells greeted each other: once you crossed the threshold of this place, you belonged.

"Yes, er, hello, Mr. Dalton . . . Edward . . . excellent journey, thank you."

"Oh, call me Ted," he said, grabbing Arthur's hand in a powerful grip. "How are you?"

"I'm fine, absolutely fine, thank you," replied Arthur, struggling to match the instant goodwill of this clubby suburb.

"Wonderful. Come on in. My wife's at the fete. She is sorry to have missed you. I must collect her in half an hour, but we have time for tea," said Dalton, rubbing his hands together and stretching his fingers, apparently unused to the strain of pushing the mower.

"Confounded machine. Mrs. Dalton won't hear of having a motor mower—too much pollution." He lit the gas under the kettle, offered Arthur a newspaper and a seat in the living room, and went upstairs to change.

Arthur took a quick look around, searching for some grounding about who this man Dalton really was. The house was a postwar, comfortable, middle-class home, with a faint whiff of furniture wax, about as distant from Arthur's dream house as a home could be. The kitchen looked out onto the two-car brick garage, covered in ivy and surrounded by clay flowerpots of the type British tourists brought back from holidays in the south of France, where, he imagined, the Daltons were regular summer visitors. Beyond the garage door was a somewhat faded, silver Jaguar. The other slot was empty, presumably for Mrs. Dalton's automobile.

The living room was filled with overstuffed sofas and armchairs, covered in matching olive green damask. There was a sunroom, an extension overlooking the garden, with wicker chairs and bright floral cushions, from a catalogue of porch furniture, a favorite of the neighborhood, he guessed. The *Daily Telegraph* was on the coffee table. Arthur sank into one of the armchairs and started to read the editorial headlined, "Putin's Russia Returns to Totalitarianism." He had almost finished it when Dalton breezed back into the room with two mugs of rich brown tea and a plate of Bourbon biscuits.

Dalton, now a vision out of *Country Life,* was wearing a cream shirt with thin brown and red stripes, a pair of gray cotton trousers, and brown leather loafers. He smelled of bathroom soap, and Arthur felt slightly grubby.

"Well, it's such a surprise to see you after all these years," Dalton said as he lowered himself into an armchair that seemed to wrap itself around him. Before Arthur could speak, Dalton continued, "You don't remember me, of course. But I remember when you and your parents came to watch Sputnik at the Boldersons', across the road."

Arthur was about to take a sip of tea and suddenly stopped. "I'm sorry, I had no idea."

"Well, no, we did not meet then, exactly. We were over at the Boldersons' and Mr. Bolderson was yelling "fucking trash"—in Russian—at Sputnik each time it passed over. But you probably don't remember that; you were a tiny tot."

"Of course, I remember," said Arthur. "It was a legend in our family . . . I had no idea you were part of it, but I suppose you . . . let's see . . . you were in your twenties then, yes?"

Dalton nodded.

"We had been watching Sputnik every night for a week by the time you arrived, and frankly we'd had enough. But I remember your father. He was very tall, if I'm not mistaken."

The mention of his father softened Arthur, threw him off guard. He suddenly imagined his father in the room, in his shaggy corduroy jacket. "Your parents had been here, to this house, several times, but you were younger, maybe not even born," Dalton continued without a pause.

"You see, my father was in the service—Russian section—and your father was working on missile design at Harwell. They weren't friends exactly, but they had things to discuss from time to time, and they did it here."

Arthur was beginning to regain his balance, but he was not here to wander through the Cold War and its secret histories.

"Your father was in MI5 or 6?"

"Yes, the service," Dalton said, adjusting himself in his chair, suggesting that the moment had come for more serious matters. "I want to talk briefly about Alastair and about his legacy."

Dalton took a sip of his tea and continued. "I don't pretend to know the whole story, but I have a piece of information. I must ask you not to say it came from me, if you don't mind."

Dalton bit off a chunk of biscuit, and Arthur prepared himself for a message from Dalton's pals, most likely dark hints at nefarious goings-on rather than facts. Then Arthur would have to work out for himself what the message really was. All too often that was how the service worked, as Merrill had said.

"You will find some of this strange, from the son of a man who spent his entire life loyally serving his country," Dalton began. "I have never been in the service myself, but I have known members, of course. My father is long gone, my mother too, but some of my father's younger friends are still around. I meet them from time to time. They are like family to me. I was in the City all my life, you see. And they looked after me during a rough patch, as family members are supposed to do."

He paused, asking Arthur to help himself to the biscuits. Arthur took one and another draft of tea. Everything about this place—even the tea and the biscuits—was from a time Arthur had left long ago, out of preference, mostly. Even so, it was seductive, and he had to keep shaking himself back to the present.

"Alastair and I discussed the patent on apomixis many times," Dalton was saying. "He was determined that it should not fall into the hands of a multinational corporation, but he was worried that he would not be able to prevent it because the government—our government—was against him. They strong-armed him. They trumped up charges of his being in the pay of the Soviets—usual stuff, taking money from Moscow in the sixties. Of course, it was ridiculous.

"Anyway, Alastair told me about the inquiry and I sent him to a good lawyer in London, name of Spigelman, Blackfriars Court, for protection, really. I also got Alastair a good patent lawyer, and they worked out some protected commons, or whatever, so that he could share his invention. It was a jolly good idea, an elegant solution, I thought. Inventions like that should be shared, with everyone, like the Internet, like open source software. We can't have one multinational company running the world's food supply. The problem now, of course, is that Scott is dead. The question is: Who owns his patents? I want to give you the lawyer's name."

He went to a desk and wrote on a piece of paper, which he folded and gave to Arthur. "David Spigelman." Dalton looked at his watch.

"Christ, I was supposed to pick up Mrs. Dalton ten minutes ago. Sorry, Arthur, but I must go. This was an awfully long way for you to come for a cup of tea, especially after your trip to Lyme Regis. Not a word about any of this, you agree? I just want to clear my friend's name. It's not right what's happening. I know you'll understand."

"Not a word," agreed Arthur, stunned by Dalton's mention of Lyme Regis. He had not told him anything about his trip to see Miss Richards.

"How did you know about my trip to Lyme Regis?"

"Somebody mentioned it, I think it was your secretary," Dalton said, suddenly a little flustered.

Arthur found himself glaring at his host in disbelief. Eva would never have done that.

Dalton collected the tea mugs and took them out to the kitchen. "I'll give you a lift to the station," he said, coming back into the room. Arthur readily accepted. A ride in an old Jaguar would be most agreeable, even if he was suddenly feeling uncomfortable about its owner.

On the way, they passed a churchyard where a fete was in full swing. Dalton gave two hoots on the Jaguar's horn and waved out the car window. He could see Mrs. Dalton, he said, but the message was meant for the congregation as a whole, Arthur felt.

As they turned into the station, Arthur tried to sound easy as he asked Dalton, "You mentioned in your eulogy going boating with Scott. Wonderful stories. I was just thinking, a silly question, but could you both swim?"

Dalton gave a smile that signaled he knew why Arthur was asking the question.

"Not such a silly question at all. Strange to say, but no, Alastair never learned to swim. But he was fearless: he didn't care. I lived in dread of Alastair falling in and drowning—and not just because we were often sloshed. I am a good swimmer, but not that good."

As Arthur was getting out of the car, Dalton said, "I don't know, but I think he did commit suicide. He had the guts to do it."

The train to London was filled with the nightclub crowd, already celebrating their evening excursion. Arthur sank into a corner seat. So, he said to himself, that was more than a cup of a tea and a phone number. In one important detail, Dalton had confirmed Miss Richards's story. Alastair Scott could not swim. But Dalton had let slip that he knew Arthur had been to Lyme Regis. Was that what the woman was doing on the train? It was at times like these that Arthur wished he had nothing to do with the service; everything they did was riddled with petty rivalries, so damned convoluted that you never got the whole story. Merrill said it right: clever shit.

When he got home to Kew, he called Eva.

"Your trip plan was impeccable, as usual. We have moved up a couple of spaces. Could you track down a Mr. Spigelman of Blackfriars Court. He's Scott's lawyer and I need to know if Scott left a will."

"Yes, Arthur."

"And could you go to Oxford tomorrow, to the university farm at Lower Witton, and ask for Bob Hendon. Tell him I need a copy of the CCTV surveillance tape of Greenhouse Six and the parking lot for the Saturday, all day, before the break-in at the museum. Stress the greenhouse, but make sure you get the other one."

"I understand, Arthur."

"You might take Mr. Hendon a box of cigars, Cuban."

"I thought you weren't giving cigars as gifts anymore."

"There are exceptions to every rule, Eva."

"Yes, Arthur. Your tickets for Zurich are on the kitchen table. Bon voyage." Then she hung up.

It was always the same on Sundays. Eva considered it her day off and she did not like to be disturbed.

Thirty-two

red Barton arrived at Heathrow dressed like a man going to a game park. Khaki shirt, khaki pants, and a slightly paler khaki vest festooned with the sort of pockets preferred by photographers and archaeologists. He was fairly bulging with public notice, as clear as a sandwich board, that he was a reporter. One breast pocket was filled with pens, the other with moleskin notebooks. An old 35 mm Minolta was slung around his neck, and a smaller, digital camera protruded from a side pocket. In the fishnet pouch on the back of the vest was a *Blue Guide* to Switzerland and several rolls of film. He carried a backpack with a change of clothes and a laptop.

"Well, no one is going to mistake you for a Swiss banker." Arthur smiled, as they met at the Terminal 1 check-in desk.

"Good morning, Doctor." Fred sounded formal on this unfamiliar territory, a good distance from the Badger. He wasn't going to admit it, but this was his first foreign assignment after two decades of very local journalism.

"It's my normal attire for jobs outside Oxford," Fred managed. "Glad you like it."

He peered at Arthur in a cleaner version of yesterday's outfit.

"I see you're in uniform." Fred was not used to being upstaged, especially this early in the morning. "Very becoming."

The flight was on time, and Arthur told Fred that he would brief him on Zurich when they arrived. He didn't want anyone eavesdropping on their conversation. Instead, he scanned the Monday newspapers, where a few articles reported on the reaction to Scott's funeral—with various degrees of flair and verisimilitude. Beside him, Fred burrowed feverishly into his *Blue Guide*.

From the duty-free trolley, Arthur bought Eva some cherry brandy chocolate liqueurs and stuffed them into his backpack. Fred purchased a half bottle of vodka and attached it to his own backpack, in the space for bottled water.

"You can never tell how these situations are going to turn out," he said, giving Arthur a knowing look.

At Zurich, Arthur rented a car and maneuvered through the lot to the main artery into the city. As his car banked on an elevated curve, he spotted a blue Audi, an A6 Quattro, right behind him.

"*Merde,*" he cried.

Barton stirred, adjusting himself in his seat with all the gear attached to his body.

"What's the problem, Doctor?"

"Panrustica. They're following us—the blue Audi. That's three hundred thirty-five horsepower and I've got this piddling Fiat."

"I'll zap 'em," said Fred, rummaging along his body for a camera.

"Not yet," Arthur hissed.

He shifted forward in his seat and increased speed so that the ride was smooth and steady on the highway. Behind him the Audi was also steady.

"Barton, write the license plate down in your notebook."

"Yes, sir," Fred snapped, recording the number on the first page in his moleskin, and putting a figure "1" beside the entry. For Fred Barton, at least, the mission had begun.

Arthur punched Marc Haber's number on his cell phone and got a recording machine.

"Marc, this is Arthur. I have a blue Audi on my tail. The number is . . . Fred, what's the number again?"

Fred repeated the number.

"Sounds familiar. I think it's the one that was outside the Monch. Marc, I'd be obliged if you would deal with it, thanks," he said just short of the closing beep.

"You know how the Audi got its name?" Arthur asked, thinking Fred might actually know.

"Of course, I do, Doctor. The company's founder was a German named Horch, which means 'Listen' in German. *Audi* is the Latin translation of 'Listen.'"

"Excellent, Fred, move up three spaces. And while you're at it, make your camera ready, we're going to have a little fun."

"Ready," said Fred, beaming.

Arthur moved into the fast lane. The Audi stayed on his tail.

"Shameless," muttered Arthur. "Bloody shameless."

The first Zurich exit was the zoo, and Arthur suddenly darted back into the slow lane. The Audi followed.

Arthur remembered the zoo, next to the cemetery. At a park where the trams ended, there was always a crowd. He needed people.

The Bahnhof Bridge took them over the Limmat—Arthur and the Audi—and up the hill. Arthur checked his companion, whose face was slightly flushed, but his hands were steady.

"When I get out, Fred, follow me and start taking pictures."

"Ready," said Fred.

When they reached the square in front of the zoo, Arthur stopped the Fiat suddenly just short of the zoo entrance, which was already filled with schoolchildren. In his mirror, Arthur saw the Audi halt on the other side of the square, its hood dipping as the driver hit the brakes.

"Let's go," Arthur shouted to Fred as he leapt out of the car.

He ran toward the Audi, yelling in English.

"What the fuck do you think you're doing? You maniac, you almost had us all killed . . . You dolt . . . Who the fuck are you?"

The driver's window was open, but as Arthur approached, the window closed. Arthur bent his long body so that his face was looking directly at the driver and banged on the glass. The driver had blond hair, was midthirtyish, and was wearing a blue denim jacket. Arthur was sure he recognized him from the Limmat Bar, the man with the Panama hat, the one he had kicked in the balls. Fred was right beside him snapping pictures of the car, and the man.

A crowd of zoo visitors gathered around the car, but not too close. The driver put the car in gear but he was hemmed in, which gave Arthur and Fred another good look at him. Arthur shouted at Fred that they were leaving.

"Would you mind explaining to me what the hell is going on?" asked Fred as they got back into the car.

"Let's get on the road first," said Arthur, turning the car back down the hill, where he could rejoin the highway to Bern.

He called Haber's office, but the Interpol agent was still not there. Then Arthur called Geiger's house in Bern, but no one picked up the phone. Slightly worrying, he thought.

Then he turned to Fred.

"I'm sorry," Arthur said. "I can't wait to see the pictures. Now, let's get back to the mission. Embargoed until I give the word, or I'll deny it, all of it, OK? And no mention of me. Still agreed?"

"Agreed, Doctor."

It was a gamble, Arthur knew.

★ ★ ★

Arthur told Fred the story of the patent application, of Tanya bringing the research material to Zurich and handing it over to Matt, and the trip to Geiger's house in Bern.

Fred was scribbling notes, and his voice rose as he followed the story line. "Shit, is this a *scoop,* or what?" He laughed out loud. "I can see the headline, 'Billion Dollar Biotech Patent behind Prof's Death.' By Fred Barton. Dateline Zurich."

Arthur rolled his eyes but managed a smile. This mission was certainly going to be different with this goofy journalist on board.

Fred fell unusually silent for the rest of the trip, for which Arthur was thankful, a small gift of time to think, and worry. As he drove into Bern, he tried Geiger's number again. No reply. Twice more and still nothing. As he turned into the street of the Physic Gardens, Arthur saw Peress's modest black Citroen and felt reassured. But when he drew up outside the house, he saw the front door wide open and no one to greet them. He told Fred to wait in the car while he checked the place, and to keep his camera at the ready.

Professor Geiger's house had been ransacked. In the living room, chairs had been turned on end, desk drawers had been opened and flung to the floor, scattering papers and pens and faded family photographs. Bookshelves had been emptied; the professor's coffee mug lay in pieces on the floor. Pictures had been torn from the wall, the glass frames smashed. The phone had been pulled from its socket. In the kitchen, china had been swept off the sideboard into the sink. Arthur surveyed the scene with mounting anger.

He cursed himself for leaving Matt and the old professor alone. He knew it was a risk, but Haber's minder had reassured him. Where was Peress now? His car was still outside. Arthur called Fred in from the road and told him to take as many pictures as he could of the ruin around them. Geiger's old jalopy had gone. The double garage doors, which led out into a small lane at the back of the house, were wide open.

Arthur felt the entire mission collapsing around him. Had he been fooled by Matt and Tanya? Were they working for someone else, for Eikel, perhaps? For the Russians? What had become of his friend Professor Geiger? And where was the so-called bodyguard, Peress?

Arthur was running the options when Fred called from the greenhouse in the gardens. A note scrawled in chalk on a small blackboard on the greenhouse door read, "Zytgloggeturm, Truffle."

"Clever old Truffle," muttered Arthur. "It seems they got out of the house, maybe in his car, and went to the clock tower. Let's go."

"Ready," said Fred.

They ran back to the car, and Arthur sped up the hill to the old city. In the square, opposite the clock tower, among the tour buses, Arthur spotted Geiger's faded red Fiat, empty. He looked around for an Audi. None. He parked the car next to Geiger's and told Fred to bring his camera. He bought two tickets at the clock tower kiosk and they climbed the steps with the other visitors—slowly, painfully slowly. Near the top, the clock started its chimes for the hour and the marionette show began, with music box jingles. Above the clock was a small platform where visitors could watch the mechanical ballet, and cowering in a corner, sitting on the floor, was Geiger, with Matt, who was clutching the aluminum case to his chest. Geiger immediately got up and pushed his way through the tourists.

"I don't know when I've been so pleased to see you," he said.

"And I you," said Arthur. "Are you all right?"

"A little excitement, it's nothing," said Geiger, stoically. Arthur wondered if the professor knew what had happened to his home; he was not eager to tell him. Not now. Matt had not got up. Arthur pulled him to his feet, the young man still holding on to the aluminum case.

"Come on, Mr. Attorney, let's go."

Back in his car, Arthur introduced Fred. Geiger said it was wonderful to have a reporter recording all this excitement, but Arthur could see Matt was not happy. Geiger told the story of what had happened to them. Matt had just finished his work and packed his case when Peress wanted to stretch his legs, as he had put it, and went outside. He had never returned. Half an hour later, the doorbell had rung and Geiger, peeping through the curtains, recognized the man who had come before, claiming to be Inspector Gallen. He and Matt ran into the greenhouse with the aluminum case. It was Geiger's idea to escape in his car by rolling it into the back lane and down the hill. He scribbled the note and they left as the bell rang again and the man outside started banging on the front door.

Arthur listened, shaking his head in disbelief. These people were not amateurs. He ordered his three companions into his car, with Fred muttering about his deadlines.

"You'll get your story," Arthur assured him, "but not today."

Arthur climbed into the driving seat beside the professor and they set off for Zurich. His phone buzzed. It was Haber.

"Are you having fun, *mon ami?*" he asked.

"I suppose you could say that," Arthur replied, nettled by Haber's mocking tone.

"Here's what I know," Haber began. "Peress left a message to say he was taking a break after lunch. We have not heard from him since. He's usually most reliable. We have our people at Geiger's residence. What a mess. Where are you now?"

Arthur explained that they were on their way to Zurich and would be there around five o'clock. They had everything they needed, he said, knowing Haber would understand.

"Then we'll just keep in touch. The Swiss weekend is over now."

"And we all are grateful for that," said Arthur.

Matt, who had not said a word since being rescued from the

clock tower, suddenly blurted, "How's Karen? Nobody has mentioned Karen."

"She's dead," said Arthur, finding himself unable to protect this
young man any longer.

"No, I mean Karen Lichfield, the researcher at the museum."

"Yes, she's dead," Arthur repeated. "She died of anaphylactic
shock after apparently being poisoned in her own laboratory."

"How? Was it an accident?"

"Nobody knows."

Arthur looked in the rearview mirror and saw that terrified look
on Matt's face, the same one he had seen in the Limmat Bar. He
hoped he hadn't made a mistake in telling him the truth. Everything
now rested on Matt's writing the patent.

"Better get some rest," Arthur said.

Matt didn't reply.

Arthur looked over at Geiger, who had dropped off to sleep.

My dear Truffle, Arthur said to himself, as he viewed the slum-
bering halo of silver hair. I hope to have your fortitude when I reach
your age.

Thirty-three

The Bahnhofstrasse was packed with shoppers, fashionably dressed Zurichers going about their lives, confounding the national image of thrifty, brown-shoe conservatives. Arthur stopped outside the World Patent Organization and took in its worthy look, a brand-new blue glass office building with the UN's blue flag flying above the entrance, like a miniature, modern version of the United Nations headquarters in New York.

Fred said he wanted to develop his pictures and start writing his story. He would meet them back at the Rosengarten in the bar. Arthur told Geiger that he did not want him back in Bern until the patent had been filed, and the professor volunteered to stay with his sister in Zurich. He'd had enough excitement for one day, he said. Arthur hated causing his steady friend so much trouble, and someday he would find a way to make it up to him, but it was not a time to think about anything except rushing Matt up to his office on the twelfth floor, where patent attorneys rented space at preferential rates.

Matt guessed it would take about five hours to file the patent, and Arthur insisted on staying with him, just in case. As they went up in the elevator, Matt was silent. Arthur was thinking how this sterile, uninviting building was about to be the site of a truly historic event, not just in the history of science, but in the history of patents. A key discovery in agriculture, worth billions of dollars, was about to be put in a protected commons, freely available to all. It was Alastair Scott's dream. And yet this youth was as gloomy as ever.

The twelfth floor was arranged like a large law firm, with a central lounge and attorneys' offices leading off it. Arthur was surprised. It was functional but pleasant. Matt punched in a code on the panel outside his office, and the door opened to reveal a small room with a window looking out onto the street. It was furnished, like Matt's apartment, with the basics—a desk and chair, filing cabinets, bookcases, and a futon couch. It was cramped but one of the tidiest offices Arthur had ever seen. No papers lying around, no books out of the bookcases. Even the cork notice board with messages and holiday snaps was arranged neatly. The oddity was a red, white, and blue bumper sticker with the word "Bushwhacked," stuck to the monitor of his desktop computer.

"Nice one," said Arthur.

"My parents sent it to me. It's about how I feel right now," Matt confessed. Arthur realized he should just accept this young man's persistent state of anxiety. Maybe he could be easier under different circumstances.

"It's almost over," said Arthur, trying to be reassuring, as he watched Matt assemble the contents of the aluminum case and prepare his desktop to punch in the information. As the patent application form came up on the screen, Matt began to relax and settle into something familiar at last, a job he knew well. Arthur, worried about how they were going to get through these next crucial hours without a hitch—or another intrusion.

He knew that the act of filing the patent was not the end of the affair. Matt would have to go to London to authenticate the copies of the lab notebooks with the ones being held by Scott's lawyer, and Arthur would have to find out what was in Scott's will—whether he had named an heir to his patents. Even with a will, there could be a messy legal battle with this much at stake. Years of wrangling with patent examiners lay ahead. He wondered whether Eva had tracked down Scott's lawyer.

"Don't mind me," Arthur told Matt, "I'm going into the lounge to make some phone calls. I'll be right outside your door."

The lounge was deserted. He found a comfortable armchair by the window and called Eva. She had located Mr. Spigelman of Blackfriars Court. He had the original copies of the notebooks, and under the "proper" circumstances, he said, he would divulge the contents of the will. Eva understood this to mean a meeting of the beneficiaries.

"Can we make a date for the reading?"

"Mr. Spigelman said Wednesday at eleven o'clock is the earliest."

"They always say Wednesday. It's the only day they do any work."

"But he means it, Arthur."

"Wednesday it is, then. Eva, Eva, don't go yet . . . Did you manage to enlarge the *Chronicle* pictures?"

"Oh, yes, sorry. You may have struck a gold mine, Arthur. The Americans were very busy on the day before the break-in, as it turns out. One of the cars, a little Fiat, was rented by a man named William Paynter. He gave his address to the car rental company as thirty-five Burlington Court, SW1. That's a mews house owned by Panrustica."

"The bastards," Arthur said, trying to contain himself and looking around the lounge. But there was still no one there.

"And then," Eva continued in her superefficient tone, "another car, also parked outside the museum, is registered with the American embassy in London."

"The embassy?"

"It's one of their fleet of Toyotas."

"Another fisherman," Arthur mumbled.

"What's that, Arthur?"

"Nothing, sorry. You've done splendidly. Give me a list of all these cars and their numbers."

"I haven't finished yet. Your Mr. Hendon is a rough one, isn't he? But he couldn't have been nicer after I gave him the cigars. I just think that should be the last time, Arthur."

"Yes, yes, but did you get the parking lot tape?"

"I got it. I have arranged for you to see it in the Kew photo lab on Tuesday evening."

"Perfect. You are—"

"Forget it, Arthur. Chocolates?"

"Already in my backpack, Ms. Szilard."

Arthur hung up as Matt appeared outside his door saying he was desperate for coffee, and Arthur, reluctant to leave him even for a moment, decided the young American could not be denied this small pleasure after all he'd been through. In any case, Arthur was in a generous mood after Eva's news.

He went down to the WPO cafeteria in the basement, but on the way back, the elevator stopped at the ground floor, giving Arthur a full view of the lobby. Through the elevator doors, he was sure he saw the Interpol policeman Peress at the reception desk. As the elevator doors closed, the man was gesticulating wildly. The elevator moved slowly up, the passengers getting off at different floors. At the twelfth floor Arthur banged on Matt's door and shouted his name, but Matt took his time. Inside, the office phone was ringing. Arthur thrust the coffee into Matt's hand and picked up the phone.

A man identified himself as the security guard and asked for Matt Raskin.

"*Il n'est pas ici,*" said Arthur.

"Do you speak English?" said the guard.

"*Oui, oui,*" said Arthur.

"There is a man here who would like Mr. Raskin to call him. It's urgent."

"*Oui, oui, d'accord. Merci.*" He paused and then said, "This is Mr. Raskin. That person who was asking for me, did he leave his name?"

"No, m'sieur."

"Thank you. If anyone else comes, please tell them I'm not available." Then he hung up.

"What the hell is going on? Matt demanded.

"You're busy," said Arthur. "I wanted to let everyone know."

Then he stretched out on the futon and picked up the copy of *Time* magazine. He must have dozed off, because the next thing he knew, Matt's office phone was ringing again. He picked up the receiver.

It was a woman's voice, with a Slavic accent. He guessed immediately that it was Tanya. She was sobbing and mostly incoherent. He just listened. She had returned from the mountains and had read about Scott's death in the newspapers. Arthur put his hand over the receiver and told Matt he had to talk to Tanya. He had to find out where she was, tell her to stay put and that he would come to her immediately.

Matt told Tanya to be calm, he would be there. He promised. She was at Gerda's Bar on the Rindermarkt.

He hung up. "But I can't go, I haven't finished—not nearly."

"I'll go," said Arthur, thinking this was the last thing he should do—for all kinds of reasons. But there was no choice. He couldn't send Matt, and he couldn't leave Tanya alone in a bar in that state.

"But you've never met Tanya."

"I've seen a picture of her, and anyway, how big is this bar?"

Matt agreed.

"You must not leave this building or answer your phone," said Arthur, as he pulled his jacket on. "Sorry, but that's an order. And how do I get out of here except through the lobby?"

Matt told him to go down to the parking level marked on the elevator button. He could walk out from there.

Before leaving, Arthur gave him another number in London—Eva's number, just in case.

Thirty-four

*G*erda's *Bar was a darkened room* in the basement of an old apartment house, three steps down from the Rindermarkt. Drinks were dispensed over a mahogany bar on one side, and the clientele sat in high wooden booths along the other. Gerda kept a clean establishment. Rowdies were ejected by her personally, and seldom had anyone protested her order to leave. By even the latest standards of physical fitness she was a strong woman, not to be challenged lightly.

The bar had its share of regulars and a handful of wayward tourists. By ten o'clock, when Arthur arrived, a few mournful drunks were squeezed into the booths, settling in for the night. A couple of hookers were sitting at the bar, waiting for clients to take upstairs, and they brightened as Arthur walked in.

At first, Arthur could not see a woman resembling Tanya in the photographs of the Oxford museum summer party. As his eyes adjusted to the dim lighting, he finally saw her, sitting alone. She was still, frighteningly still, her head in her hands.

Arthur approached and began softly, "I'm a friend of Matt Raskin. Matt sent me to look after you. You must be very upset."

She looked up. The face was Tanya's. He saw the Slavic cheekbones, the long blond hair, tied carelessly in a ponytail. She was wearing an oddly festive cotton dress, a mass of bright yellow and green flowers, as though she had come to celebrate the arrival of summer. Now, even in the dim light, he could see that her big, dark eyes were half closed from too many drinks and too many tears. Arthur slipped into the seat opposite her.

She looked up at him, and Arthur winced at the pain showing so openly on her face.

"Upset?" She repeated the word, "Upset?"

She looked away, toward the room and the door. The profile too was like so many Russian faces he'd seen before—in crowds during the Cold War—faces of classical beauty hardened by years of abuse. Tanya's face was not there yet, but it seemed to be moving too fast in that direction.

Arthur tried again. "I have come to tell you that . . . that everything will be all right," he sputtered. "I work at the Royal Botanic Gardens at Kew." He offered her his card, which she snatched from him and put in her pocket.

She stared at him, coldly.

"*Ya vas nikogda ne videla.*" She was spitting at him in Russian now and shaking her head. "I've never seen you in my life."

Arthur understood, of course, but decided not to reply in Russian. That would surely have made matters worse.

"I am a botanist, like you," he said. "Matt has written the application for the patent from the materials you brought from Oxford. Everything is in order. Everything will be fine. The application will be filed, and the patent will be granted. There is nothing to worry about."

Tanya looked at him, her eyes now filled with tears, overflowing down her cheeks.

"You can't know about me. We were all afraid something would go wrong. That the companies might win."

Her body fell forward, collapsing onto the table. Arthur reached for her hand, he hoped in a fatherly way. She was beautiful, and many men must have been tempted to offer other forms of comfort. She shook him off, brought her hands up to her face, and pressed them against her eyes to catch a new wave of tears.

"Let me take you home," he said gently. "To your hotel."

"I don't know who you are. Why should I go with you?" she sobbed. "Are you from Moscow, from Lubyanka, or from the vice-chancellor, or the British government, or the CIA, or Panrustica? How do I know who you are?"

"You don't know," he said calmly. "But you phoned Matt. He would not have sent me if I had been unfriendly, would he?"

"I don't know. I don't know anything anymore."

As she waved her hand, it caught her glass of wine, lifted it slightly, and emptied the contents across the table.

"I'll get you another one," he said, knowing she didn't need it.

As he reached the bar, he looked back at Tanya, but she was already fleeing for the door. He rushed after her. Behind the bar, Gerda was yelling, "Police, police, he hasn't paid!"

In the street, he saw Tanya in her yellow and green dress running down the Rindermarkt and behind her the blond man, wearing his denim jacket. The man must have been waiting outside the bar, Arthur realized.

It had started to rain, a steady, warm, summer rain. Arthur wiped it from his face enough to see Tanya running toward the river. Others had joined in, running alongside her, shouting and yelling. He could still see the bright yellow and green dress, and the blond man steadily gaining on her. He sprinted in an attempt to catch up, but they turned a corner and he lost sight of them. Then he saw

Tanya again, and others, heading for the river and the tram lines along Limmatquai. The man was almost upon her, but he suddenly slowed, and Arthur began to shout as he saw why. A tram was coming along the tracks.

"Tanya, stop. Stop, Tanya, for God's sake, stop!" he yelled, but she did not turn or even slow as he heard the clanking of the tram on the tracks, the screech of its brakes suddenly applied.

As Arthur ran on, still trying to shout her name, he felt something—a foot maybe, or a hand—knock his feet from under him. As he went down onto the cobbles, he saw the face of the blond man above him, the face bearing down on him. Then everything went dark.

When Arthur regained consciousness, he had been propped against a wall, courtesy of some dutiful Swiss citizen, no doubt. There was blood on his hair from a blow to his head. The lights from an ambulance and a fire engine lit up the quai. Slowly, unsteadily, he stood just in time to see a body in a green plastic bag being strapped to a stretcher and lifted into the ambulance. Arthur began to ask people in the crowd what had happened. They looked at him, surprised at his question.

"Dead," a woman said. "Fell in front of the tram. The tram killed them," she added in precise, studied English.

"Drunken tourists," said another woman. "It happens every year."

Thirty-five

For several minutes Arthur stayed in the crowd growing around the tram, watching as police cordoned off the Limmatquai. The rain had eased and the onlookers were talking now in hushed whispers, pointing to where they said the tourists had fallen, their grim faces lit by the flashing lights of the police cars. A few were giving their names as witnesses. Arthur would make his statement later—at a better time and to Marc Haber, a more crucial listener.

As he retreated, along the quai and back to his hotel, his legs felt as though they were wading through thick mud. He moved slowly, testing his bruises, quickening his pace as his limbs gathered strength. When he looked at his watch—it was almost midnight—he saw that the back of his right hand was grazed and bloody. He put his fingers to his head where it hurt and they came away covered in blood.

He struggled up the hill past the Grossmunster. In the lobby of the Rosengarten, the desk clerk stared at him but said nothing. Arthur shook his head as he walked to the elevator. It must take special training, strict Swiss hotelier training, to see a wet and bloodied hotel guest in the middle of the night and act as though nothing had happened. He went straight to his room and phoned Matt.

"How's Tanya? You've taken your time."

"She's fine," Arthur lied, trying to sound calm. He had no idea whether she was dead or alive, whether she had been killed in the tram accident, or whether she had escaped from the blond man. "She's . . . she's back at the Monch, drying out, you might say."

"What's the Monch?"

Arthur suddenly regretted what he had said. He did not want Matt to know the name of the hotel, but it was too late.

"It's where she's staying," he said. "And I'm at the Rosengarten, as you know. You can call me here. How's the filing?"

Matt reported all was fine. No more calls. He had finished the application, but there was another computer glitch—the same trouble they had after the break-in two weeks ago.

"What the hell does that mean?" asked Arthur, suddenly alarmed.

"I never knew then and I don't know now; I'm not a computer expert," said Matt in that competent but annoyingly flat voice of his.

"I'll have to wait until the engineers get here—around ten this morning. The application is on a disk, ready to go. Maybe I should go and see if Tanya is OK."

"That's not a good idea," said Arthur firmly, then adding, "given the goon population of this city. Stay where you are; I'll check on her. Keep the disk in your pocket, or locked up. And lock up the papers."

"But how was she?"

"She was drunk, what do you expect?" said Arthur, trying to remain firm, trying to pretend that an emotional Russian woman had been drunk, nothing more. He disliked the deception, but there was no other way. He told Matt to stay put, stretch out on a couch or something.

"If you have to pee, do it in a bottle," he said and hung up.

Then he phoned Marc Haber at home, apologizing for calling so late. He was going to tell him Tanya's story when Marc interrupted.

"I was about to call you," he said. "We have your Russian; she is asking for you."

Arthur was silent.

"Arthur?" Haber said into the phone. "Arthur?"

"Tanya is with you," Arthur managed finally. "Thank God, I thought she might have been in the tram accident . . . The body bag in the ambulance . . . They said drunken tourists had died . . ."

"A tourist was killed, maybe a drunk, but your Russian wasn't one of them. Ms. Petrovskaya is sleeping it off, shall we say. The police found her semiconscious, a few streets from the tram accident, and took her to the hospital. When she came round, she asked for you . . . You must have made an impression. I arranged for her to be moved, here to my office. Whenever you would like to collect her, she's yours. No questions asked."

Arthur was silent, thinking.

"Are you still there, my friend?" Haber asked.

"Yes, yes, I'm here. I'm still trying to take this in." He let out a long sigh.

"I don't remember you ever being quite like this, *mon ami*. Are you hurt?"

"I don't think I've ever been quite like this," replied Arthur, trying to pull himself together. "Must be getting old. A few scratches, that's all."

Haber told Arthur to take it easy, get some sleep, and they would talk in the morning. He would look after Tanya.

Arthur looked at himself in the mirror and wiped the blood from his face. Behind the mirror there was a small medicine cabinet and on the shelf a tiny bottle of yellowish liquid that smelled like disinfectant. He let the bottle drip onto the graze on his hand, wincing as it burned into the cut. Then he poured the rest onto the wound on his head. It stung like hell. His whole body ached, from his head down. He slipped into the shower and let the hot water soothe the pain. His right elbow was starting to throb; he must have gone down on his right side.

When his body had warmed up, he put on the hotel's cotton wrap, lay down on the bed, and closed his eyes.

Thirty-six

Haber called Arthur at dawn. Tanya was awake and asking for him.

"Tell her I'll be there as soon as I can," Arthur said. "And for chrissake don't let anyone near her . . . Sorry, I know you better than that."

"Don't worry," Haber said in his best avuncular tone. "I thought you would like to know another good ending to your story. The Audi A6 outside Tanya's hotel and the one that had followed you from the airport were both from Panrustica's fleet. They have been listed as stolen cars."

Arthur asked for a copy of the Audi report to be sent to him at his hotel, and Haber promised it would be there in half an hour.

"One more thing, Marc. I'm sure I saw the Frenchman Peress at the WPO, trying to get into the office where we're filing the patent. Do you know anything?"

"Only that he's gone missing, we can't find him anywhere. He lives alone."

"*Der'mo,*" exclaimed Arthur. He used the Russian expletive for "shit" when he was really upset. The thought of a hostile Peress on the loose at this stage was unnerving. "I'm sorry I'm causing you so much trouble, Marc."

"*De rien,* my old friend. Watch out for yourself."

Dressing meant as much tending his injuries as finding a cleaner shirt. His hair covered most of the head wound, which had stopped bleeding, and his hand looked better, now that it was cleaned. But the elbow was sore, and he worked it back and forth several times, wincing with each swing. At least it was not broken.

Unable to face another smorgasbord at the hotel, Arthur walked two blocks to the Café Munch. Low clouds hovered but the rain had stopped, leaving a musty, bitter smell of soaked city streets, even in well-scrubbed Zurich. There was no Audi outside the hotel, at least none that he could see.

At a table facing the Kunsthaus he drank his tea greedily and stared across the plaza. The art museum on a normal day would have his full attention, but Arthur's mind was on the innocents caught in this brutal contest. He thought of Tanya and the treasure hunt she and Scott had set up for Matt; the naïveté of it, a meeting without contact at the Rodin statue and a note in a bouquet of flowers at Joyce's grave, and then a man in a Panama hat, all the props of a fifties thriller.

Those soulless bastards at Panrustica, Arthur mumbled to himself, that efficient cutthroat, Eikel. Surely the blond man was his foot soldier, chasing cars and people all over Zurich. Maybe the same blond man had been at the break-in at the museum. Arthur wondered who paid this man—a government, a law firm, or Panrustica? And then there was the self-satisfied Sir Freddie, above it all, safe in his big office, posing as the creator of a kinder, gentler corporation. A boss with a winning smile—and a mistress, apparently.

As his anger at Panrustica rose, Arthur began to summon the energy he needed to finish his job in this deceptively calm city. He had to get Matt and Tanya to London to deal with the lawyer. And he had to arrange for a reading of Scott's will. He could escort Tanya, but Matt needed a minder.

As he walked back to the hotel, Arthur called Kew and found Eva in the library.

"I've been thinking about your chocolates."

"Yes, Arthur, cherry brandy liqueurs."

"I bought them already, but I'm not sure they're your brand. How would you like to come and choose them yourself?"

"Is that a joke, or an invitation?"

"An invitation, a genuine invitation. I want you to leave Kew right now and go to the airport. Get the first plane, first-class, if necessary. You don't need anything, not even a sweater. It's a day trip."

"Just what I've always wanted, a day trip to Zurich." He could see Eva smiling, raising her eyebrows.

"How kind of you, Arthur," she said, with just a hint of sarcasm. "Obviously, you're in a bit of a pickle. I'll call you from the airport."

It would take her about four hours to reach Zurich, he guessed, if she was lucky. The thought of her coming made him feel better, like a besieged commander knowing his best outfit was on the way. Eva adored adventure, especially unscheduled adventure. It was in her genes. Her father's favorite advice, she had often told Arthur, was "Keep a bag packed."

The computer glitch at the WPO had given Arthur a little extra time. As he walked back to the hotel, he started thinking of Sir Freddie. The chairman was always complaining to Ag & Fish about a lack of cooperation. By the time he had reached the Rosengarten, Arthur had decided to call on Sir Freddie—to say goodbye. Sort of.

Back in his room he phoned the chairman's office, and the redoubtable Mrs. Winchester answered, with great and proper efficiency. The chairman was not in yet, she advised, with her forced upper-class English voice. Sir Freddie had meetings all morning. He might have a window at three, she suggested, but frankly, even that looked improbable, given the luncheon guest list. Wednesday the delegation from India would be in town. Thursday morning seemed to be the earliest possibility.

Arthur listened patiently then said, slowly and firmly. "Kindly tell Sir Freddie that I will be there at eight o'clock. He will want to be there, too. I have important information for him. No, make that eight fifteen." Then he hung up.

In one of those business magazine profiles, Arthur had read that Sir Freddie arrived promptly at eight each morning. Giving the chairman fifteen minutes to settle in was the decent thing to do. Besides, it allowed Arthur time to walk to Panrustica instead of taking a cab. He was best at marshaling his thoughts on foot.

As he prepared himself for this encounter, he exercised his sore arm, as best he could, wincing as he moved it to less and less pain. Then he reached for the phone—too fast—winced again, and dialed Fred Barton's room. Poor Fred would think he had been abandoned. But he answered as he always did, asleep or not.

"Barton here . . . Ready." Arthur could hear the fumbling as Fred struggled with the phone. "So, what happened to you last night?"

"Fell among thieves, sorry," said Arthur. "How are the pictures?"

"Great. Nice ones of the blond man at the zoo and plenty of Geiger's trashed house. Some arty shots of marionettes in the clock tower, if you're interested. They'll be better when I get them home and I can play with them."

He asked Fred for two photos, one of the Audi incident at the zoo, and one of Geiger's house. He said he had an errand to run be-

Day of the Dandelion

fore going to the airport and would like to show someone the pictures, not another journalist, of course.

Within a few minutes, a rumpled Fred was in the lobby with the photos in a brown envelope.

"Not for publication."

"Promise," said Arthur, pulling out the pictures. "Good shooting, Fred. If all else fails, you could always get a job as a photographer."

Fred ignored him. "What's the story with Matt?" he asked. "I'm ready to file as soon as you give the word."

"It's taking longer than he thought. Computer glitches, but should be around midday," said Arthur. "I'll keep you informed. You're getting the ten o'clock plane as arranged, right?"

Fred confirmed the flight.

"Meanwhile, why don't you indulge the smorgasbord?"

"No, thanks," said Fred, "I saw it simmering before I went to bed."

"Then I recommend the Café Munch, down the street, opposite the Kunsthaus."

Thirty-seven

*A*rthur set off for *Panrustica* at a brisk pace, telling himself he must resist the temptation to lecture Sir Freddie on the ethics of multinational corporations, though that was what he felt like doing. This was an opportunity to find out something—from the very top. He crossed the Limmat at the Munster Bridge and at 8:14 precisely was riding the elevator to the chairman's suite.

Mrs. Winchester, he guessed, would be of medium height, with hair in a permanent wave and red-rimmed spectacles. She would be wearing a black pantsuit with a brooch on the lapel, a golden sheaf of wheat that Sir Freddie had given her to commemorate the merger of Transgene and BIC. She would give Arthur a look of withering disdain, especially because he was, by her standards—by most standards actually—shabbily attired.

In reality, Mrs. Winchester's pantsuit was an alarming scarlet and her hair a dyed blond. But she wore a gold brooch, a sheaf of wheat.

At least he got that right. And her stare was more withering than anything Arthur could remember since his schooldays, when the Rev. Farrell's wife had caught him in the bathroom with the cleaning woman.

"The chairman has been waiting for you," said Mrs. Winchester, making a big deal of looking at her watch. It was 8:17, Arthur noticed by the clock on the wall.

"Clock's fast." Arthur smiled as he strode past her to the door marked "Chairman."

Sir Freddie got up as Arthur came into the huge corner office with a panoramic view of Zurich. In this setting, Sir Freddie seemed smaller than in J. B. Foster's cramped embassy conference room. The overly cheery handshake was the same, but Sir Freddie's natural bonhomie was at odds with the office suite, where everything was gray—the armchairs, the sofa, the carpet, the drapes, even Sir Freddie's suit. The modest gold rim of his Patek Philippe deco watch and his gold cufflinks, miniature versions of Mrs. Winchester's sheaf of wheat brooch, seemed out of place in this studied neutrality. Arthur felt the chairman did not quite fit into his new surroundings.

"Arthur, great to see you again," Sir Freddie said, but with only the briefest of smiles. "Rum business about Scott, eh? Any news of the autopsy?"

Arthur said he hadn't heard anything. He wasn't about to be the coroner's messenger boy. Why didn't Sir Freddie ask about Karen Lichfield? Perhaps the chairman didn't know or didn't care.

Sir Freddie insisted Arthur take in the view across the Limmat.

"Marvelous, isn't it? I remember Zurich in the sixties during the sterling crisis. You're too young for that, of course. Times have really changed. Now Zurich is a bustling modern city with its own distinct culture. I opened Panrustica's headquarters here to ride along with that revival."

Arthur assumed these thoughts of Chairman Freddie were part

of every visitor's introduction to the new corporation. He resisted the temptation to say Zurich was still a nice quiet place to have a mistress. Frankly, he didn't care about Sir Freddie's personal foibles; it was the morality of his business dealings that made this saccharine exchange so emotionally fraudulent.

Straining to be polite, Arthur agreed that Zurich had changed a lot. But as his eyes swept the cityscape, they caught a more important sight—a stack of photographs on Sir Freddie's desk. The top picture looked familiar: it seemed to be the front of the Oxford museum, but it was partly obscured by papers.

"Well, let's get down to business, shall we?" said Sir Freddie. "You have some information, you told my secretary? You've been very busy. Williams said you were good—and that you would be sure to find Ms. Petrovskaya. Have you found her? Zurich is, after all, not a very big place."

"Yes, I found her."

"Excellent, where is she?"

"In the hospital," Arthur lied.

Sir Freddie stopped his pacing and returned slowly to his desk.

"In the hospital, you said?"

"I'm surprised you haven't heard," said Arthur. "Your man was the cause of her being there."

"I don't know what you're talking about. My people haven't told me anything."

"Why don't you ask them? Your man was right there. Saw everything."

Sir Freddie frowned.

"I don't know what you're trying to say, Hemmings, but you may be going too far."

"On the contrary, Sir Freddie, your company is the one that has been going too far. One of your men has been following me ever since I landed at the airport," Arthur said, looking Sir Freddie in the eye. "I thought it was the Russians."

"Perhaps it *was* the Russians." Sir Freddie's eyebrows shot up, sensing a welcome detour.

"No, it was not. It was your man. I checked the license plate. The car was from your fleet of blue Audis. See for yourself."

Arthur let the police memo from Marc Haber fall on Sir Freddie's desk.

"The Zurich police report on the car that followed me. It's from your Audi fleet in the basement of this building."

Then Arthur added Fred's picture from the zoo.

"Interfering with the work of a government investigator from Ag & Fish may not sound like much to you and your intrepid Mr. Eikel, but at home the ministry would regard it as perverting the course of justice."

Sir Freddie stared at the police report and the photos like a man who was not overly surprised.

"Of course, Arthur, of course, my dear boy. Apologies. Following you was just silly. We're on the same side, for heaven's sake. Eikel gets overexcited about such things. He's a corporate lawyer, what can I say? But fine. It's agreed. No more of that."

Sir Freddie got up and walked to the window.

Arthur picked up the police report and Fred's photo from the desk and deliberately knocked the papers off the top of the photo he had seen of the museum.

"Just a minute. I recognize this picture," Arthur said, realizing that he had started something that would very shortly get him thrown out.

"This is from a collection of photos taken by the *Oxford Chronicle* of the outside of the museum on the day before the break-in. It was taken for the cherry blossoms, but the only possible interest for you—and for me—is that the photo shows a car outside that was hired by an employee of Panrustica. Now what would that car be doing there, Sir Freddie?"

The chairman whipped round and faced Arthur.

"Williams will hear about this," Sir Freddie hissed. His neck was turning puce, just above his very expensive shirt collar.

"You bet he will, Sir Freddie," Arthur hissed back, "and now if you'll excuse me, I have other business to attend to."

Arthur turned on his heel, marched out of the office and straight to the elevator, passing Mrs. Winchester's desk without looking at her. She would soon be frantically placing calls for her boss, he guessed. The first would be to Eikel, to establish Tanya's whereabouts. The second would be to Williams in London. He'd like to eavesdrop on that one. Merrill would be calling any minute. Arthur took his cell phone out of his pocket, pressed the off button, and watched the tiny screen of Big Ben and the Houses of Parliament flutter to a safe, blank gray.

The elevator stopped at the ground floor, but Arthur kept going down to the basement garage.

It was full of company cars, blue Audis of varying models, presumably gauged to the status of the employee. A uniformed chauffeur was running a feather duster over the gleaming body of Audi's top-of-the-line Quattro, the A8, nearest the exit. Arthur approached him.

"Sir Wilfred told me to tell you he'll be down in a minute. You are his chauffeur?"

"Yes, sir."

Arthur kept going toward the exit, moving swiftly but not so swiftly that he missed the car's license plate. ZU5500C.

He walked past the security guard and out into the crowded street. ZU5500C. It sounded more like a telephone number than a license plate; perhaps it was both. He jotted it down in his notebook, then folded into the rush hour crowd on the Bahnhofstrasse.

He looked behind before each turn, but no one seemed to be following him.

At the Limmat he sat on a bench beside the river and called Haber. The number was engaged.

"Another car, Marc. To add to the list," Arthur told the answering machine. License plate ZU5500C."

Then he walked to Matt's office.

Thirty-eight

t the entrance to the World Patent Organization, visitors were being held up at the security desk. Extra precautions after the computer glitches, Arthur hoped, but anything that slowed things down was ominous. He walked to the front of the line, flashed Haber's Interpol card, and to his surprise, the guard waved him in. He was taken aback by his own audacity, but time was short.

At the twelfth floor, he knocked on Matt's door, but there was no response. He knocked again and called Matt's name. Still nothing. He dialed Matt's office number on his cell phone and then he punched in Matt's cell number. No reply. He called the guard, who opened Matt's office, but he was not there.

Arthur had only one thought: Matt had gone to the Hotel Monch to find Tanya, who, of course, would not be there, but Eikel's thugs were still at large. They might be there watching for her return. He jumped into a taxi, gave the driver a hundred-franc note, and told him it was an emergency. They were held up crossing the Limmat because a tram had broken down. "All this bollocks about Swiss efficiency," Arthur muttered to himself. As the taxi turned into Brunngasse, Arthur could see the entrance to the Monch. A blue Audi was parked outside the hotel, and Matt Raskin was being pushed into the back seat by the blond man. Arthur jumped out of the taxi and yelled at the cab to wait. As he sprinted to the Audi, it took off. He got back into the cab, and the driver nodded and smiled over the challenge as Arthur promised him another hundred francs. As they raced after the Audi, out of the Old Town and onto the Seilergraben, Arthur called Haber.

"We are following the car," Haber said, as if he were watching the whole scene on television. "The Fiat in front of you is ours. Enjoy the ride." Then he hung up.

The Audi was heading for the main intersection at the Bahnhof Bridge, where it had several choices—up the hill to the zoo, along the quai by the river, or across the bridge to the railroad station. As it neared the bridge, a flower seller was pushing his stand across the road, and he jumped back, just in time to avoid being hit. The Audi gave the flower stand a glancing blow, sending blooms everywhere, forcing the police Fiat into a wall and sending the Audi down onto the quai. A tram blocked the exit to the Bahnhof Bridge, and the Audi continued along the river. At the next bridge, police cars blocked the two exits. Arthur braced himself for the impact he knew would come.

Somehow, the cab driver managed to avoid a collision; even so, the sudden stop catapulted Arthur into the front seat and he felt a sharp jab of pain as his right elbow, the injured elbow, hit the dashboard. He yelled at the driver to wait for him and kicked open the door of the taxi in time to see Matt fall out of the Audi's back door, just before it piled into the police car. As police surrounded the Audi, Arthur dragged Matt away, carried him back to the taxi, laid him out on the back seat, and told the driver to turn around and head back up the quai to the Rosengarten. Matt was moaning on the seat beside him, and Arthur had to control himself. He wanted to yell at the youth, but instead he told him everything was all right.

"I filed the patent," Matt was mumbling. "I filed the patent. It's over. It's over."

It was not over, Arthur knew, not nearly. At the hotel he half carried Matt across the lobby and into the elevator. Again the clerks at the desk ignored him. In his room, Arthur opened the cocktail cabinet and poured two miniature brandies into a glass.

"Drink this," he told Matt, who gulped down the contents.

Arthur fetched a towel from the bathroom and thrust it into Matt's hand. "Now take a hot shower and hurry up. We have work to do."

Matt gave Arthur one of his baleful looks, and Arthur yelled at him.

"Now."

Arthur called Haber. Calmly, Haber reported that two men had been arrested from the Audi, the Frenchman Peress and the blond man, an American named William Paynter. The charges on the American included assault, harassment, burglary, and illegal entry into Switzerland. "The U.S. embassy has been informed," Haber said, with obvious satisfaction, adding that his next stop was Panrustica.

"I apologize about Peress; he used to be so reliable. I guess they paid him more than we did."

"There's a lot of money being paid out around here," Arthur observed acidly. He was relieved that the two men were now in custody, but he had to force himself to thank his friend. The Peress episode had almost unraveled the entire enterprise. He told Haber that he had to go to the patent office and he would then collect Tanya.

"Don't worry, Arthur, she will be fine with me."

"I know, Marc, I know."

★   ★   ★

Arthur bundled Matt into a taxi and headed for the WPO. At the entrance, Matt suddenly came to life. He led the way to his office, sat down, and pulled up the front page of the application on the computer screen. Arthur began reading the abstract, slowly, proofreading, checking every word.

Matt had done an excellent job, as Arthur had expected, but this had to be perfect. Every lawyer in the food business, especially Richard Eikel, would be searching for any loophole, the smallest error.

The Abstract, or summary, was titled "Apomictic Plants and Methods To Produce Them." Arthur began reading.

Apomictic maize/*Tripsacum* hybrids having a ratio of maize chromosomes to *Tripsacum* chromosomes of at least 35:3 are disclosed. These hybrids produce stable inherited characteristics without the need for continuously producing hybrid seed by repeated crossing of selected parental lines. DNA primers for use in assaying maize/*Tripsacum* hybrids for apomictic reproduction behavior are provided. Genetic sequences causally associated with the apomictic trait are provided which can be used to convert any sexual plant to an apomict.

Inventors: Scott, Alastair (Oxford University, UK) and Petrovskaya, Tanya (St. Petersburg, RU).

Arthur then flipped to a separate attachment in which Matt had laid out how the patent would be assigned jointly to Scott's heirs and the Crucible Foundation, the legal mechanism for the protected commons, set up by Arthur's friend Tom Franklin in Boulder.

"Impressive. I'm proud of you," Arthur complimented the young lawyer.

The only problem, they both knew, was Scott's will. Who was

the heir? And would they honor Scott's desire to have his invention made available to all through the protected commons?

"Why is your name not on the patent?" Arthur asked.

Matt shook his head. "Alastair offered, but they did the work," he said. "I'm just happy to see it through."

Arthur approved. A fine gesture. In contrast to the instincts he'd been encountering recently, this one seemed almost saintly.

"This is a great moment in the history of botany. Is there somewhere we could get a glass of champagne?" Arthur beamed. But the young American could only manage a tight smile.

Arthur was thinking ahead. He wanted a place that would get Matt out of the office, a place where Eva could come, a crowded lunchtime bar. The Zeughauskeller, where he used to drink with Haber during the wine scandal, was only a block away. They could walk there.

The bar was filling up, but they saw a table in the corner. Arthur ordered two beers as he walked in, and the waiter brought them as they were sitting down.

"To the patent," said Arthur, raising his glass.

"To Alastair and Tanya," said Matt, clinking his glass into Arthur's and taking a sip. Only a sip, Arthur noted. Pity this young man had never learned to drink, he lamented, as he considered his next move—persuading Matt to go to London with Eva as his chaperone. Matt tipsy would have eased the problem considerably.

Thinking of Eva, he switched on his phone and it buzzed immediately. She had just arrived at the airport. He gave her the address of the restaurant. Then he turned the phone off again. Merrill would be calling, but he would have to wait.

Then he turned to Matt.

"My assistant, Eva, is coming to escort you to London while I find Tanya. You will be in good hands."

Matt was staring down at his beer.

"I don't need a fucking nanny," he snapped, exactly the trouble Arthur had expected.

"Yes, you do," said Arthur, raising his voice. "I need one myself, most of the time. You've got to do this for Alastair and for Tanya. Don't screw it up. Eva is the best in the business." He paused.

"Would you like to eat something?" he asked, more softly.

Matt looked at him, sourly, a look Arthur understood to mean no.

Arthur ordered two more beers, and they sat in silence for an endless quarter of an hour until he saw Eva coming across the crowded restaurant. She was wearing a light summer dress, beige, the color of a soft beach, and a matching straw hat, an outfit he seemed to recall from an outing they had once made to the Henley Regatta. He let out a whistle of relief, drew another chair up to the table, and made the introduction. Eva took immediate command, as he knew she would.

"Now, we have a plane to London at five this evening, first-class," she was telling Matt, her hand on his. "And we're all booked into the Savoy for the night, Tanya included. What time should we leave for the airport?"

"I don't believe this," Matt was saying, shaking his head.

"You'd better believe it," said Eva, now with a firm grip on his arm. She had become his keeper, instantly.

"And we don't want any slacking on the way, Mr. Raskin," she said, throwing a quick glance at Arthur, who was stifling a bout of irritation.

This young man was being treated to a trip to London, first-class, and an evening at the Savoy, free of charge, with a lively, good-looking older woman, and all he could do was mope. Why the hell couldn't he loosen up? Just this once.

Eva sensed the risk in Arthur's brooding, and fearing an outburst, she quickly intervened.

"What's that on the back of your hand?" she asked, spotting his wound.

"Nothing," Arthur replied. "I slipped on a wet sidewalk."

"And there's a nasty something on your head."

"I slipped and fell."

She smiled at him, an understanding smile.

"Well, put something on it," said Eva, moving into her matronly best. "And I thought you had things to do."

Eva was now in total control. Minutes after her arrival he had been dismissed, he realized, not without some relief. He bowed to this remarkable woman, and as he got up to leave, he turned to Matt.

"Just hold it in, young man, until you get to London, OK? We'll throw plates at the wall tomorrow."

Matt didn't reply.

Eva stood up with one hand still on Matt's shoulder. "I forgot one thing," she said, rummaging in her handbag and bringing out a folded sheet of foolscap paper, which she handed to Arthur.

"You'll want to look at this, carefully," she said. "And now you must go."

Arthur took the piece of paper and gave her a peck on the cheek.

"I'll see you in London tomorrow, *mit* Tanya."

Out in the street, Arthur unfolded the paper. It was in Eva's handwriting. Mr. Spigelman had confirmed the reading of the will for ten o'clock tomorrow and given her a list of the invitations. Besides Tanya and Matt, there were Miss Richards, Mr. Simpson, Panrustica, and Karen Lichfield.

Karen Lichfield? Panrustica? Mr. Simpson—of MI5? Arthur was stunned.

Then Eva had written, "The tapes from the farm are at the Kew photo lab. The technician will wait there this evening until you come. Here's the list of the cars and numbers you wanted. The Toyota embassy car outside the museum was assigned to J. B. Foster. Interesting, eh?"

Arthur stopped on the sidewalk, looked again at the piece of paper, folded it carefully, and put it in his wallet. J. B. Foster, or someone driving his car, was in Oxford on the day before the museum break-in.

Thirty-nine

Marc Haber was calling.

"We have a problem, my friend. The Russians somehow found out Ms. Petrovskaya had been in the hospital and they are claiming her."

Russians? Arthur wondered. How about Richard Eikel?

"Of course, we have not granted them access," Haber continued, "but it is up to a judge. She entered the country illegally, and we do not have an argument to keep her. The judge's decision could come at any moment. I think we should take precautionary measures."

"Which means?"

"Which means you should come to my office immediately."

Arthur took a taxi to the Lindenhofstrasse, where, he reminded himself a trifle wearily, this Zurich excursion had begun, only five days ago. It seemed like five weeks. Haber met him at the front door

of the Interpol house in a somber mood. No schnapps today, when
he could have used it.

"We really had only one option," Haber said. "Arrange for you to
take Tanya out of the country—if she'll still go with you. She's here,
fully conscious but not in great shape. I did not tell her anything
about the Russians."

"You really think it's the Russians who want Tanya, not Panrustica?" Arthur asked.

"Arthur, it doesn't matter," Haber replied, suddenly impatient.
"Whoever it was, they are trying to spoil your plan and we have to go."

Arthur dropped the subject. They went up in the elevator to
Haber's office, where Tanya was sitting upright in one of the uncomfortable armchairs. She got up slowly as she recognized Arthur, who
gave her a firm but respectful hug. She had made a remarkable recovery, with no outward trace of her binge and its traumatic end the
night before. She was wearing the same floral dress, which the hospital had apparently washed and ironed, her hair was tidy, and her face
calm, her large, round eyes open and bright, the eyes Arthur had first
noticed in the photo at the museum party.

"Thank you, Mr. Hemmings," she greeted Arthur quietly.

Arthur stepped back and looked into those eyes.

"I made a mistake leaving you . . . It was my fault. I apologize.
I'm very glad to see you."

"No, you saved me," she said, sitting back in the chair. "And the
inspector, of course."

"We haven't got much time," Haber interrupted. "In fact, we
should leave immediately for the airport, if you don't mind, Ms.
Petrovskaya."

Arthur quickly explained to Tanya that the patent had been filed
at the WPO, that Matt was on his way to London already, and tomorrow morning they had an important date to keep with the lawyer in
London to verify the lab notes. He did not mention the will.

"You know about the notebooks, of course," he said.

She nodded. "I took the originals to Mr. Spigelman two weeks ago."

Haber was impatient. He said he would drive them to the airport in his own car, and they would have to leave now.

"We have already left too much to chance."

At the airport, Haber drove down an alley beside the departure terminal, to a door marked "No entry, officials only." He ushered them up a flight of stairs and opened a door that led into the main terminal.

"Here is where I leave you. Here are your tickets. You go straight to the SWISS departure desk. Have a safe flight."

"*Merci,* Marc." Arthur realized he had already overstayed his welcome.

There was no sign of Eva and Matt; Arthur hoped they had caught an earlier flight. Just before they boarded the 6 p.m. plane, Arthur left a message for Eva to meet them at Heathrow, if she could.

As they strapped themselves in, Tanya in the window seat, Arthur sitting protectively on the aisle, he turned to her.

"You must be looking forward to seeing Matt again."

"Yes, it will be nice to see Matt again. Thank you, Mr. Hemmings. Thank you." She turned her face to the window and closed her eyes.

Arthur ordered a double brandy and wondered what the next twenty-four hours would bring. There were still so many questions to which, annoyingly at this late stage, he simply did not have answers.

Forty

Eva was at Heathrow arrivals, as Arthur was confident she would be. She was still wearing her straw hat, and Matt was hovering behind her, smiling for once, his sulk apparently dissipated under Eva's full-throttle charm. Arthur walked out of customs beside Tanya, who took a quick breath as she spotted Matt's tangle of brown hair. As she got closer to the barrier, Matt reached out for her and they hugged, gently rocking each other in relief.

Eva shook Arthur's arm to get his attention. Her face spoke of trouble, and he could imagine the source all too easily. Minister Williams had heard about the patent filing and was in a fury, she told him. Merrill had been calling, hitting the redial button every ten minutes.

"I simply told him that he would have to wait until you returned," Eva said.

"OK, I'll deal with Merrill."

"Fred Barton has also been calling."

"No surprises," said Arthur. "I'm sure he wants to tell me his scoop is in tomorrow's paper."

"It is in tomorrow's paper. And Harry Torrens has found . . ." —she hestitated as she referred quickly to her notes—"abrin . . . *a-b-r-i-n,* in Karen's samples from the hospital."

"Abrin?"

"Did I get it right, Arthur?"

"You certainly did. Thank you."

"And Harry says it's the variety found in Florida. He's quite sure about that and insisted I should not forget to tell you. He found a sliver of a seed, hang on . . ." She looked at her notes again. "A sliver of a seed of, yes, a *j-e-q-u-i-r-i-t-y* seed, in the Band-Aid."

Arthur deposited the three of them into a taxi. Eva bustled her charges inside, promising to call when they reached the Savoy. He watched until they were out of sight, got his own cab, and settled into the back seat. So Karen Lichfield died from abrin poisoning, but not from abrin in her own lab, not the material she was working on, which she said had come from Thailand. And the inflammation on her hand was not from a shard of broken glass, as she had imagined, but from the sliver of a jequirity seed containing abrin—from America. The poison had been cleverly chosen because the symptoms were similar to those caused by trichothecenes. The source would be hard to trace. Whoever did this could not have known she was so allergic. They might not have intended to kill her, just scare her into silence. Very clever, Arthur thought, but not clever enough.

As the cab turned onto the highway, he called Merrill at the office, but he had already left. He found him at home.

"Where are you, Arthur?" Merrill demanded.

"In a taxi coming from the airport."

"Williams heard about the patent application with the WPO, and yes, he had to be scraped off the ceiling," Merrill began.

"Of course, he thinks you organized the whole thing," he went on. "Secondly, an apoplectic Sir Freddie was almost arrested by the Swiss police at a fancy Zurich restaurant named Zunfthaus whatever, for being in possession of a stolen vehicle. He knows you were behind that little prank. Thirdly, you never have your cell phone on. I am going to take it away from you."

"Merrill, calm down. Number one. I don't see why anyone should be upset about the patent. The invention is now available for everyone to use, just as we discussed. It's called sharing. A new concept for life science corporations, I know. But what could be a better outcome for you politicians—you guardians of the public trust? You have invested public funds in a public good."

He imagined Merrill grinding his teeth as he listened to Arthur's responses.

"Number two. Guilty as charged about the stolen vehicle. And it couldn't have happened to a more deserving person. I'm only sorry they didn't put Sir Freddie in jail. It's where he ought to be.

"Number three. Guilty as charged. Cancel my cell phone, please."

"It's more complicated than you think, boyo," said Merrill. "Scott is bloody dead. Dead men can't own patents. And no one knows whether he named an heir."

"Really?" said Arthur, playing dumb. "I never thought of that. We'll have to work out something in the morning. In the meantime, there is something I can tell you."

"How gracious of you."

"It appears that Karen Lichfield was killed by abrin, not trichothecenes. And the abrin did not come from her lab. It came from America. It may not have been an accident."

"What the hell is abrin?"

"It's the toxin in *Abrus precatorius,* which is a perennial ornamental

vine with attractive but very poisonous tiny red seeds, used in rosa-
ries and necklaces. It grows in the tropics, including Florida. Abrin
is a phytotoxin, like ricin only considerably more poisonous, if taken
through the skin. Quite well known as a murder weapon in ancient
India."

"So, what are you saying, Arthur?"

"Karen Lichfield's death was not an accident."

"Shit."

For once Merrill had fallen silent, but only for a few seconds.

"You didn't mention anything about Tanya," Merrill said.

"Tanya is staying in London, in a hotel around the corner from
the ministry. Very safe."

"She's what?"

"Staying in a hotel around the corner from the ministry. I'll arrange for you to meet her in the morning."

"What hotel? Where?"

Arthur closed the phone and stared out the window. It was almost dark, and he knew it would be another night short on sleep. As
the taxi took the Kew Gardens exit, Eva called to say they had arrived
at the Savoy.

"How will you get Matt and Tanya to the lawyer?" Arthur asked,
still concerned about her charges, especially Matt.

"Arthur, please don't worry about such things; you've got enough
to do. Our suite here is very grand. Matt is already asleep, and Tanya
and I are having a nightcap. Nanny is not going to sleep tonight. She
has a good book."

Arthur managed a smile at the thought of Merrill's face when he
saw the expenses. First-class airfares to and from Zurich, and a suite
at the Savoy. That should turn up the gossip level at the ministry.

Forty-one

*I*t *was dark* when Arthur's taxi drove into Kew, and as the beam of its headlights swung onto his cottage, he asked the driver to go around the green one more time. It was a ritual: arriving home at night, he always liked to check the neighborhood. Then he asked the cab driver to wait while he opened his front door. The key turned easily in the lock. Arthur switched on the lights and dismissed the cabbie. On the door mat was a pile of letters, one handwritten, in a woman's hand, he guessed—small, neat letters. He picked up the letter and studied the postmark. Oxford last Wednesday, the day Karen Lichfield had died. "Took its time getting here," Arthur muttered as he sat at the kitchen table and unfolded the white foolscap.

The letter was addressed to "Dear Mr. Hemmings" and signed "Yours sincerely, Karen Lichfield." He shuddered. The last time he had read a letter from a dead person was when his parents were killed in the car accident. His mother had written him the day before.

"As soon as you had left," Karen's letter began, "I realized I should have told you everything, as I have no reason to protect Scott anymore, and every reason to protect myself.

"Three months ago, I met Richard Eikel at a mycotoxin conference in London. We talked about my work on T3; I told him more than I should have. He flattered me by offering me a job at a very good salary in Panrustica's R & D labs, and of course, I was interested, but in return he wanted me to supply him with seeds from Scott's apomixis research. I told him I would never do such a thing. In any case, I told him the lab work was under lock and key, literally, in a safe in Scott's office. Eikel said he could arrange for someone to open the safe—if I could arrange access to the laboratory.

"I was outraged. I couldn't believe what I was hearing; it reinforced everything I had ever suspected but had been unwilling to believe about Panrustica, and I told Scott.

"What happened next will surprise you greatly, but you must understand that the professor was a strange man, arrogant and paranoid at the same time. He mixed the innocence of a purist with foxlike cunning. Scott suggested I go along with Eikel's plan. He would arrange for the wrong seeds to be in the safe—those coded NS and SP, instead of LG. SP were tobacco seeds, as I'm sure you've discovered by now. He thought his plan would create confusion at Panrustica about the state of his research, delay the company's offer of funds, and give him time to file his own patent. He even suggested the timing of the supposed break-in—during the guard's supper.

"I knew of Scott's plan to file the patent in Zurich and approved of it, so I agreed to play the game. Matt and Tanya did not know of my role. They thought I was in favor of the Panrustica deal. It was a perfect cover for me. I let Eikel's man into the museum but made sure he had the wrong seeds.

"I was devastated when Scott died. I don't believe it was suicide because he had this elaborate plan. But I am now in a very difficult position. The patent has not been filed and Eikel will find out he has the wrong seeds. He will blame me. Mr. Hemmings, I need your help. Please contact me as soon as you get this letter.

"P.S. My hand has swollen up where the man from Panrustica held me. Perhaps it wasn't glass from the broken window in Scott's office. I'm scared."

Arthur put down the letter.

"All this for a tiny bag of seeds," he muttered to himself, "the wrong seeds."

Karen's fear had been justified, he now knew. It was not a shard of glass; it was a splinter from a jequirity seed containing abrin—from America. He put the letter back in the envelope and headed for the photo lab.

He had made this journey many times, and even in the dark, the route was familiar—go past the monkey puzzle tree, bear right at the Orangery, and enter the herbarium from the south gate. To-night the shadows he knew well seemed strangely menacing. At the photo lab, he showed his pass to the security guard and walked down the corridor to Room 7C, the showing room.

As he opened the door, Merrill was standing in front of the view-ing screen talking to the technician.

"You're late, boyo."

"What the hell are you doing here?" asked Arthur.

"Looking after the minister's interests—and yours."

"Conflicting interests."

"Are you saying you're not glad to see me?"

"No. I just thought I was going to be alone. How the hell did you know I would be here?"

"Before we spoke ten minutes ago, I had been looking for you and found out that Eva had been at the farm reviewing videos. I called the Kew lab, naturally, and—unlike you—they answered the phone."

"Hendon told you about Eva?"

"Yes, Hendon. He works for the ministry, Arthur, not for you. But he didn't rat on you, if that's what you're thinking. I called him trying to find you, and he offered the information that Eva had been there. Why did you want the tape?"

Arthur was actually glad Merrill had come. He should have thought to invite him. Merrill should witness the tape he was about to see, now a crucial piece of evidence that he expected would expose an even darker side to this already sordid story. Seeing the tape would help Merrill explain to the minister what was really going on.

"I asked Eva to get the tape after I had interviewed Miss Richards in Lyme Regis. The police had seen her. Inspector Davenport said they had learned nothing. She had insisted that she didn't know anything, except some stuff about Scott's milk bottles. But with a little prompting, she told me a story about Scott committing suicide on the Saturday before the break-in at the museum."

Merrill was now sitting down, arms crossed and resting comfortably on his belly.

"You haven't been frightening old ladies, have you, boyo?"

Arthur ignored him. "Ms. Richards said that she and Scott had gone for a walk by the Thames, just above Queen's Lock, and that Scott was consumed by depression over the Panrustica offer, by visits from officials from the U.S. embassy, and by an accusation by MI5 that he had once taken a bribe from the Soviets. So he had wandered off, like Captain Oates, and drowned himself. Committed suicide. It was a good story, well told, with a plausible ending, but I didn't believe her: it didn't sound right. On that Saturday, Miss Richards said she and Scott had left their car in the lot opposite the farm. The parking lot is covered by CCTV from the farm because of the demonstrations by the greens, but the cameras are well hidden. Then I found out that J. B. Foster had been in Oxford on that Saturday, something he had not told me. My nasty mind started to churn. And here we are."

Merrill was silent.

"Why don't we watch the movie?" said Arthur, turning to the technician.

"Joe, there should be two DVDs marked Saturday and Sunday. We'll start with Saturday."

The film was typical CCTV video, black-and-white, slightly fuzzy, but there was a good view of the parking lot. In fast forward, two cars and a delivery van came and went, apparently workers at the farm.

Then at 10:38 a.m. a small car, an old-model Mini, came into the lot and parked with its license plate showing clearly.

"Stop right there, Joe. Go in on the number."

Arthur took the piece of paper Eva had given him at the airport out of his pocket.

"That's Miss Richards's Mini, Merrill. OK, let it run."

Two people got out of the car; a small woman, who had been driving, and a taller man, dressed in what looked like a sports jacket. They took a rug and a shopping bag out of the trunk and walked off toward the left of the picture.

"That's them, Miss Richards and Scott walking toward the river."

At 10:39 three more cars arrived in the lot. Two cars, apparently together because they parked side by side, were family cars. Parents and children spilled out of these bulky vehicles. The third car parked a short distance from the others.

"Stop. On the license plate, please, Joe."

Arthur checked the number against Eva's list.

"Let it run."

A large man got out of the car from the passenger side, and the car immediately left the parking lot. For a split second the man faced the camera.

"Stop. Enlarge."

"Bloody hell," cried Merrill. "It's J. B. Foster. What the fuck's he doing there?"

"Watch him," said Arthur.

Foster turned toward the river, pausing at Miss Richards's Mini to take a picture with a small camera.

"What's he trying to prove?" asked Merrill.

"He wants to be able to show his bosses that he was there. He wants them to know every detail," replied Arthur. "He's only following orders. He feels perfectly safe. He does not know he's on camera because the cameras are so well hidden. In any case, he has diplomatic immunity.

"You can fast-forward, Joe," Arthur said, watching the flickering video carefully. Cars came and went, most if not all of their occupants going to the pub.

"The Badger opens at noon," Arthur explained to Merrill.

But there was no sign of Miss Richards, the professor, or J. B. Foster.

At 1:03 a small woman came scurrying into the picture from the left, the river side.

"Back up . . . Stop. Forward, slowly."

The video showed Miss Richards moving, almost running, toward her Mini. She got in and drove away.

"Let's stop right there, Joe."

Then Arthur turned to Merrill.

"In her story," he said, "Miss Richards claims that the professor went for a walk along the bank, she heard a splash, knew what he had done, but was petrified and couldn't do anything to stop him. She remained for a while on her rug and then she left."

Merrill interrupted, "She's old. They are both old. She's a close friend, by all accounts. She might have had a suicide pact with the professor— because he couldn't take the strain anymore. It would not be unheard-of. And J. B. Foster could have just been going for a walk by the river."

Arthur shook his head.

"Except, my dear friend, for one thing. He did not come in his own car. He was driven to the farm by a man, another American, named William Paynter. That was Paynter's rental car. Mr. Paynter was arrested yesterday in Zurich after a police car chase and charged with assault, harassment, and burglary. We don't know what J. B. Foster did after he walked off the video screen, but the chances are that he was up to no good."

"Next DVD please, Joe."

Sunday's video opened at 6:20 a.m. The parking lot was empty when the same car that had brought J. B. Foster returned. A short, stocky man got out and headed toward the river.

"That's Paynter," said Arthur.

Twenty minutes later he returned, got into the car, and drove away.

"This is the same car that brought J. B. Foster to the parking lot on Saturday," said Arthur. "I suggest Paynter was returning to the scene of the crime, to remove any incriminating evidence that might have been left behind, and to check if there was any sign of the body. There wasn't, as we now know. The body did not surface, or rather was not brought to the surface, until Tuesday morning."

"Well, the only person who would be able to add information would be Miss Richards," said Merrill.

"Right. Tomorrow morning at ten I am due to meet Miss Richards in a lawyer's office in the City of London, where there is a reading of Scott's will."

"What?"

"Yes, Merrill, isn't that what you wanted me to find out? Who owns the patent?"

"So, you won't be coming in to see the minister before then?"

"No, Merrill, I won't. I think you have enough information to brief Williams yourself."

"This is a cowardly act," Merrill protested. "Why do I always have to cover for you? Why do I always have to take the brunt of Williams's anger—all of it these days, without exception, caused by you?"

"Because, my dear friend, that is your job. And secondly, and more importantly . . ." Arthur paused, thinking of a way to end the sudden bitterness between them. "Because you are Welsh."

Merrill managed a half smile and shook his head.

"OK. We're both tired."

"And now I will escort you off the premises, if you don't mind. I need to finish some work at my cottage, alone. Not even a nightcap tonight, I'm afraid."

Arthur took Merrill to the main gate.

He needed to prepare for the meeting with Mr. Spigelman. He also wanted to congratulate Fred on his scoop—even though he hadn't seen it yet.

Barton was panting to relay his news.

"The vice-chancellor will announce his resignation in the morning, and there's a rumor that he's going to join the board of Panrustica," Fred said, breathlessly.

"A perfect match," said Arthur.

"And the autopsy is also out tomorrow."

"And I may have a certain something to add, Fred, so listen out." Then he hung up.

Of course, that certain something depended on whether Miss Richards would now tell the truth.

Forty-two

The next morning, fortified by several cups of strong, bitter tea, Arthur took the detour past Sydney's cottage on his way to Mr. Spigelman's office. She was in her front garden, transplanting primulas. Her hair was tied in a haphazard knot that to Arthur made her look young and fragile, an image that he knew Sydney would find, at best, insulting. He watched her fold the pale yellow plants into her front flower bed until she looked up and saw him. She let out a yelp, brushed her hands against her jeans, and rushed up to him. Maybe she had really missed him. He smiled contentedly as she reached up, gave him a kiss, wrapped her arms around him in a prolonged hug that signaled friendship, or at least relief that he had returned safely.

"What news?" she asked impatiently. "I want to know everything."

Arthur was pleasantly surprised at her urgency.

"No time. I'm on my way into town. How about dinner tonight? I have two very fine Dover sole in the freezer."

"You bet. What's a Dover sole, again? A flounder?"

"No," Arthur said firmly, resting both hands briefly on the garden fence. "A flounder, Sydney, is a related but quite different species, often passed off as a sole but, frankly, inferior . . . I'll tell you the rest of the story tonight."

"Nice to know there's something superior about English food," Sydney shot back, but Arthur was already jogging to the tube station.

As the clock on the tower of St. Andrew's struck ten, Arthur walked through the covered passages of Blackfriars Court to the law office of Jacobson, Allen, Knightley & Spigelman. Eva, Matt, and Tanya were already in David Spigelman's second-floor office, sitting in the front of three rows of chairs.

Eva, showing no sign of her sleepless night, was engaging the lawyer in her seductive small talk as Arthur introduced himself and looked over at Matt and Tanya, both of whom appeared pale and uncomfortable. Matt nodded, and Tanya barely managed a smile. Arthur reached over and gave their shoulders a comforting squeeze. The office radiated comfort, reassurance. Legal volumes lined the walls. Embossed invitations covered the white marble mantelpiece, over which hung ancient photographs of men in frock coats and top hats, the law firm's founding partners, Arthur presumed. There was a view of the courtyard through the mullioned windows, chestnut trees in full flower and a lawn stretching down to the Thames embankment. It was the sort of law firm Arthur would have expected Edward Dalton to recommend for his former college companion. Mr. Spigelman was a jolly man with a permanent half smile and a ruddy face, not unlike Dalton's. In fact, he and Dalton had a lot of the same airs, as if they were members of the same club, perhaps the same very private club. Perhaps Mr. Spigelman also lived in Tunbridge Wells.

At the back of the room, in the third row of chairs, three men in dark suits sat in silence.

"Panrustica," whispered Eva.

"*Three* representatives?"

"It's a big company, Arthur."

In the second row sat an attractive young woman who gave Arthur a knowing nod.

"Have we met the young woman?" he asked Eva.

"She's also a lawyer, representing Mr. Simpson. You probably have come across her, at some meeting or another."

Arthur didn't remember her, but he looked back and gave the young woman one of his best smiles.

A man in an open-neck shirt and a golfing jacket sat beside the young woman.

"He's from the Australian Embassy," Eva said softly. "Apparently he's looking after the interests of Scott's sister."

"Where's Miss Richards?"

"No sign of her."

"Damn."

"I thought you didn't like her."

"I don't, but I need to talk to her."

At that moment, Mr. Spigelman cleared his throat, and looking toward the back of the room, said, "Do come in, Miss Richards. Do come in."

Arthur looked around to see the small figure of Miss Richards peering around the half-open door. She was dressed in a blue suit and carrying a navy blue handbag. In this large room, she looked even smaller than Arthur had remembered. He went to greet her. She was obviously surprised and somewhat irritated to see him, although she contrived not to show it.

"Mr. Hemmings, how nice to see you again." She smiled, but her eyes were as cold as the stones on the Cobb at Lyme Regis.

"I wonder if we might have a word after the proceedings," Arthur said. "Only a few minutes."

"Loose ends?" she asked, looking him in the eye.

"Only one or two," said Arthur.

"Of course, Mr. Hemmings. I don't want to be unhelpful."

Mr. Spigelman cleared his throat again, apparently a signal that the reading was about to begin. As he untied the pink ribbon around the will, he explained that he would skip a full reading and go straight to the legacies. If anyone wanted to examine the will afterwards, they were welcome to do so, he said.

The will had last been updated by Professor Scott, in Mr. Spigelman's presence, six days before he died. There were several beneficiaries, including persons who were unable to attend today but had sent representatives. These were Mrs. Emily Mitchell, of Sydney, Australia, and Mr. Everett Simpson, of Cheney Walk, London. A third person, Ms. Karen Lichfield, of Oxford University, had unfortunately passed away only last week, Mr. Spigelman noted. Then he cleared his throat again.

"To his sister, Mrs. Mitchell, represented by Mr. Alexander Mitchell, no relation, of the Australian embassy, the professor leaves the sum of five thousand pounds."

Eva gave Arthur a quizzical glance. Arthur shook his head to counsel patience.

"To Mr. Everett Simpson, represented by Miss Anna Lawley, he leaves his collected works of Lenin, Karl Marx, and his first edition of Trotsky's *History of the Russian Revolution.*"

Arthur looked around at Miss Richards, who was certainly the only one in the room who appreciated the black humor of this bequest, and she gave him another of her instant smiles.

"To the global life sciences company Panrustica, of Zurich, here represented by the firm of Altringham Whitley, he leaves a bound copy of his lecture series, *On Ethics and Agriculture,* published by the Oxford University Press."

Mr. Spigelman paused, giving proper effect to the grand insult Scott had just handed the company he so loathed. Arthur turned to look back at the three men, but they were looking straight ahead at Mr. Spigelman. They were really here to find out who would inherit the patent, of course. He looked over at Tanya, expecting her to be smiling as well, but her gaze was directed beyond Mr. Spigelman, through the window and toward the Thames.

"To Matthew Herman Raskin, here present, he leaves his collection of antique microscopes and the sum of twenty thousand pounds."

Matt, who until now had kept his head down, suddenly straightened up. Eva put out her hand and he took it in his.

"To the estate of the late Karen Lichfield, not represented, he leaves his library of scientific reference books and twenty thousand pounds."

A pity that she didn't know how much she had been appreciated, Arthur thought.

"To Miss Ida Molly Richards, of Oxford and Lyme Regis, he leaves the sum of fifty thousand pounds and his house in Squitchey Lane, Oxford, and his volumes of poetry."

Arthur drew in a quick breath, but it was what he had expected, a reward for a devoted friend who had provided succor in his final days of depression. He resisted the temptation to look back at Miss Richards. He felt sure she would be showing no reaction, in any case.

Instead he gave Eva a nudge.

"Here we go," he whispered.

"All remaining items in the estate, approximately two hundred and fifty-eight thousand pounds in cash and securities, the contents of his house in Squitchey Lane, except for the volumes of poetry, and the other books already mentioned, and . . ."—here Mr. Spigelman paused again—"the right and title on his patents . . . Professor Scott leaves to his daughter and heir, Tanya Ivanova Petrovskaya, here present, of Oxford and St. Petersburg, Russia."

Eva chirped a simple "Hurray" and put her arms around Tanya, who buried her head in Eva's bosom.

There was an immediate rattling of chairs, and Arthur looked around to see the Panrustica lawyers filing out. Miss Richards had already left.

He pushed past the lawyers and ran down the stairs to the ground floor.

Miss Richards was walking briskly out into the courtyard.

He called after her, but she quickened her pace.

He called again, and she stopped and turned.

"Oh, Mr. Hemmings, I completely forgot. You wanted to ask me something."

"It will only take a few minutes," said Arthur, trying to control his irritation.

"We could sit on one of the benches in the courtyard," he said, leading her over to a double wooden seat on the lawn. Clutching her handbag on her lap, she sat staring straight ahead, down to the river. It was a familiar rendezvous with this tricky old woman.

"I want to go back to that Saturday," Arthur began, "when you and Scott drove out to Lower Witton and left your car in the parking lot at the farm. It was just before midday, I think."

"Yes, that is what I told you."

"And then you walked to the river and eventually sat on the bank in a secluded spot and drank some coffee from a flask."

"Yes. I told you."

"But you didn't tell me that an American, the man from the embassy, came along the path by the river."

"I see . . . You know this man from the embassy then, Mr. Hemmings?"

"I do. And I also know he saw you and Scott that afternoon."

Miss Richards drew in a long breath and turned toward Arthur, but her eyes were not looking at him.

"It is true that the American did talk with Alastair, on the bank of the river. Alastair saw him coming and told me that he was the American diplomat he had seen before. He was a very large man. I didn't catch his name."

"And then they walked off along the bank, didn't they, Miss Richards."

"Yes. I forgot about that. They did. Towards the woods."

"What did Scott say to you?"

"I told you last time. He said he was going for a walk and when he came back, we would go to the Badger and have lunch."

"And then you heard a splash, didn't you?"

"Yes."

"And you waited, but Scott didn't come back."

"Yes, I waited, but he didn't come back."

"And did the American come back?"

"No, I never saw the American again."

"So, the last person to see Professor Scott alive was the American?"

"I presume so."

"And you waited for a long time . . . more than an hour?"

"I don't know, maybe. I thought the American would come back. I didn't know what I was going to do."

"And that's why you didn't tell the police your story, because—"

Miss Richards interrupted him.

"Yes, Mr. Hemmings, because I am still scared the American might come back."

"So, why did you tell me this now?"

"Well, Mr. Hemmings, you seemed to know it already."

She looked at her watch and got up.

"And now, if you'll excuse me, I really must go and catch my train."

She did not say goodbye. She simply walked off across the court-yard, the same purposeful stride that he remembered from Lyme Regis.

Arthur wanted to call after her and offer to take her to a taxi, but he knew she would refuse. In any case, Eva was beckoning.

"Are you finished, Arthur?" she called out. She was standing with Matt and Tanya at the bottom of the steps leading to Mr. Spi-gelman's office.

"These two young things want to go to lunch."

Arthur held up his hand, a plea for a moment to himself, and called Merrill.

"J. B. Foster appears to have been the last person to see Scott alive. Miss Richards confirmed that Foster and Scott walked off to-gether along the riverbank."

"Bloody hell," said Merrill.

"My next stop is the American embassy," said Arthur.

"You will be disappointed, boyo. Mr. Foster has been recalled to Washington. Left on the morning plane. And just so you know, the autopsy is due out this afternoon, and it will say Scott probably committed suicide by drowning himself—of course."

"Of course," repeated Arthur. "There'll be another time," he as-sured his friend as he looked across at Eva, who was waving her arms at him. "Any news of Eikel?"

"He and Sir Freddie are apparently assisting the Zurich police with their inquiries," said Merrill.

"If the police ever get past Mrs. Winchester," said Arthur. "I have to go now." And he hung up.

Eva was telling Matt and Tanya where to go for lunch—politely, of course.

"May I suggest El Vino's on the corner of Blackfriars Bridge. It's a short walk—that way," she said, pointing along the embankment. "You can meet us back at the Savoy, in a couple of hours."

They nodded, both of them understanding that this was an order, not a suggestion.

"Arthur and I have some catching up to do, don't we, Arthur?" she said, glaring at him.

He nodded obediently and said, under his breath, "Personally, I'm in need of a stiff drink."

"What a good idea. Then we can discuss my latest discovery . . ."—Eva moved closer—"the name of the American who came to Kew library to look up the Russian material. I found out this morning, it was J. B. Foster. Now isn't that interesting?"

"Interesting, yes," said Arthur. "I definitely misjudged that one."

Eva began telling Arthur how Matt and Tanya had authenticated the laboratory notes, and what a nice man Mr. Spigelman was, and how well he had handled such a tricky situation. But Arthur was not really listening. He was thinking instead about Tanya, a little girl growing up in St. Petersburg during the Cold War, her mother keeping them both warm with stories of Mendel and her great-great-grandfather, and how her father, a brilliant British scientist, was unraveling mysteries that the abbot himself would be working on, if he were alive today.

Author's Note

Gregor Johann Mendel 1822–84
Ivan Fyodorovich Schmalhausen 1849–94

In 1865, Gregor Mendel, the abbot of the St. Thomas Monastery at Brunn, Moravia, published his celebrated essay on crossbred peas, *Experiments in Plant Hybridization*. This work formed the basis of the Mendelian laws of heredity, but it was ignored, or unread, by the biologists of the day, including Darwin.

The one exception was Ivan Fyodorovich Schmalhausen, a botany student who in 1874 completed his master's thesis, *On Plant Hybrids—Observations on the Flora of St. Petersburg*. After his thesis had gone to press, he read Mendel's 1865 essay in German. In an appendix to his thesis, he added, "I consider it necessary to refer to Mendel's study, for his methods, particularly his way of expressing his results in formulas, merit our attention and deserve to be further elaborated."

Mendel, lonely and saddened by the lack of attention given to his work and never knowing that one day he would be famous, died at two o'clock in the morning on Sunday, January 6, 1884. His housekeeper, Frau Dupouvec, was at his side. In the early 1900s, almost forty years after the publication of his original essay, Mendel was acknowledged as the father of a new science, which would be called genetics.

Ivan Fyodorovich died after a brief illness in St. Petersburg on April 19, 1894, at the age of forty-three. A German translation of his thesis had been published in 1875, but without the appendix. His reference to Mendel went unheeded in Russia until 1925 and was not made known in the West until 1965.

Although Ivan Fyodorovich traveled as a student to Zurich and Strasbourg, there is no evidence that he ever corresponded with Mendel or that he ever met him. As far as is known, none of Ivan Fyodorovich's relatives was named Petrovsky.

I learned of Mendel's household and his final days from Robin Marantz Henig's charming biography *The Monk in the Garden*, but the version here is my own.

Some of the places and organizations in England, Switzerland, and the United States do exist but have been rearranged or adapted to create my story. The characters and their actions are fictitious. Any errors, historical or scientific, are, of course, all mine.

Acknowledgments

My good friend Richard Jefferson introduced me to the idea of apomixis and the ways that it might someday revolutionize agriculture. We had many conversations, often into the wee hours, about science, especially botany, and about the need to make sure that the world's poorest farmers have access to key discoveries. Michael Carlisle, my agent, encouraged my fascination with the strange reproductive system of the dandelion. Michael Korda gave early and invaluable advice, and several friends were extremely generous in spending time as critics of the first draft. Alice Mayhew applied her inestimable combination of enthusiasm and wisdom, and the great production team at Simon & Schuster again made it go so smoothly. I thank them all. As with my other storytelling, I would not have completed this venture without the love and counsel of Eleanor Randolph.

About the Author

Peter Pringle, a veteran British foreign correspondent, is the author and coauthor of several books, including the bestselling *Those Are Real Bullets, Aren't They?* He has written for the *New York Times,* the *Washington Post, The Atlantic Monthly, The New Republic,* and *The Nation.* He lives in New York City.